A Boom to preserve the French Ships

A Plan of the
CITY & FORTIFICATIONS of
LOUISBOURG
1745

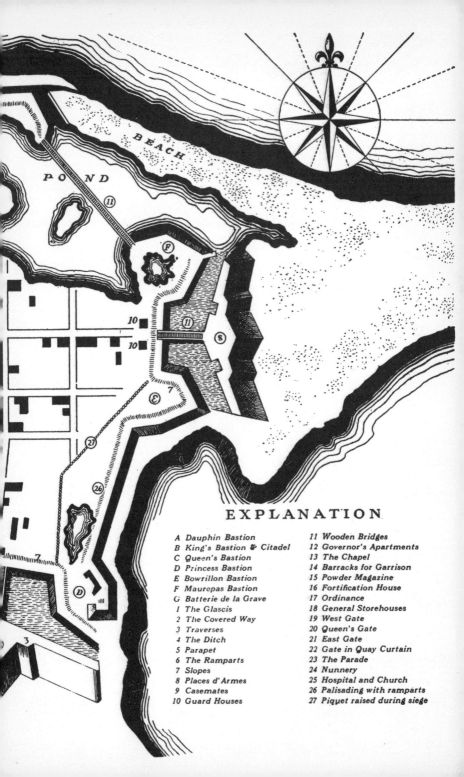

BEACH

POND

EXPLANATION

A   Dauphin Bastion
B   King's Bastion & Citadel
C   Queen's Bastion
D   Princess Bastion
E   Bowrillon Bastion
F   Maurepas Bastion
G   Batterie de la Grave
1   The Glascis
2   The Covered Way
3   Traverses
4   The Ditch
5   Parapet
6   The Ramparts
7   Slopes
8   Places d' Armes
9   Casemates
10 Guard Houses

11 Wooden Bridges
12 Governor's Apartments
13 The Chapel
14 Barracks for Garrison
15 Powder Magazine
16 Fortification House
17 Ordinance
18 General Storehouses
19 West Gate
20 Queen's Gate
21 East Gate
22 Gate in Quay Curtain
23 The Parade
24 Nunnery
25 Hospital and Church
26 Palisading with ramparts
27 Piquet raised during siege

Prisoner in
LOUISBOURG

Zillah and Colin Macdonald

MACMILLAN OF CANADA   TORONTO

To George Neilson Bayne
Also a Gatherer of Acadiana

AUTHORS' NOTE

This is the story of the First Siege of Louisbourg, Cape Breton, in the spring of 1745, when a little band of three thousand New England men besieged and captured, with the aid of Admiral Warren's British ships, a fortress which the French had erected after plans by Vauban at a cost, according to Parkman, of "thirty million livres."

Our authorities have been in the main *The Pepperrell Papers* as published by the Massachusetts Historical Society; Francis Parkman's *A Half Century of Conflict;* Winsor's *Narrative and Critical History of Boston; Louisbourg Journals, 1745,* edited by Effingham de Forest; and the work by a Canadian author, Senator J. S. McLennan, *Louisbourg from Its Rise to Its Fall.* We have also had the help of the Canadian Archives at Ottawa.

The main character in the forces, General William Pepperrell, is an attempt at a portrait. The incidents of the siege, numbers of men, conditions, the buried guns, the names of the bells, the scene where the colored servant bears the wounded Morpain into the fort, the taking of the Royal Battery, the quoted material, the thirteen streets, the letters of the admiral — all are matters of record. The *Vigilant* was a real ship and was captured as we have pictured it. On a visit to Louisbourg we even saw the secret passage which appears on no maps.

Sir William Pepperrell, who lived from 1696 to 1759, was the first native American to be created a baronet.

The Siege of Louisbourg in 1745 was the first battle these New England men, later to form the United States of America, ever fought. It was accomplished against great odds. In it they became unified as a nation and convinced of their ability to fight successfully. Some have referred to it as the Cradle of the American Revolution. It is a significant fact that Pomeroy of Bunker Hill was at Louisbourg, and several who raised the earthworks on the famous hill had seen and learned from the earthworks of Louisbourg thirty years earlier. Few have taken note of the fact that Bunker Hill followed Louisbourg exactly thirty years to the day.

ZILLAH AND COLIN MACDONALD

CONTENTS

PART ONE

Bostontown

1: Roll of the Drums

" ZOOM-M-M-M-M-M-M! " A salvo of guns echoed from the water front.

It shook our small cottage so that the tall goblet sitting on a plate, by Aaron's bed, tinkled softly, and I wondered how it would feel to be on a frigate's deck in a running fight — such an experience as I had heard told and retold in the sailmaking shop of Feathertale John near the Long Wharf.

As the reverberations died away, there was borne faintly to our ears the voice of the crier, announcing his news in another lane.

But opposite me, in the old four-poster bed, my big brother, Aaron, just past nineteen, sat up suddenly. His fingers clenched the bedclothes. His eyes blazed.

" The Proclamation! " he cried. " They will read the Proclamation and I — I may not even hear it, tied to my bed like an old woman." Then he sagged limply back, seized with a fit of the weakness, and I ran for the draught which frequently brought him relief.

When the seizure had passed, Aaron's eyes still shone. " Run, Eben, run," he cried excitedly. " Only by your hearing can I hear."

I turned away that he might not see the eagerness in my own eyes. For this, above all things, was what I would wish to do. " Mistress Merrie bade me stay with you," I said reluctantly. " And I doubt not, Aaron, you need me sorely."

" Aye," whispered Aaron, " but this is an event, I believe, will be writ large in the history of Bostontown and I would hear of it firsthand."

" Zoom-m-m-m-m-m-m! " A second salvo echoed from the water front.

" Haste, Eben, haste," Aaron admonished again. " I will tell Mistress Merrie I sent you, though I doubt it will help much."

Now in my heart, great seventeen-year-old that I was, was desperate fear of Mistress Merrie's sharp tongue. Nevertheless, I journeyed forth into the empty lanes, for no soul was abroad in our part of the town, the crier having summoned all to the Dock Square.

Once there, I sought vantage from a flight of steps and took careful note of the assemblage. It was a mixed company. For mingling with the gay uniforms of the governor's staff, the rich fabrics affected by the gallants, was the plain homespun of the soberly clad Puritans. The Proclamation was about to be read.

I made no doubt that it was a notice that a state of war existed between England and France, and glad I would be to hear it. For then our men could sally forth and privateer on the French, who were firmly established at Louisbourg, Cape Breton, in the New World — a work of depredation that the French, better informed than we New Englanders, had already started.

So intent was I on the proceedings that I did not note who my neighbors might be until I heard a familiar voice beside me.

" You are not looking, Paul. You would come and now you look only at the ground."

I glanced around quickly and saw a tall girl, about my own age, with a mass of amazingly fair hair. I had had some small conversation with her at Feathertale John's shop, and I understood that she was niece to him. Beside her was a young boy about nine. It was to him she had spoken.

" But I am seeing something of great interest, Dogood, truly I am," the boy replied. I realized he was gazing with love and admiration at my silver shoe buckles.

" He would come," Dogood complained, and now she was speaking to me, " and I doubt now if he will even listen when the Proclamation starts."

" But, Dogood," the lad persisted, " I am looking at something very beautiful, more beautiful than even the gallant's swords. I cannot think where they were made."

4

I smiled at his eagerness. " They came from France," I told him, " to my father, who is a Huguenot, the Captain St. Jean de Gervais." Then seeing Dogood's look, and mindful in what regard some of the Puritans held all French, I hastened to add, " but my mother was a Puritan."

" I am a Huguenot too," the lad hastened to inform me, and I knew I was right in my judgment of Dogood when I saw her frown darken. " My name is Paul Revere. My father is the silversmith, and I will be one too. I will make a pair of shoe buckles someday myself, but I doubt if they will ever be as beautifully chased. I have much to learn."

" You will make them," said Dogood, " if the crown does not forbid the colonists' working in silver."

" Oh, no, Dogood! " the boy cried quickly. " It will never do that! "

" It forbade my father to make felt hats," she said darkly, " that we might not spoil the trade of the English hatmakers."

I had heard of such an order and I said quickly, " It was a great pity to have one's work taken away from one."

" But I must do my work in silver," Paul cried determinedly. " Such things as I have in my head to make."

" The crown will have something to say to that," said Dogood bitterly, " though it is folly the crown will yet pay dear for."

I looked around me quickly, for Dogood's words savored of high treason, but no one seemed to have remarked it, and I said quickly, " It is a declaration of war against France we are to hear today, I wager."

" Indeed, it is not! " said Dogood sharply and closed her lips. I did not wonder that Dogood knew what it was all about, for I have often noticed that news gets ahead of itself along the water front, and Dogood's father's shop was a rendezvous of many men.

Further talk was interrupted by the announcer, who began loudly:

" By His Excellency, William Shirley, Esquire, Captain General and Governor in Chief in and over His Majesty's Province of the Massachusetts Bay in New England, Proclamation,

" Whereas at this juncture of affairs it will be of dangerous consequence to His Majesty's interest if the French King's subjects in America should be supplied with any kind of Provision or ammunition from this Province,

" I have therefore thought fit with the advice of His Majesty's Council to issue this Proclamation hereby strictly forbidding all Persons whatsoever within this Province from carrying or sending to any port, place or harbor in any of the French Islands, Colonies, or Plantations, any sort or kind of Provision, ammunition or warlike stores or other goods or merchandise whatsoever or to supply any Person or Persons with any of the things before mentioned for the use of any of the French King's subjects, as they will answer the contrary to their peril. . . ."

I glanced at Dogood. Her face was become a thundercloud. Little Paul was still engrossed with the beauty of my shoe buckles and haply, I thought, not listening.

The announcer's voice ended, " By order of the Governor with the Advice of Council, William Shirley, God Save the King."

Instantly Dogood's anger burst forth. " 'Tis as monstrous unfair a decision as ever I heard," she cried. Her eyes were dark with fury. I heard a low " Aye! Aye! " from those around me. " If we are not at war with France, and no one has thought fit to inform us we are, the crown has no right to forbid us to build up a legitimate trade with the French."

" It will mean a hard thing for your father, no doubt, Dogood," I said.

" It is ruination," stormed Dogood. " And he with a great merchantman even now loading at the dock and no place to sail to. 'Tis a cargo especially chosen for Nova Scotia and Quebec. The people of the south and the West Indies will not stock the warm woolens we sell to the French. 'Tis monstrous folly and the crown shall pay well for it, you will see," she finished. Then, as if fearful she had said too much, she cried hastily, " Come, Paul, I am going home," and stalked off.

Paul started to follow at once, but, going, took a last long look

6

at my shoe buckles. " I have seen what I do not wish to forget," he flung at me quaintly, and ran after Dogood.

I felt that here indeed was something to think about, and that I should hasten at once to Aaron with it. But I knew that Mistress Merrie had already returned before me, and I determined to climb the hill ere I should return. I knew that the big ships were still firing their guns, and I had wish to see it, unobserved.

From the hill I could see the harbor. Ever and again the great white sails disappeared beneath a curling wreath of smoke as the earth rocked in the roar of the great guns, busy with their practice firing.

So absorbed was I, I was again like to overlook what was happening about me, and I almost missed the sight of a small maid in a purple pelisse trimmed with white fur, hurrying hither and thither and pausing now and then as if afraid.

She was a good hundred yards away, and instantly I forgot the great happenings about me in wonder as to her plight and indecision. It seemed to me if I were to accost her it would but add to her fear. As I hesitated, a menacing figure, clad in an old blue coat, appeared before her and made a snatch at the little fur bag which hung from her wrist. I hastened toward her, but to my surprise the young girl drew herself up with great dignity — an act which caused her assailant to withdraw quickly several paces — and her clear, ringing tones reached me across the ground.

" For shame," she cried, " to take that which does not belong to you! " I noted now that the cringing figure was a dark-haired ruffian, and I hastened closer. The little maid went on: " If you would but ask, I might give it to you, for I make no doubt your need is much greater than my own. Here," she held out her white mittened hand in which I caught the glitter of coin.

The ruffian, noting my approach, whispered hastily: " Throw it, missie. Throw it."

The little maid, before I could stop her, somewhat disdainfully I could not but notice, threw it on the ground, and the ruffian, stooping with lightning speed, caught it and made off with it.

The girl, left alone, sank down on a bench, and covered her face with her hands. I could see that she was trembling all over, but I had to admire her courage that she had not let the ruffian see her plight.

I wondered what she was doing out all alone and approached timidly, whereupon a stone dislodged by my foot went rumbling down the hill. Instantly my little maid was alert. She started and jumped up, facing me. For a long time we remained thus, saying nothing. Then at last with a sweet dignity she spoke.

" Perhaps, you would be so kind as to tell me, sir, where I am."

Much pleased that she should take me for a man grown, I hastened to tell her that if she would but let me know where she wished to go, I would help her to go there.

"Perchance then," she said, " you would know the way to the Province House."

" It may be that I would," I said soberly, though much amused, for all Boston could show you the Province House, which was the governor's residence. Here indeed was matter of interest to tell Aaron. " Are you by chance kin to Governor Shirley? " I asked.

The little maid shook her head. " I am no kin of his, although I live with him, and address his wife, my lady, as Aunt Margaret. My father is agent for the mast trees and is even now gone to New Hampshire to look into the sources there. I am but late come from Londontown."

I could scarce believe it that one so young should have made such a long trip, for Londontown was a good six weeks by fast sloop from Bostontown, and a hazardous undertaking even at that. Anon we fell to talking. She insisted that, now she knew how to find her way home, there was no need to hurry. It was well to wander up the hill and see what was to be seen.

" But will not someone miss you? " I inquired. It seemed strange to me that she could be thus unattended. I was fearful no good would come of this escapade for either of us.

My little maid made a face extremely comical, so that I must needs laugh with her. It would seem that all were abroad save only the governor's lady, who was still abed, and the usual house serv-

8

ants. She herself had been left to her own devices and had promptly slipped out of the gate and at once had been frightened by the crowds, and then she had lost her way. She had, once off the crowded lanes, met no soul to whom she could confess her plight.

Finding she had no mother, I told her how I had lost my own with the black sickness. How father was even now sailing the seven seas in *The Golden Lily* and like to become a great merchantman. How Aaron also had suffered from the black sickness and was being nursed by Mistress Merrie, who had us in her care — a most honest woman, but a terrible stern one too.

I showed her my silver shoe buckles, which were my father's and which Aaron insisted I should wear, taking great delight in keeping them bright, but Mistress Merrie thought it great vanity in one so young and was like to punish me by cutting them off, big lad that I was, and she likely would if this day's doing came to her ears, as no doubt it must.

Then my little maid made me stand back so that she too could look at them from all angles. She said they were wondrous beautiful and not even at court had she seen aught more lovely. At mention of the court, I must know all about it. So we sat on a bench and my small maid discoursed on things I had never heard of. It came to me then that she was very beautiful, her dark hair like gay tassels about her face, and her cheeks so red and her skin so white.

I must needs tell her all about Aaron: how all that she had told to me would I tell to him. At once she was for going to see him. When I would not take her, for Aaron wished to see no one, being ashamed of the fact that he was light as a woman and not able and manly like my father, she stamped her foot in rage and ordered right regally that I should take her.

Whereupon I said I would do no one's will but Aaron's, and we were like to have had a great quarrel, forgetful of all the wondrous time we had had. A salvo of guns recalled us, and my strange comrade, changeable in mood as the winds that dimpled the harbor water, was all for seeing the sights of the town. I pointed out the great ships of the harbor, many of which I knew by name, and informed her that even here we could see much of interest.

9

Instantly she cried out on that. " Ships! " she said scornfully. " I wish I might never see another. They are beautiful to look on, I grant you, at this distance, but frivolous, evil-smelling things to encounter closer. I would I might never see a ship again," she repeated, and then a sigh it was hard to hear rent her. " Although I would see Londontown," she ended wistfully. Her small mouth quivered, and I was in haste to take her hand and run with her through the lane to Cornhill. There we found the gallants returning from the Assembly, and she must take her place on a horse block and watch them go by, insisting I come up beside her and see all that she saw — for Aaron, she said. But to me that seemed scarcely fitting, although I at last gave in, with many misgivings as to where this day would lead me, both with Mistress Merrie and with His Excellency, Governor Shirley, should he discover me.

Thus it was I saw many a fine figure and I bethought me that, arriving at their age, I would like to have such a wonder of velvet and fine lace and linen cloth myself. Then I remembered that under Mistress Merrie's tutelage I was fast becoming a simple Puritan and must close my ears to such extravagances.

There too I caught my first glimpse of Master Pepperrell, a great merchant of Maine, my little maid knowing him also, since he was a man much with the governor. I liked his hobnobbing with the English governor and holding fast on occasion to his sober suit of homespun, such clothes seeming more fitting for a well-to-do colonist.

I thought his was a face to trust, little knowing that I would be but a few months older when I myself would be putting my whole life in his hands.

My little maid kept me well acquainted with the name of each officer, for already she had learned the governor's guests by heart, and here and there one catching sight of her upturned face, framed in its white-edged bonnet, gave her recognizance. She returned it with great dignity, the while my heart had more misgivings still concerning this day's doings. When the governor passed I was like to slide down and bury myself in the crowd which had gathered, except for very shame in face of my companion. But the governor's countenance was set as he passed, and he looked neither to right nor left, as, of course, befitted the dignity of his office.

At last, well knowing it was high time I myself reached home, we slipped through a cross lane and came to the Province House. My comrade, holding tight to my hand, drew me within the gates. Though loath to follow, I could not help thinking that this would be news to tell Aaron. So we walked up under the trees, to the red-brick house with its cupola. We climbed the long stair to its great double doors.

But when I would have left her there she started to hold me back, then as suddenly desisted. " Very well, Aaron's brother," she pouted, " perhaps it were as well you returned home."

At which I reminded her, " I have a very good name of my own, mistress."

She made a grimace. " Is it so? " she said teasingly. " I thought you were but Aaron's brother."

" My name is Eben Chadwick St. Jean de Gervais," I said proudly.

Instantly my little maid's head came up angrily. " You are a Frenchman! "

" Even so," I said standing as tall as I could and glancing down at my silver shoe buckles, " it is a name held in some esteem by the Puritans of Bostontown. And I am a Puritan too on my mother's side." I knew that the English and the French were by way of being enemies most of the time, and most certainly were at war now if all reports were true. I could not but understand her anger.

At that my little maid's face smoothed out. " That you are most truly," she mocked, then added: " My name is Antoinette Cyr Stuart. It is Scotch. And I would have you know," she sighed softly, " it is a name not held in much esteem among the English at present."

And, not thinking, I said the Scotch were a hard race. Feathertale John had always told me so. My little maid instantly grew furiously angry again. She cried, " They are a finer race than the English, and the English are finer than the Puritans, and the Puritans are finer than the French, and now where do you find yourself? "

She being a woman and I a lad just entering manhood, and not being able to fight her, I said, " I find myself just on the point of bidding you adieu, Mistress Antoinette Cyr Stuart." And I wished her a very good afternoon.

At this her small face must needs crinkle up again. " Go then, Aaron's brother," she said with great dignity, " go, and mayhap I will stand here all night, not being of a size big enough to reach the great knocker."

Now this I doubted, for in spite of her slenderness that made her look very small indeed she was of a height equal to my own. I came back instantly and was immediately rewarded by a smile so sweet I must forget her seeming unreasonableness. I stood before the great doors and raised my hand, wishing that I might have a riding crop in hand to use as I had seen the gallants do. I beat a rat-tat on the great lion's head which was the knocker. At once the door swung open. A man in gold braid and silk stockings looked sternly at my little maid, and frowned openly at me.

" I did not know you were from home, mistress," he said reprovingly. My companion tossed her head and said very distinctly, " There is no need that you should, Digby, my lady not needing me this morning."

Now all the while her hand was close clasped in mine, so that I needs must follow her into the great hall with its winding stairway of which I had heard much and never hoped to see. She took me at once into a large room on the right. There was a huge fire burning there. I saw little furniture but many portraits. A single deep divan faced the fire, and two ladies in flounced silks, seated thereon, looked around as we entered.

" Why, Antoinette! " one exclaimed, and her voice was like the trickle of the little brook in the Pond Lane. " What is this? Were you abroad? "

I made sure that the first of my hours of reckoning on this day's doings was speedily come upon me.

Mistress Antoinette curtsied unabashed. " It is a case for congratulation, surely, my good Aunt Margaret. I went out to see the great sights and was lost, and this lad has brought me home, and if

he had not, it is wonder what would have happened to me, for —
I have been attacked."

At this I wondered if my comrade was as innocent as she seemed,
for at once both ladies forgot her shocking conduct in hearing of
her adventure. They threw up their hands and demanded immediate satisfaction of their curiosity. My Lady Shirley murmured:
" These young people of today! They are so very venturesome."

Then both must know what had happened. Mistress Antoinette
cast down her eyes and told them how the dark ruffian had demanded her purse, but she did not tell them that she had given
him its contents. They, seeing it still in her hands, as she held it up
to them, instantly thought that I had had something to do with her
retaining it. Unused as I was to their quick chatter, and fearing to
be thought rude, it was not possible for me to do more than deny
any part in it, which they only took for proper modesty on my
part. In spite of the fact that I knew I was allowing a false impres-
sion to get abroad, I could not correct it.

My puzzlement was interrupted by My Lady Shirley's guest, a
sweet-faced woman with hair so white I suspected it was powdered,
and features of great beauty. " And what is your name, lad? " she
asked me.

Then, though I was plainly clad in homespun of Mistress Merrie's own making, I bethought me of the silver shoe buckles which
had belonged to my father, the Captain St. Jean de Gervais, and I,
sweeping off my wide hat, bowed low as I had seen the gallants
do, and said, " I am Eben Chadwick St. Jean de Gervais, ma'am,
an' it pleasure you."

Whereupon my lady's guest cried: " I was sure of it! Your mother,
lad, was Charity Chadwick and your father is commander of *The
Golden Lily*, and even now at sea. I knew them both very well,
when I used to live here in Bostontown before you were born."

I, all eagerness, must hear more of my mother. My Lady Shirley,
having things to attend to, most kindly left us alone, and, sitting
there in the firelight, her guest told me much of my mother with
whom she had gone to school.

Meantime, I found my eyes resting on the great blue tiles of

13

the fireplace where was depicted many a tale of Bible times, so that ever afterward the picture of my mother seemed bound up in the picture of David and Goliath, for that especial tile fixed itself on my memory. As for Mistress Antoinette, she sat very still and seemed as interested as I was.

When, at last, I wakened to the fact that it was more than time I was on my way home, I said good-by to the gracious lady, and Mistress Antoinette took me into the great hall. Here we found the governor and many of his staff gathered. Mistress Antoinette must needs introduce me to the great William Shirley, whereupon I made again my great bow, but with less success this time, for it seemed to me I could hear a trickle of laughter somewhere, and I at once became the center of all attention, greatly to my own confusion.

" Who is this? " the governor demanded.

Mistress Antoinette made ready answer: " It is Master Eben Chadwick St. Jean de Gervais, son of the Huguenot Captain St. Jean de Gervais, master of *The Golden Lily,* but on his mother's side, a very proper Puritan. He is to take me to the docks, for I would see the new frigate but lately anchored in the stream."

I, knowing nothing of the plan, but mindful of her great aversion to the ships, was thrown into even greater confusion.

" Oh, ho! " said the governor, " and what does my good wife say to this? "

Mistress Antoinette, smiling sweetly, said: " Indeed, sir, she knows nothing of it. I had hopes she would hear it first from you."

Whereat everybody laughed and someone said: " By my faith! A very proper witch."

Good Lady Shirley, overhearing it all from the grand stairway, said, " O Will, do you think it is wise? "

The governor, looking at me slyly, said: " It is probably most monstrous folly, but it is good politics too. The child will fall into no harm. Of that I am assured. These Huguenots are most trustworthy."

Then did I feel most immeasurably proud, but My Lady Shirley was like to take the wind out of my sails, for she said quickly: " But,

14

Antoinette, have you forgotten, dear? Tomorrow, we go to Roxbury."

Then did Mistress Antoinette lift a frowning face which cleared
almost immediately. "To be sure!" she answered and added
quickly, "We will have to make it tomorrow week." At that the
officers seemed much amused again.

So Mistress Antoinette, whispering to me, "Three of the clock,
Eben, tomorrow week — tell Aaron," sent me on my way, and I
was amazed to find it was long past the time I had set for returning.
And seventeen years old though I was, I had sudden fear of what
Mistress Merrie would say to me for my desertion of Aaron. I
stumbled over the cobbles as fast as the dark would allow me.

2: A Summons from a Fair One

On leaving the Province House, I slipped into Milk Street
and down the Long Lane to Crooked Alley where Mistress Merrie
had her modest dwelling. My shoes made noise on the cobbles as
I could have wished they did not, for the lanes and the highways
of Bostontown were none too safe after dark. Even Mistress Antoinette, I recalled, had been importuned in broad daylight. But
greater than danger from chance thieves was danger from the press
gangs of the British navy which now and then roved the thorough-
fares. For, while I had great desire to go to sea as a free man, I had
little taste for the fate accorded to those "impressed." But on this
occasion at least I came safely to my own dwelling.

Hardly had I shut the door when Mistress Merrie — she being
very different from her name — fell upon me, scolding me long
and terrible severely for my desertion of Aaron, and telling me of
the red fire which would most surely consume one who acted as
I had. As though I were a twelve-year-old I was sent to my chores
supperless, and then ordered to bed. I did not mind the going to

bed, for I was much wearied with the excitements of the day, but it was hard to go without seeing Aaron when my head was so brimming with the adventures I had been through.

I managed to bespeak him, nonetheless. I whispered I had had a marvelous time and would forget nothing before morning, which I fervently hoped would be true.

Aaron whispered back: " I can wait, Eben. I mind not, so long as I know there is something interesting to tell on the morrow. 'Tis terrible wearisome lying here with nothing to think about."

Then did I know that although I had disobeyed Mistress Merrie and had likely put my soul in torment for it, still much more would I do for my brother who had not the strength to do aught for himself but must lie helpless days on end. I often thought that if only I could make Aaron eat, his strength would come back to him, but no rich broth or snowy curd seemed like to tempt him.

Next morning I was very busy. Mistress Merrie was more than ordinary needful of many things. There was the feeding of the chickens, and I must turn the churn, a wearisome task, for never was butter so long in the making. Then must the butter be taken to her various customers. This I did not mind. It took me out where I could see the ships in the harbor, and no task was heavy which led me thither, for ever I would be a sea captain like my father. Mistress Merrie, unfortunately, was not of the same mind, and threatened that I should be bound out to a shoemaker immediately, which I did not think my father, master of *The Golden Lily,* would approve, but being gone on such long voyages he could not be much help to me. This was my great fear.

All morning I wondered what I was to do about that afternoon a week hence when I was bidden to the Province House. I could not think that Mistress Merrie would believe me were I to tell her that I, Eben Chadwick St. Jean de Gervais, simplest of the colonists, had been commanded to the governor's house to escort his guest to the docks. It seemed that I had surely dreamed the whole incident.

But soon I had evidence of the forethought of my little maid. For just as I was sitting at the bare kitchen table with my bowl of porridge there came a great rat-tat at the door. Mistress Merrie, all excitement, took time to put on her best bonnet and a new apron. When she opened the door there stood a manservant in livery of His Excellency, Governor Shirley, and very impatient methought he was.

"Is there one by name of Eben Chadwick St. Jean de Gervais abiding in this house?" he demanded.

Instantly I made answer, but Mistress Merrie frowned me down and would conduct the interview in her own way. So she made a curtsy and said there was.

"Then," said the courier, and I thought he was not overly proud of his errand, "I am to command him to appear at the Province House at three of the clock on this day week, the governor having need of him."

Mistress Merrie, looking much puzzled, said: "Very good. I will see that he comes, although I understand nothing of it. I hope he has not been up to a mischief."

The courier, disdaining to answer, rode away.

Then Mistress Merrie, turning on me, demanded what I had done.

Rather confusedly, at first, I made answer that during my wanderings I had rendered some small service to the governor's ward. Belike she would wish to thank me for it.

Mistress Merrie frowned deeply and said: "I like not the whole proceeding. Still an order from the governor is an order from the king. I suppose you will have to comply with it." She then went soberly about her business, and at last I was free to fly to Aaron.

I found him hard at work on the map of the great fortress at Louisbourg. The peninsula of Nova Scotia, just to the north of us, was in English hands, but the Island of Cape Breton, close adjoining, had been given to the French king by treaty, and here they had built a great fortress, designed by no less an engineer than the famous Parisian, Vauban. It was said to have cost 30,000,000 livres.

Fantastic tales were told of its strength and the wonder of its embattlements, of its imposing buildings and secret passages.

Aaron was making the map from information I had gathered, from time to time, from the sailors who frequented Feathertale John's. Many of them had traded there. Some had even been hired on the building of it. It was said the Normandy stone which France had sent out for the façades and the erection of the gates was of the gleaming whiteness of alabaster.

Louisbourg was an important base. From it the French were becoming daily a great menace to the shipping of New England. Already the privateer Morpain had sallied out of it and seized some New England merchantmen and sloops, whereby the astute argued that England and France must be at war. But no notice to that effect having come to the colonies, the men of New England were restrained from retaliating. It was a hard situation for our side, and I had great sympathy for them. I had thought for long that such negligence on the part of the crown was impossible, and that the French were spreading the rumor of war to cover their own misdeeds. But I was fast beginning to think it must be so and that the French and English were indeed at war.

Aaron had started the map a year previous, before my father sailed. He was greatly interested in the project. "Learn all that you can, my lads, about everything," my father had exhorted us. "In some emergency of life, I do not doubt, you will have sudden need for just such knowledge. In my own life I have frequently noted it."

But now Aaron swept everything aside to make place for me on the bed beside him.

"When our father returns in *The Golden Lily*," he cried, "Mistress Merrie will no longer keep us apart. We will have a great house then and slaves of our own, and I will be of an age to be the master myself when he sails abroad again."

Aaron was like this, always very brave to undertake a thing but finding it difficult to endure. Wherefore I think he found his illness more difficult than most.

I had my lantern with me and as I talked I polished its glass windows diligently. It was not long until Aaron offered to help, and I let him take his turn at it, thinking it was good for him to do some small task. I found it strangely enjoyable myself to talk with idle hands. For Mistress Merrie chid me most unmercifully whenever she saw me at rest, thinking it sin to let the hours pass without some gainful toil.

As I told him the tale, Aaron's eyes shone brightly. He asked many questions concerning my little maid and seemed much set up that she should be interested in him.

Then I, thinking to pleasure him, told him that Mistress Antoinette would surely wish to come and see him.

At that Aaron grew all in a panic.

" You are not to do it," he cried. " I will not see her. What manner of man would she think me, forced to lie here all my days? "

" Indeed," I said without thinking, " she would find it vastly entertaining to talk with you."

But Aaron cried out: " She would! She would! It would seem monstrous amusing to her, no doubt, that I should have my meals brought to me like a small child. You are not to bring her. I will not see her."

Then I told him how sweet she was, and how lovely to look at, her face being like the sea, never the same two minutes running.

Whereupon Aaron cried out: " I will not see her. I do not want to hear more of her. Stop it at once! " And with that he flung the lantern crashing against the opposite wall. Then he buried his face in the pillow and sulked like an eight-year-old. And he a lad passing to manhood.

I was sore puzzled what to do. Retrieving the lantern, I found to my consternation it was much injured. The door had been quite torn off. I did not know what Mistress Merrie would say to it, but I bethought me that it would have to be mended before dark. I would not dare enter the dusky barn without it; nor would I go in with an open candle, so great was the danger of fire in our small town, many having lost their barns and sheds and even their very houses in like manner.

Then I bethought me that I could take it to Feathertale John's and maybe mend it myself without cost of any kind, which would please Mistress Merrie.

" Go away! Go away! " Aaron was demanding. I knew he was ashamed that I should see him thus weakly giving way. So with a sore heart I gathered up the map and placed it neatly to his hand, hoping the sight of it might take his mind off his own troubles. Then I slipped away. I sought Mistress Merrie and explained to her that I had had a small accident to my lantern and I would like to go to Feathertale John's before night and have it mended. To my surprise Mistress Merrie seemed very anxious I should be gone at once.

" I have but this minute been speaking to a neighbor," she said, " and it would seem that the French privateers have captured two more of our vessels. It must be that England and France are at war. See, Eben, if there is news there of *The Golden Lily* — when she may be expected."

I could not help smiling at her anxiety. The ships taken by the French had been for the most part small merchantmen, not of a size or speed to compare with *The Golden Lily,* which was in effect almost an East Indiaman. I knew that Mistress Merrie's small savings were all invested in her, but it amused me that she should feel anxiety for my father's great ship. I felt quite sure that Captain St. Jean de Gervais would not let his fine ship be captured by such as they, even should the great Morpain himself give chase. Both he and his ship were a match for any French privateer. Besides, I doubted that either of them would be in these waters for many a long day.

3: Feathertale John's Shop

Feathertale's shop was in the Winan Shipyard. To reach his loft one must wend one's way between huge stacks of lumber, and cradles of ships, and men working happily in the open sunshine. Near by too were several lots of mast trees, fir and pine, bearing about them the odors of their native forest. I could not but pause here and admire their monstrous length and think of them — where they were going and what they would see. For the masts were intended for the tall English men-of-war. They must be very strong to stand up in battle, so that a ship when in action might maneuver quickly, unhampered by broken spars and cluttered decks.

While they fascinated me, they made me thoughtful too. The mast trees were a great source of anger to the colonists. It seemed that, having conquered the land, they should be permitted to cut the trees thereon; that all these should belong to the crown or — as so often happened — the crown's unworthy agent was a source of continual discontent. So much I had gathered in the talk at Feathertale John's. And I felt sorry that my little maid's father should be engaged in a task so distasteful to most of the New England men.

Feathertale's shop stood at the very edge of the water and up a ladderlike flight of stairs. It was a great room of such size that the biggest sail might be spread flat on the floor. Its oak floor was polished by much walking and the particles of wax which drifted abroad when Feathertale smoothed his thread. The loft had several features of interest to me. Its huge rafters were not unlike the cradles of the ships I saw in building outside. On each side were windows. On the sea side, however, was a big door filled with a window of many panes. In summer Feathertale was accustomed to swing it wide. Through the opening shone the blue of the harbor and the white sails of the lateens and sloops, the tangle of masts of the West Indiamen with their golden figureheads facing into the breeze. Always out of the great opening was movement, from the ships to the shore and back again, the whale boats and skiffs bringing strange people and stranger cargoes. Now and then the boats would hold nought but bundles of brown ausnaburg of all shapes and sizes with tall characters painted on them in red or black, for ever some vessel was unloading in the stream because of haste or lack of dock space. Winter or summer, Feathertale's window door had a great fascination for me, for always it seemed to bring the outdoors indoors in a way that filled me with a sense of strange magic.

All down one side of the shop were bolts of duck and canvas.

Near Feathertale's seat in the doorway to the sea were several balls of heavy twine and a trough for needles. There were no chairs in the room and no benches, save only Feathertale's, which was long and low. In his bench was a drawer. It always interested me to watch Feathertale stooping down between his knees to pull out the drawer and abstract therefrom a long piratical-looking knife with which he cut his thread. There were, however, in the place several coils of rope on which one might rest luxuriously. One in especial was much in request, having in its midst an old anchor which made an excellent back. There were ship's lanterns and ratlines and royals suspended from the dim rafters.

Perhaps the spot which held my attention most was in the middle of the side wall. There a massive wooden figurehead, in form of a woman, loomed out of the shadows. I thought of all she had seen in the days she had sailed the seven seas.

It held great fascination for me for yet another reason. On the day he had sailed away, the Captain St. Jean de Gervais, on a visit to Feathertale, had paused before it. Drawing my attention to the thing, he had placed two fingers on the eyeballs of the woman, releasing thereby a hidden spring, cleverly concealed inside. Immediately, a whole section of the left side swung out, showing a secret recess.

And I, all filled with the wonder of it, found my father looking soberly down at me. " Ah, Eben," he murmured, " a woman who can hide things in her heart is a great thing in a man's life. For to be able to store a thing in the heart of another is often to heal one's own hurt. Your mother was such a one. I have missed her sorely."

Then when I had cried out on the ingenuity of the thing, my father had smiled at me, " 'Tis not the only secret the old body hides, but one were enough for a lad of your years." Somehow it had been a moment of intimacy between us I loved to recall.

Feathertale's shop held still other things. In one corner was even an eighteen-pounder of French design, and happy indeed was I when some gunner from the king's navy was present and would explain to me its workings while running his hands caressingly along its cold sides.

On nails along the wall was an array of twelve earthen mugs bearing strange pictures. It was Feathertale's custom to allow the men of the yard to come here with their rum and drink from his mugs on occasion, the whiles he carried on his trade. In this way he gathered much information of all that was happening in the great world across the seas.

Now I have not mentioned the forge which Feathertale had in the back of his shop, for unless it were lit one might well miss it in the shadows of the "back shop" as he called it. Feathertale himself did no forging, but the tools hung neatly to one side, the anvil was ready, so that a chance visitor from the ships could do an odd job for himself at the old hearth.

I understood from Feathertale that the forge was there when he came, and certainly he found it handy himself for the occasional cup of tea he was forever brewing himself and for the light and warmth it afforded the loft. Often I have lain flat on my back on the floor, fascinated by the grotesque shadows which played hither and yon among the rafters.

It was so now, and I judged that Feathertale had but just sought refreshment at the forge. Then I noticed that he was sewing a small patch on a moonraker and would soon be through. Belike he was fixing the sail for a ship at that moment ready to embark, so I decided to wait to ask him about my lantern until he should be more interested in my presence.

There were several figures in the shop when I entered, and two men sat talking opposite Feathertale. Their weather-beaten faces and necks looked like old wood in the red light. I recognized one as Asa — I knew no other name for him. He was an accountant in one of the great warehouses on the water front, a kindly man who had more than once brought me an odd gift. The other was Adam Peddling, master of a small fishing vessel. Near the great window, sitting as immobile as the figurehead, I espied Thundercloud, an Indian whom I understood was in confidence of His Excellency, Governor Shirley. He spent many an odd hour in and about Feathertale's shop. I had never heard him take part in any conversation, but his eyes seemed to miss nothing in the long room, and now and then he would punctuate the talk with a loud grunt. Whether it signified approval or distaste I could never be sure.

" 'Tis a great fortress they have in Louisbourgtown," Adam was saying.

" Aye," Asa responded, " I have been inside of it."

It seemed to me that all within the shop, even Thundercloud, leaned eagerly forward. I myself felt a sudden thrill of interest, as never failed whenever the subject was mentioned. Tales of the huge fortress were many and seemingly fantastic. Here was a man of sober sense who had been in Cape Breton and had actually seen that whereof he spoke.

" Is it as strong as they say? " Adam demanded.

" It cannot be taken." As if to set finality to his remark, Asa finished his draught in one long pull.

" Is it so? " Adam murmured wonderingly.

" What would you? " Asa continued. " Its walls alone are thirty feet in thickness. And it faces the harbor where no ship may enter unwanted because of the Island Battery bristling with thirty cannon and seven swivels, twenty-eight-pounders all. It is set squarely in the harbor mouth. On the shore opposite the mouth is the Grand Battery with its twenty-eight guns, all forty-two-pounders. Set as it is on a rising slope from the water's edge, the back wall of the fortress commands the harbor also, having six bastions and three with platforms for one hundred forty-eight cannon and six mortars. Below the rampart is a moat eighty feet wide running down into the sea itself. From the top of the moat on the far side the land drops sharply away into an impassable morass. Not only that, but the whole coast is so bleak and wave-thrashed that, save for this one harbor, no boat of any size may land in many miles."

" But the town," insisted Adam. " I should think the town might be taken."

Asa shook his head. " The fortress cradles the town. The ramparts line the water's edge and climb the hill and surround the town. 'Tis in all a quaint place with a set of bells prettier than any in Bostontown."

24

"I should like to hear the bells," I said, having heard that they were the sweetest outside of France itself.

Asa nodded. "At sunset the waters of the Chapeau Rouge are copper-gold, and the spires of the hospital and the citadel pierce the sky like golden rapiers, and the bells of St. Louis, St. Jean, and St. Antoine-Marie ring sweetly across the waters. It is not a thing to forget."

"They tell me," said Feathertale, "the French have built into the town just thirteen streets."

"'Tis so," Asa made answer. "Some there may be that think it a bad omen. But I — I would wish nothing gayer than its little lanes. I think the flowers in the governor's garden are brighter than any I have ever seen. 'Tis said it is due to the fog."

"They say the French are planning to come down upon us from the Lake Champlain region in great force in the spring." Now I knew that this rumor was rife and was matter of great concern to those who were responsible for the safety of the colonies. I listened more eagerly than ever. "Heard you aught of that when you were there?" Adam Peddling continued.

"Aye," said Asa. "There is no doubt they are planning it. And when word comes in that it is started, prepare ye here in Boston-town for a bombardment from the sea. That also is part of what is to happen."

Now Feathertale paused in his moistening of the thread which he was running through his lips. "These French of the New World fight only little battles. It will not happen."

"Listen," in his eagerness Asa leaned forward. "It is not a thing to go to sleep over. The fishing around Cape Breton is worth millions of kentals a year. It comes for the dipping in of a net. Think you France is going to let that go to the adventuring New Englanders who continually invade her waters?"

"But this Louisbourg," said Feathertale. "They tell me there is nought there but a bunch of paid Swiss mercenaries, a disloyal guard under a drunken governor, Du Quesnel."

Asa frowned. "It is a thing I cannot understand. A fortress that could withstand a king's navy, and within a drunken, disloyal, mutinous garrison."

Others had dropped in, and I noticed their interest in the discussion, many punctuating a sentence end with a loud " Aye! Aye! " of agreement.

" 'Tis maybe where the French are crafty," said Adam. " When the spring comes you may well see they sing a different tune. Louisbourg, I have heard, needs not five hundred loyal men to hold it. It is drenched in fog most of the year. When the ice moves off next spring, you will see, France will land a loyal garrison. 'Tis said a great fleet is even now gathering along her shores for conquest of the New World. The fleur-de-lis, it is said, is to fly over all the colonies."

" Where heard you that? " Feathertale demanded sharply.

Adam sucked in his lips and regarded the empty tankard. " 'Tis what Randy O'Hara was preaching from the poop of the *Good Intent,* only this morning."

Thundercloud gave one of his sudden and unexpected grunts. And, as if it marked the end of something, silence descended upon the gathered company.

Now this Captain O'Hara was not altogether a stranger to me, although he was a comparative newcomer amongst us; but I had conceived for him a profound dislike.

On each occasion when I had been where he was I had heard his voice before I had been aware of his presence, and it had made me vaguely uneasy. Having been warned many times by Aaron that I was possessed of an impetuous tongue which would, sooner or later, most surely get me into trouble, I had great fear of talking where I did not know my company. The sudden interpolation of the strange voice of Captain O'Hara, when I had thought no stranger present, confused and upset me. I felt a man owed it to his fellows to enter among them boldly, and not insinuate himself as if by stealth into their company, as Captain O'Hara seemed addicted to doing.

But perhaps his quietness of approach was at the root of his great interest for us, for when he did talk he almost always informed us of some event of great interest several hours in advance of its publication from official sources. I did not doubt that his habit of slipping in and out of gatherings gave him access to much knowledge he would not otherwise have had, and to which he was in no way entitled.

Perhaps, however, there was another reason for my dislike of him. He was becoming a bone of contention between Aaron and me. Always when I related some choice piece of news, Aaron demanded: " But what manner of man is this Captain O'Hara, Eben? Is he tall or short, fine appearing or ill? What does he look like? " And all I could reply was, " He is dark and stooped and possessed of a wooden hand," which did not seem to satisfy the inquisitive Aaron at all.

Only recently I had come to the conclusion that this same wooden hand was perhaps responsible for my seeming lack of perception in regard to his physical appearance. For one never was aware of his presence until he talked, and he never talked without waving his great wooden hand aloft, whereupon I was so completely fascinated by its curious weaving gyrations that I could see nothing else of him. After each such encounter I promised myself I would not allow myself to be distracted by it again, but each time was exactly like the last. There was something so large and menacing about its gestures that one found oneself ever on the alert for its next move. I strongly suspected it affected us all alike.

I often wondered why, having need of such an appendage, he had chosen such a giant-sized, spread-eagled model, but one day I came upon him winding a line over his elbow and through the stiff fingers and I realized it had its uses.

I must admit also that he could be, on occasion, an entertaining talker. I had heard him questioned twice on the cause of his injury, and had been somewhat startled to hear him relate a different version of the accident on each interrogation, but both explanations, I had to admit, were equally diverting. I could not but admire his courage in thus making a mock of his deficiency. For the rest, he was supposed to be the master of a ship and as such a man of authority amongst us. My truant thoughts were suddenly recalled by Asa's voice. It rang out clearly in the still room:

"I tell you it will not be long until you hear the guns of the Lilies in Bostontown."

"Never!" I cried fiercely.

The men looked up surprised and then, seeing it was but a youth speaking, laughed aloud. Their merriment stung, and a strange sailor's remark did not improve my temper. "That's it, laddie. But don't look for the crown to do anything about it. 'Tis my opinion the English are weary of the colonies and would as soon France took them in exchange for some good louis d'or."

Now I had borne much that day from Aaron, and this thought that we were to be sold by the crown like the black slaves advertised in *The Boston News-Letter* — "For sale, an able-bodied slave and a grate for coals" — fired me anew. "It is not true," I shouted. "When my father returns in *The Golden Lily* he will show you what a New England privateer can do to the papists of the fortress. He will not wait for England's help. He is a man himself."

Now in referring to the defenders of the fortress as papists I was but quoting a term used far and wide in Bostontown, but I thought Feathertale John threw me an odd look. And I noted that no man made answer, but all stared at me so intently I had a strange, creepy feeling down my back. At the same moment a shadow rose menacingly before me on the ceiling. I whipped around, determined to see what manner of thing was behind me. Silhouetted against the red forge fire and looking taller than ordinary was Captain O'Hara, his wooden hand raised angrily above him. Of a sudden I recalled hearing that Captain O'Hara was by way of being a papist himself. I was instantly sorry I had used the term, for even my father, the Huguenot, believed that, if we were to have lasting peace in the New World, the freedom to worship where and when we pleased should apply to one and all alike.

I was treated now to the taunting cackle I had heard Captain O'Hara use before on the rare occasions when he had allowed himself to be stirred to anger. It always sent shivers down my spine.

28

" *The Golden Lily* is it that is to teach us to be men? Much good it or its master will do anyone now. He and his ship are gone to Davy Jones's locker, prey of the great Morpain."

His hand continued to wave excitedly, and an army of shadows capered sinisterly over the raftered roof.

Now this Morpain was one of the most daring of the privateers operating out of Louisbourg, proof, we felt sure, that a state of war existed between the French and the English, and that the French had knowledge of it though we had not, as Dogood had suggested. Then a dreadful thought possessed me: it might well be that my father was nearer home than we had thought.

Nevertheless, I saw fit to deny his remark quite stoutly.

" It's a lie! " I cried and looked at Feathertale. He made no answer.

Captain O'Hara's eyes took in the whole assemblage. " Cease your idle boasting, all of you," he warned. " Morpain is cleverer than any of you. And the fortress at Louisbourg is untakable. 'Tis not a place to pit puny strength. The crown is wise to that! "

Now suddenly a great fury possessed me. " We are not children. We do not need the crown's permission to defend ourselves. If I were a man I'd take them both." And then the full significance of what Morpain had already done to me struck me sharp as a blow. " O Feathertale! " I cried. " It is not true. Tell me it is not true and my father will still come back."

Feathertale looked at me sadly. Of a sudden he turned on Captain O'Hara with a fury that matched my own. " Cease your baiting of the lad. Can you not see what it means to him? "

Captain O'Hara made no answer, but with a quiet, " Come on, lads," strode to the stair well. They followed as if at the command of a master; somehow their going was the hardest part of all. They went as men leaving a new bier. They went with bent heads in absolute silence. It was true. I knew then it was true.

And when from the foot of the stair Captain O'Hara's cackling laughter rose like a last amen, I flung myself down, shaken by an emotion which was terrible. I had no inclination to cry. My eyes were hot and dry. Still great sobs shook me from head to foot, and seemed to rack my body and spirit. I could not bear to think that I should never see my father again.

Then Feathertale, to divert my attention no doubt, said, " What have we here, Eben? " and pointed to the lantern I was still clutching. Mutely I surrendered it, and Feathertale without a word took it to the forge and neatly mended it, a feat I would not have thought him capable of. Later he put it back into my hands. " There, there, lad," he murmured. " I would *The Golden Lily* could be made whole again as easy as this lantern. Hasten home with you before Mistress Merrie hears the news from outside. It will be a hard blow for her."

" 'Tis possible she knows a'ready," I informed him, still shaking. " I think now she had heard rumors of disaster and sent me down to find out the truth of what she heard."

" Poor body! Poor body! " said Feathertale. " We have both lost a great friend this day." Then with a blaze of anger, he added: " If England's men-of-war had been in these waters, this would not have happened. Why do we pay such taxes, if we are not to be given protection? "

It was the second time that day that Feathertale had surprised me. I realized then how completely moved by the event he had been, for Feathertale was ever a stanch royalist.

I took the lantern from Feathertale's kindly hand and stumbled off home, much confused as to how I should break the news to Mistress Merrie. But I need not have worried, for my face was ample messenger. On sight of me she flung her apron over her head and let out a loud wail, and the spectacle of this stern woman so broken up shook me anew. A sense of catastrophe overwhelmed me afresh. I thought at first she was but mourning her money until I caught a chance word or two. " He was a good man. A fine man. There is not his like left in Boston-town."

Then Aaron must needs be told. To my surprise he showed no grief, only a great abiding anger. " This brute, Morpain," he shouted with flashing eyes, " must be taken along with their mighty fortress. I too will become Captain St. Jean de Gervais someday.

I will avenge my father's death. You will see, Eben. I will grow strong now."

And it is always strange to me to think that from that day Aaron did seem to grow stronger. Much of it, I know now, was due to Mistress Antoinette and her odd wisdom, but always afterward I was sure the change began with this moment.

The loss of Mistress Merrie's wage made it imperative that I get work soon, for much of my father's means was invested in the ship he sailed in. There was now no talk of apprenticing me to a shoe-maker, for which I was most heartily glad. As an apprentice I could not hope to earn for some time.

Now it happened that I was ever a wizard at figures, and it was Mistress Merrie's thought that I should find a place in some of the great countinghouses on the docks. I was not averse to the change, for the chores about the place irked me considerably, and always I felt I could do them in half the time if only Mistress Merrie would permit me to do them in my own way and not under her direction. When I found my place in the countinghouse I would have to do these things long before even Mistress Merrie had begun her duties for the day.

My father, it so happened, though turned captain, was determined that his sons should lose no whit of the knowledge he had himself acquired from a scholarly father. He had been at much pains to see to it that I wrote a fine, legible hand, and this with my adeptness at figures would undoubtedly secure me a good place.

It seemed to me that Dogood's remarks when she had knowledge of my sorrow were entirely in keeping with her character. She looked at me shrewdly. "You have had trouble, Eben," she said. Then she frowned darkly. "It is thus we will all go. If I were a man, I would show the crown whither it was riding."

At the same time I had ample proof of the understanding of my little maid, for, long before the week was up and I could see her, she had heard of the matter. A little note was delivered into my hands.

"Do not weep, Eben," she had penned in a large, fine hand. "I

31

doubt not your father, the good Captain St. Jean de Gervais, is much nearer than we think. Watch, Eben, that you do nothing of which he would not fully approve. Antoinette."

Somehow it turned my thought of my father from a bitter mourning into an endeavor to do all things as he would have me do them and, I doubt not, helped me much over this hard period.

4 : Of the Adventure That Befell Me on the Water Front

It was with some perturbation of heart that I entered the countinghouse of Master William Pepperrell, of Maine, albeit Mistress Merrie accompanied me. His proper title was Colonel William Pepperrell, for he was an officer in the Maine Militia, but I preferred to call him by the title that Feathertale John always used — Master William, or Master William Pepperrell — as more indicative of the intimate regard in which he was held by all who knew him.

His first words were such as to set me at my ease. And always afterward I thought what a wise man he was so to secure the allegiance of his workers from the very first moment.

Getting hastily to his feet, he greeted Mistress Merrie and made her sit beside his great desk. Then, turning to me, he said kindly: " I hear, Master Eben, you would like to work for me. It would give me great pleasure to have a son of the Captain St. Jean de Gervais in my employ. He was a rare man of great fineness of heart."

I soon learned that Master Pepperrell, besides being a most upright man, had great knowledge of how to draw others toward him.

Having discovered that I wrote a fine, legible hand, he seemed to think I had all the qualifications necessary and should be hired at once. The terms of my contract seemed to me very fair indeed. I was to work only on such days as cargo was coming or going, but, inasmuch as on such occasions my labors would be long and arduous, I was to be paid as if I had worked all my time.

Now my one regret in going into the new environment had been in the thought that I must now forgo my visit to the Province House, but I had reckoned without Mistress Merrie. Immediately on the contract's being settled, Mistress Merrie informed Master Pepperrell that there was but one delay to my starting. I had been commanded to appear at the Province House on Wednesday of the next week and must needs fulfill my obligations. Master Pepperrell smiled slyly at me. He said such an order could not possibly be overlooked and that if I would start at once — they were even then unloading a full cargo — he would permit me to leave even though on that day a ship was going out. Whereupon I had evidence that Mistress Antoinette was indeed a very thorough person, for I could not doubt that she had already informed him of my engagement. I knew that Master Pepperrell was a great friend to His Excellency, the Governor, and a regular frequenter of the Province House. At once I was much relieved. I had counted much on seeing her so soon again.

Mistress Merrie now took her departure, and I found that my duties were to begin at once.

Master Pepperrell himself took me through a wide, low door into the biggest roofed-in place I had ever been in. Far ahead as a forest glade it stretched, dimly lighted and filled with elusive shapes and bundles and even more elusive odors.

The merchandise was piled high on low trestles to keep it off the floor. Now and then, down an aisle, we got a glimpse of a window, but so dirty was it, so incrusted with spiders' webs, that only a dim light filtered through it. I learned later that this was not altogether lack of cleanliness on the part of anyone. Many things in that hoard of miscellaneous merchandise would have been sadly injured if exposed to strong sea light.

"You will soon get to know your way around by the smell," Master Pepperrell informed me. "See what think you is in this lot, Eben." It was evident they were kegs and, sniffing obediently, I said at last, "Molasses, sir."

Master Pepperrell nodded with great satisfaction. " You have a merchant's nose already, Eben. It is half the battle."

A little later he put the same question. " Take your time," he said and seemed more than ever eager I should guess right. " Think what image it brings to your mind." Then I sniffed, and there rose before me a corner of our barn where an old saddle was powdering to pieces from age.

" It is surely leather, sir," I said, " but not hides."

" Bravo! " Master Pepperrell said. " You will make a fine merchant one day, Eben."

Then we moved on through aisles and aisles of merchandise, and once again he paused and pointed to some packages scored all over with strangely painted red characters.

" Someday we will open one of these, Eben. They contain rare ivories. I have much money invested in them which I may never get back, but it is well to bring the rare products of one country to another. We men of the New World are apt to think too well of ourselves until confronted with the fine, rare handiwork of an older people."

Now up to this time I had thought there was no life but the sea, but that day I caught something of the adventure and romance of trading.

Also I was much surprised at the length and breadth of the great warehouse, for among us Master William Pepperrell was accorded to be " the merchant of Maine." I was to learn later that his real property and his fishing business were indeed at Kittery Point, and that this was but a small portion of all that he owned in both places. He was a man of great means.

At last we came to the end of the warehouse, and here Master Pepperrell had no need to question me concerning the contents of the various hogsheads, the rude boxes. Our noses told us they were filled to overflowing with the salt cod.

At the extreme end two patches of sunlight flung on the floor a golden nugget where the great doors opened on a wide expanse of wharfage. And here was continual movement, men going to and fro, heavily laden, for a fishing schooner was even then at the wharf, lightening herself of her cargo. At one corner, high on a stanchion, a bell was hanging. I did not need to be told it was for use in case of fire. We had lost much in Bostontown already by its cruel ravages.

Returning my gaze to the inside of the warehouse, I saw just back of the great doors a long counter with two raised places. Behind each was a high stool and on a sloping shelf in front a huge volume. There, quill in hand, bending over one of the volumes, was Asa. I was glad, indeed, to see one I knew.

" Here, Asa," Master Pepperrell accosted him, " I have brought you a helper, Eben, son of the Captain St. Jean de Gervais. I make no doubt you will find him a willing and honest servant."

Asa greeted me kindly and Master Pepperrell, nodding to us both, swung back into the shadows of the aisles of merchandise.

Asa, having first tried out my ability to write legibly and seeming well satisfied, made haste to show me where I would sit. It was behind the second of the high ledgers, and it was my duty to write down, as he would call out, the kind and quantity of each hogshead of fish that the seamen were bringing ashore. At night we would check opposite each item, he explained, its cost and any duties to be collected on it. Each day the value of the merchandise must appear in the great books.

As the time went by I found Asa unfailingly kind but for the most part silent. There was no doubt but that he thought that as his time was Master Pepperrell's it should not be wasted in idle chatter. At Feathertale John's I had been wont to find him ready to talk aplenty. But, indeed, when next day came and the great *Lady of Glasgow,* a merchantman with a cargo of mixed stuffs, hove into the stream and started to unload, I found there was little time for anything but the exciting business in hand.

Perhaps the need for work at this time was not altogether a hardship, for it took me away from Mistress Merrie and Aaron and their mourning, and threw me into surroundings where I had little time to think my own sad thoughts.

I had been with Master Pepperrell four days and already it seemed I had been there all my life. I left each night with Asa, who was most careful to see that no one was on the wharf when he locked up. I found that a small runway, half hidden under the gable of the warehouse but open on the sea side, formed a separate passageway to the thoroughfare on which the place fronted. At the wharf and at the street end it was cut off by a heavy gate. When a ship lay along the runway, and her crew must needs come and go after dark, Asa was in habit of leaving the front gate unlatched and posting a guard. But on ordinary occasions both gates were kept securely locked at night.

It happened on the fourth night, just as I was leaving, that Asa was called into his master's office. He left me to close and lock the great doors of the warehouse and the wharf gate to the passage, placing in my hands a small key with which I could let myself out of a side door leading onto the passage and then lock it and the front gate behind me. I might return the key the next day.

Much pleased with the trust imposed on me, and eager to do all things as he did them in return for the great kindness he had shown me, I sighted down the runway from the wharf. Nothing was there, so I latched and locked it. Then I entered the warehouse and secured the great doors opening onto the wharf. Not being used to doing it I consumed some time. Also I noted some stray boxes which I thought could be tidier, and it was a matter of some minutes before I started back through the dusky shadows of the silent warehouse.

I was perhaps halfway toward the front of the great place when I seemed to hear a strange sound. It was like a bird song, but such a gay trillip as I had never heard bird sing before. I rushed to one of the murky windows and was quick to note a missing pane in the glass. I did not hear the gay sound again, but I did hear voices in the French tongue. I could get but a word now and then, but there was that in the guarded quality of the tones which led me to believe something untoward was afoot. There was, I noted, frequent repetition of the words " Lady of Glasgow," the ship we had but just unloaded. She was even then in the stream, under orders to sail as soon as she could be reconditioned and loaded with a suitable cargo. When the voices died away, I hurried through the warehouse, hastily locked the great doors, and opened the small door onto the runway, being careful to lock it behind me. I took a last look down the runway toward the wharf, and was surprised to see a shadowy figure so tall I at first took it for Master Pepperrell himself.

I determined to investigate, and as I moved toward it a voice greeted me: " Ah-ha! 'Tis my brave boaster, young Eben." Then I knew it was none other than Captain O'Hara and trepidation filled my heart. Some trick of the light had again made him seem taller than he was.

" Have you taken the great Morpain yet? " he scoffed. " I would not wonder but you might find him concealed in some of those huge chests you are but now stowing away." His voice rose on the last note, ending on the hollow cackle which was to me so fearsome.

" I am about to lock up," I informed him, trying to conceal my feelings with an assumption of dignity, " and I cannot do so as long as you remain here, Captain O'Hara." I endeavored to pass him on the runway, intending to put him between me and the thoroughfare gate. I had hopes I might persuade him toward it. But this Captain O'Hara would not permit, thrusting out a foot most adroitly just in time and was like to have sent me headfirst into the water so close below us. With great difficulty I recovered myself, but it occurred to me then a more evil expression I was not like to see in a month of ships.

" An' if I tell you," he murmured softly, " that I am but waiting for Asa, having matter of importance to discuss with him concerning his master's business, what would you say to that? "

Now I, well aware this might be true, was uncertain what to do, but determined I was that I would not leave him there, when I heard again that strange trillip, like no bird song ever heard in Bostontown. Seemingly Captain O'Hara took no note of it, perhaps because at this moment he appeared to change his mind about staying. He stepped quickly past me and began to back toward the thoroughfare gate.

" I shall take myself off, my little general," he mocked, " but if Asa is much put out and your master loses a rich bargain, the blame be on you, Master Eben St. Jean de Gervais." No words could express the contempt he threw into his remarks.

With unexpected alacrity he covered the rest of the distance and slipped through the gate, closing it so softly behind him I must needs check that he was not still there. I was greatly relieved but not a little puzzled to find, on sighting into the thoroughfare, no trace of his small, stooped figure.

Now it occurred to me that truly Asa might have wished to see him and that perhaps I had better inform him of my encounter. Not liking to disturb him then, I decided to wait quietly where I was, and so crouched down in the shadows.

Darkness had fallen when my thoughts were interrupted by voices again. This time they seemed directly below me, among the great piles which held up the wharf. I made out the lapping sound of water, such as might be made by a moving boat.

A voice muttered sibilantly in French, " *Voilà, monsieur!* Three ships go out of here in the next three days. A rich prize comes in on the fourth."

Excitement raced through me. For some time it had been thought that information concerning our arrivals and sailings was being obtained by the French right here in Bostontown. Had I accidentally hit on the source? I measured the distance to the wharf gate at the end of the runway and to the like gate at the other end. I decided I was nearer the latter, and shot for it. I knew the clang of the fire bell on the end of the wharf would bring both Asa and Master Pepperrell to the scene much quicker than any explanation I might make. Doubled low, I ran and was nearing the gate. Silence had overtaken both the boat and the water beneath me. I was but a yard from my goal, the key in hand ready, when something like a thrown stick caught me between my legs, and threw me forward on my head, temporarily stunning me. When I picked myself up, I knew by the worried gossiping of the water against the piles of the dock that the hidden boat had gotten hurriedly away and taken shelter beyond one of the many hulks that peopled the harbor. Pursuit was now hopeless. I hastened back and finding Master Pepperrell and Asa together made report to them.

Master Pepperrell looked at me shrewdly, and for the first time I saw grave concern in his face.

" It is a pity they got away," he said, " but at least we know what they know and will delay our sailings. I wonder if word can be gotten to the ships coming in. You have quick ears, Eben, as well as a fine sense of smell. I am deeply grateful for this night's work."

Then I told them about Captain O'Hara. Asa indignantly denied any business with him. " It is maybe Captain O'Hara who is giving information," he hinted darkly. " I would not wonder that he were in pay of Morpain and Dolorboratz both." I told myself Asa shared my suspicions that Captain O'Hara was undoubtedly a very proper rogue, but Master Pepperrell would have none of it. " He is become a braggart, poor fellow," he insisted, " on account of the deficiency in the matter of a hand, but he is an honest servant of the crown, of that I am sure." Master Pepperrell was ever a generous man.

Now having told my tale and being free to leave, I became conscious of something which had been claiming my attention all the time they were talking. I have said that what struck me was sticklike. But at the moment of striking me, I now found, it had left a curiously odd and rather clear set of impressions. There is always to me at all times a certain friendliness in the touch of wood. But as I recalled the blow there was something hard and cold about it, something nonresilient, more like a gun's barrel. And yet I did not think it had hit the planks with the thud that a gun's barrel would make.

I decided to investigate and found it without difficulty. It lay where it had fallen, and proved to be much smaller than I had thought. In the light of the wharf's lantern I scanned it eagerly. I surmised it was an instrument for making sweet music. Although beautifully fashioned of some highly polished wood I was not familiar with, its mouthpiece was rimmed with thin silver, an exquisite piece of smithing. And it had six keys.

Then because I was overly late already I hurried home with it. I needs must lay it aside while I did my chores, but I kept it secret, being fearful of what Mistress Merrie would say to it. When I finished my chores Aaron was asleep. Nor could I show it to him in the morning, for, waking late, I needs must rush to the warehouse.

It was the day I was to meet Mistress Antoinette, but when I saw how fast the cargo of the *Good Intent* was coming ashore I gave up all hope of being spared. I spoke to Asa about it and told him whereas I had permission to go, and had been commanded by the governor, I was much troubled at leaving at such a time.

Asa promised to speak to Master Pepperrell concerning it and did. Master Pepperrell admitted it was in the agreement and by all means I must go, but, said Asa, " He was much pleased to find you reluctant to leave your work, and I doubt not, Eben, you have made a good friend this day."

So, shortly after noon, I returned home. Mistress Merrie bade me don my best, which to me meant a fresh suit of gray homespun of her own weaving, a fresh collar at my throat, and my silver shoe buckles. Although she looked somewhat scornfully at the latter, she did not forbid me to wear them. Mistress Merrie, having obtained a bit of work sewing, was leaving a little ahead of me. She turned up the hourglass on the mantelshelf and said if I were doubtful of the time, I should go by the church and consult the clock. I was not to be late for any reason.

Then was I at last free to go to Aaron. I took him the strange instrument. He raised it to his lips. At once the room was filled with the most marvelous little trills and pipings. It was become a wildwood filled with bird songs. I forgot the adventure ahead of me and was away to the strawberry fields on the warm sunny slopes of the Roxbury hills. Then Aaron must stop for breath. He lay back weak, but in his face was an eagerness I had not seen since his sickness. " Take it, Eben," he murmured. " You try it. I would hear the music I have made, if it be surely true."

So I took the strange instrument and placed it between my lips, but never a sweet sound could I make — only gruntings and moans and squeaks of hideous and incongruous effect. Whereupon Aaron was strangely happy.

"See you, Eben!" he cried excitedly. "Think you a man is worth nothing when he can make such sweet sounds the which even you, Eben, cannot?"

I assured him it was a monstrous happy gift which he had, and Aaron looked gayer than I had seen him for many a day.

Then Aaron said: "You will, of course, have to take it with you when you go for the little maid, for the governor must know of it. Mayhap some of his entourage will recognize to whom it belongs. For it may well be the property of some Massachusetts man who has contact with the French and is giving information."

Now this I had not thought on, but it might well be true. Still, I was sorry that Aaron should not have it and said so. To my surprise, he answered quietly: "I make no doubt Mistress Merrie would never allow it in the house, music, to her, being such an evil thing. Perhaps it is. Mayhap that is why I take such joy in it. It is the attempt of the Evil One to send my soul to eternal damnation."

In spite of my Puritan upbringing, I would have none of such sad talk. I was of an age to think. My little maid had shown herself in all things a brave woman and indeed a compassionate one, and I knew in the chapel she attended, the house of the Episcopates, they had music. I had great wish to hear it, but feared I never would on account of Mistress Merrie's being so strong a Puritan.

I was about to leave when Aaron called to me excitedly. He had made out on the flute a fleur-de-lis with a motto beneath it. The motto was "*J'y suis, j'y reste*," which I knew meant "Here I am, here I stay." And of a sudden I had great desire that this same motto might prove prophetic.

When I entered the Province House, His Excellency, the Governor, was standing again in the great hall, this time with only two gallants. He spoke up kindly and sent a man in livery to inform his guest of my presence.

One of the gallants was reading *The Boston News-Letter*. "Listen to this, Your Excellency," and he read, "'The gentleman who borrowed a blue coat at the Great Swan, about three weeks past, is desired to return same herewith, the person of whom he borrowed it thinking he has had it long enough.' Is it not quaint the manner of these Puritans' telling a man he's a thief? "

I could not help thinking that better manners on his own part would have restrained him from speaking thus in my hearing. These English sent out by the crown to govern us were not always careful of our feelings.

At this point the servant returned, and I was taken up the great winding stairway into an upper room where My Lady Shirley told me all manner of things to be careful of, and informed us that a manservant would accompany us, which did not please my little maid at all, but there was nothing we could do about it.

On the way downstairs I handed Mistress Antoinette the flute and explained the miracle which Aaron could accomplish on it and the strange manner in which it came to me.

She frowned as if thinking deeply and said, " It is, I am sure, of some value, and should be brought to the governor's attention." But, arriving downstairs, we found His Excellency had already departed.

The hall was empty save for the servant who tended the door.

So we started off with our escort a few feet behind us and when we reached the garden gate I noticed that Mistress Antoinette was still carrying the instrument. Now she put it to her lips, but no more than I could she make a sweet sound out of it. At which she said that she doubted its value after all, and she added most sweetly that as for Aaron's ability to use it she did not believe a word of it.

When I insisted it was true, she replied quickly, " Take me then to Aaron and let me hear this thing for myself." And of a sudden I saw whither she was sailing, witch that she was. I told her solemnly that this I could not do, reminding her we had come for the express purpose of seeing the ships.

" Poof! " cried Mistress Antoinette. " 'Twas for me but an excuse to see your marvelous great Aaron. I told you I cared nought for ships."

Now this veering about hither and thither I would have none

of. I insisted we go to the ships, and to the ships we started. Then, having gotten my way, I must show her the fleur-de-lis and the strange motto, being proud of my knowledge of what it meant. I said again I feared it was stolen. At that my little maid responded: " Such being so, it is fair reckless to parade it about the town. We will leave it with Aaron before we go to the ships, Eben." And I, knowing what company it would be to him, hesitated and was lost. My will was as water under the persuasion of her witchery. However, I made sure to tell her that I would not take her into the house. To which Mistress Antoinette said, " If he can make this music, which seems fair incredible, you can open the casement and I, outside, may hear it."

And so we arranged it. I left her standing outside, with His Excellency's servant respectfully in attendance.

When I went in and told Aaron, it gave him great pleasure. He snatched up the stick and I, stationing myself at the open window, described to him how amazed she was, and how the manservant was like to break his neck staring heavenward, thinking it was birds, but finding none.

When I rejoined Mistress Antoinette, she said sweetly: " It was all that you said, Eben, and your Aaron must be a marvelous fine lad. It is shame that he cannot go abroad like other men." All of which I treasured to tell him when I should return.

After that we went to the docks, but I am afraid we neither of us saw much of the ships, Mistress Antoinette thinking it great adventure to sit on a bench on the Long Wharf, outside one of the shops, the whiles I talked of Aaron and of the strange tales of the great fortress of Louisbourg. She had great wish to visit the sailmaker, but this I was reluctant to do, for fear she might hear there that about the royalists she might not like. I told her about Dogood and of the small boy, Paul Revere, and how much he wished to be permitted to follow his trade of silversmith, and of his great fear he might not be permitted to do so through order of the crown.

Mistress Antoinette shook her head over that. " It is not right, Eben," she murmured. " The making of beauty is a rare gift. No one should interfere with it. Least of all they who have not such gifts. But I do not think England will interfere so cruelly, Eben. The matter of the felt hats is quite different."

I did not ask her in what way, but I said I hoped indeed it was.

Then, the manservant having betaken himself into a near-by shop temporarily, Mistress Antoinette moved closer to me, put her hand on my arm, and said softly, " And now, Eben, I would hear about your father."

I had purposely not spoken of him, because I had not wanted to air my great sorrow, but at once I found strange joy in pouring out to her my loneliness and in acquainting her with the desire to avenge his death which was growing steadily in me. At that she chid me and, sighing softly, murmured: " It is but human to want to avenge a wrong, but I doubt, Eben, if in the end it accomplishes what is intended. It cannot bring the good captain back."

Then she must know all about Master William Pepperrell and the strange treasures in his dark warehouse upon the wharf.

At last, having talked overmuch, I must needs do my share of listening. She told me of her voyage and of the Old World, and when I took her home, the manservant having rejoined us, I thought it was the best day ever I had had, although so large a part of it had been consumed in memories of my father. But somehow sharing them with her had softened the hurt, and I thought again of the words of my father beside the old figurehead in Feathertale John's shop — the heart of a woman was indeed a great strongbox in which to store away hidden things.

Next day I brought the strange instrument to the governor, who informed me it was a flute. I consulted with him as to what I should do with it. He made earnest search for its owner through the columns of the news sheets, and also by means of his gallants, but so far as we could tell it had not belonged to anyone now living in Bostontown. This confirmed us in the thought that it was indeed property of one who was not eager to have his presence known among us. So with great joy I bore it back to Aaron, who took much interest in it. And as the days passed we pondered often on its strange motto, which seemed to be coming true: " Here I am, here I stay."

5: Mistress Antoinette Is Prolific of Ideas

Now my work at the warehouse being dependent as it was on the coming and going of the ships, Mistress Merrie let me do my chores as I was able, wherefore I found myself with more time on my hands than I had had when working for her alone. Feathertale John's drew me as a needle to a magnet, and I spent many an odd hour there, since Aaron was so overeager to have me go.

Flitting about were rumors as wild and as fitful as the firelight shadows among the high rafters of the sailmaker's shop. It was said that the English fort of Annapolis Royal was going to rack and ruin, that Governor Mascarene had appealed to Governor Shirley for aid in manning and repairing it. Many were of the opinion that should the French take it into their heads to attack and capture Annapolis Royal, we might well have a new Louisbourg almost at our gates. I shivered to think how easily the French privateers, quartered so close, might wipe out our overseas trade — trade on which truly our lives depended.

The situation there was doubly serious. Acadia had belonged to the French, but, without consent of her people, had been given by treaty to the English, and was now become Nova Scotia. But there were still at the gates of Annapolis Royal a great many French people who had been persistent in their determination not to take the oath of allegiance to the English crown. It was well known they were friendly to the Indians. And should a force of any size arrive from Quebec or France to lay siege to the place, they were capable of giving food, shelter, and information. They were become a source of great anxiety to the defenders of the fort.

Therefore, it was good news indeed when Mistress Antoinette informed me that a detachment of one hundred men, including some Indians, were being sent posthaste to the relief of the fort.

However, Mistress Antoinette, having ever a mind of her own, was not too jubilant. "They are border troops," she said, "and understand well fighting in the forest, but Governor Mascarene asked for two hundred men, well-equipped, and I doubt they will be enough. I am afraid he will be sorely disappointed."

Chancing to meet Dogood soon after in Feathertale John's I passed on to her the good news, saying that Mistress Antoinette of the governor's household had imparted it to me. I was surprised to find that Dogood took another view. "If word gets abroad that a force of New Englanders is on the way to reinforce the garrison of Annapolis Royal, be assured that the Indians, who supply the French with all their information, will double and triple the number. It will be a thousand men, I do not doubt, when the news comes to French ears." It might well be, I reflected, and felt a bit comforted. Then Dogood demanded somewhat abruptly, "Who is this Mistress Antoinette?"

Now a strange thing happened. Though my thoughts were rarely absent from my little maid, I found myself tongue-tied regarding her, and could only explain briefly that she was daughter of the agent who had come to inspect the mast trees and was at present abiding in the governor's household.

I could see that Dogood was far from satisfied, but I made haste to leave her before her shrewd mind could achieve other questions.

One morning not long after this when I was at home, there came a sharp rat-tat-tat at our door. No friend of Mistress Merrie's rapped so imperiously. I was up in Aaron's room and rushed to the window. From his shelter of rugs, for Aaron was always cold and it was still spring, his voice pursued me. "Who is it? What is it? Do not leave me, Eben. There are tasks to do, remember you that. I will not be left alone today," he finished peevishly.

Now as I looked down I could hardly find voice to answer.

"'Tis Mistress Antoinette!" I whispered and marveled at the noise she was making with her riding crop — such a to-do by one so seeming frail.

"She can't come up. I won't see her. She must stop her fuss.

46

It's — it's making my head ache. Go down and tell her so at once," ordered Aaron.

So, great loathing in my heart for the thing I would have to do, I hurried downstairs and prepared to open the door. I drew myself up with great dignity and opened it with a flourish such as I had seen the velveted man do at the door of the Province House.

" I give you good day, Mistress Antoinette," I said. " Will you be pleased to step inside? "

Mistress Antoinette greeted me with a peal of laughter.

" O Eben," she cried, " you looked out of the casement. Did you think the French had arrived to take Bostontown? "

" Be good enough to step inside," I repeated, overcome with embarrassment, and yet conscious of a sweet jingling sound, like that of tiny bells, and I wondered if it was all part of my delight in seeing her.

" I thank you kindly," she said, making a sweeping curtsy before she stepped over the threshold, but I thought her dark eyes flashed dangerously. " I've come to see Aaron."

I was much put about to know what to say, so churlish it seemed to deny her, but I feared for Aaron's peace of mind.

" It gives me great sorrow," I said with dignity, " but my brother is not feeling so well today. He bade me tell you he could not have you come up. It is a great pity, but he suffers overmuch."

" O Eben! " cried my little maid impatiently. " Think you I've come pushing myself upon your great Aaron for my own entertainment? Come with me," she said imperiously, and waved me out the door and round the corner of the house into a side lane. Then was I fair amazed. For standing there with great impatience were two saddle horses, shining sorrels, a black slave holding the heads of them, while another slave larger than I had ever seen stood by a horse and small carriage. The carriage horse seemed as gentle as the others were restless. Never had I contemplated such a rich abundance of Indian shawls and rugs as lay ready in the carriage. With each toss of the saddle horses' heads the bridles with their silver decorations jingled softly. I knew it instantly as the source of the musical tinkles I had heard.

"Look!" Mistress Antoinette proudly pulled back the lovely materials. "Think you Aaron will be comfortable?" There under the rugs were great pillows, and even a couple of hot stones, which made it all seem like a nest of cosiness in the brisk sea wind.

"Tell your great Aaron," said Antoinette disdainfully, "that a courtier never refuses a lady's invitation. I am now going on my way. I shall take it as very bad manners, indeed, if Aaron does not accept my invitation, for, believe it or not, I was at some trouble to maneuver it all." And suddenly she smiled her witching glance, and I knew that what trouble she had been put to had surely been in the conception of it only, for no man living could deny her anything, and yet — I reflected sadly — Aaron was likely to, not having seen her.

"But — " I began, thinking of the long stair which Aaron could not possibly negotiate.

"I do not wish to hear your 'buts,'" Mistress Antoinette replied sharply. "Did I ever start aught I could not bring secure to an end? Jonah!" she summoned the giant slave, who, throwing the reins of the carriage horse to his mate, hastened toward her. "Attend Master Eben inside. Take up the Indian shawl, and carry Master Aaron down with care. He is ill, and I would he had some amusement."

"Yes, ma'am," the slave was prompt to answer, his face beaming.

To me she said, "Go boldly, Eben, and do not forget to tell him I have gone away."

I was a little worried at leaving her to wander off alone, but I did not attempt to stop her, well knowing that Aaron, if he were to come at all, must know that she was gone.

With trembling knees I climbed the stair with Jonah. I wished that I had the gift of Mistress Antoinette for bending folk to her will. But I entered boldly, as she had counseled. "Aaron," I said, "Mistress Antoinette has come to take you to drive."

I saw Aaron's face light like morning sun upon the waters. I knew then how great the denial of his sickness had been. Then he scowled. "I can't go. I won't go. O Eben, I cannot even stand

48

alone on my feet." He turned his face to the wall. I called Jonah, who had waited outside. Aaron turned in curiosity and then sat up bewildered. "Mistress Antoinette," I murmured hurriedly, "has an errand elsewhere, but she has left the carriage for you, and this servant will carry you down."

Before Aaron could object, Jonah's broad smile was beaming down upon him. "It's all right, little massa. You come along. Jonah not gwine let yo' drop. Uncle Jonah strong — strong — strong as hawser lines. That's how strong he is. Yo' sho' see soon 'nuff, Massa Aaron." I rushed for his stockings and shoes and a greatcoat.

So for the first time in three years, Aaron, hastily bundled up, went down the stairs. It did not seem that lying in the carriage in the deep, warm rugs he was any different than in his own bed. Only the air was all around him. It whipped color into his wan cheeks; his eyes shone at the musical jingle of the harness and at the sloops and the frigates at anchor. The carriage moved easily on its fine springs with never a jolt or jiggle. Aaron breathed in great draughts of the fresh salt air with evident enjoyment — an enjoyment he had not displayed in anything since he was sick.

"It minds me, Eben," he cried, "of a place on the poop deck with the flying spray all around one." Aaron had made two short voyages with my father before he was sick. We flew down to the Long Wharf with its long row of shops on one side, its ships on the other — shops where all manner of things were bought and sold, ships with their gay chatter of many tongues, and the salty reek of the broadest street in all the world, the open sea. We turned and passed Paul's house at the head of the wharf, and went up the Cornhill Road where I showed him the Province House, and new Faneuil Hall. All too soon it was over, although dimly I sensed that in this also Mistress Antoinette was wise.

Once again, Jonah carried Aaron upstairs and, wonder of wonders, I heard Aaron laugh. Jonah was saying, "Nothin' the matter with you, Massa Aaron. Yo' just plum lazy."

Then, Jonah having departed, Aaron cried: "O Eben, I'm so hungry. I must have something to eat."

49

Wondering if this was a good sign, I went downstairs. I bethought me that a nice drink of milk warm from the cow would surely do him no harm and went outside toward the stable. There sitting on the back stoop in the midst of the sunshine, all scrunched up in a little heap, chin on knees, was Mistress Antoinette. Instantly she jumped up. " Did he like it? What did he say? Do you think it harmed him? "

I told her then I was sure it had not and that he was most hungry. Mistress Antoinette was jubilant. " It is a good sign. Now he'll get well. I'm sure of it. And cow's milk is just the thing. Can I come too and see what happens when you get the milk? Never have I seen anyone like you with a cow before."

I was well aware she was but poking fun, yet could not be angry for all she had done for Aaron. So together we went to the little barn. Glad was I that I had kept it swept and clean as no other cowshed in our town. Then did I see someone had been there before me, for in the stall next to Daisy a new animal snorted impatiently. It was one of the sorrels. Of a sudden I knew that having dismissed the groom, Mistress Antoinette had probably brought the animal in here by herself, for she did not hesitate to go into the stall with him and quiet him. I marveled again that one so small should be so fearless.

Daisy gave her milk readily enough. I hastened back, fearful that Mistress Merrie might have returned and would openly disapprove of what I had done, for to milk a cow at other than her time is not a good thing to do. When I went up to Aaron I found him fast asleep. I returned to Mistress Antoinette immediately with the milk untouched. She said at once that the sleep was a fine sign, but that I must go back and waken him and make him take the milk. This I did, though somewhat doubtfully. Aaron took of it sleepily, scarce knowing what he was doing, and was at once off again, the moment I laid his head back on the pillow. When I returned to my guest she seemed much pleased at my report and let me prevail on her to take a little of the fresh milk herself. She smacked her lips over it and then said it was bad tasting enough to do one a lot of good, ending with a peal of silvery laughter I thought rivaled the bells of Christ Church.

When I led out her horse for her and put up my hand for her to vault into the saddle as I had seen the gallants do, I marveled at the fairy lightness of her, for her weight in my hand was as thistledown.

Holding in her impatient steed, Mistress Antoinette blew a little whistle with her lips, whereupon the slave I had seen Jonah leave with the carriage horse reappeared, and I knew he had not been far away any of the time. " Come and see me, Eben," she commanded. " I shall wish to know how Aaron is doing. And be sure to give him his flute when he wakes up. He should make fine music after such an outing."

She went clattering up the lane, leaving me with a sudden sharp pain within. Her whole thought, it would seem, had been for Aaron. Then I took shame to myself for being jealous of one who was so weak. I should rather be glad, indeed, he had found a friend so well fitted to help him to get well.

Mistress Merrie, upon arrival home, did not take the doings of that day any better than I had expected she would. I continued to insist the rugs had kept Aaron as warm as his own bed.

Mistress Merrie looked at me sternly. " Things of evil," she said. " The pomp of the Devil. Master Eben, it is not this way I would have brought up children of my own which the Lord never gave me, but what the governor commands a poor woman must needs do, not that I would have let you do it had I been here," she ended somewhat inconsistently.

I was glad then of her absence. " But," she added grimly, " if harm comes to your brother, it will be your fault, Eben."

That evening I visited Aaron often and not always on tiptoe. He continued to sleep, and it continued to worry me. He slept the whole night through.

During the days that followed I was like to agree with Mistress Merrie our adventure had done Aaron no good. Never had he been so peevish. But when I later told Mistress Antoinette about it, she laughed merrily. "Why, Eben, that is the best sign yet," she cried. "Don't you know that people who are very ill don't care what happens to them. If he is peevish, it shows his strength is returning."

Leaning as ever on her wisdom, I went joyously to my duties in the warehouse.

There my joy was soon quashed. Asa was sitting idle in the doorway. I soon learned the news. The *Lady of Glasgow,* due that day from the West Indies, had been taken prize by the French. A swift packet had bespoken her but a day's journey away and had brought news of the rich cargo she was carrying. And now she was gone. All her great store of rum and spices and sugar and molasses was lost to us. There was nought for either of us to do that day.

I sat down stunned. My alliance with the firm of Master William Pepperrell had made me feel part owner of all his ships. It was like losing *The Golden Lily* again. I remembered the day the *Lady of Glasgow* had sailed, idling down the stream, dependent on her royals to catch the meager breeze. It had seemed to me then she was like a beautiful woman, regal in her carriage, all-conquering. Now she was gone:

Then I marked a new ship riding at anchor, a ship's distance from the wharf end. I noted her golden decoration, the rich carving of her poop, the elaborate catholes.

"What is yon, Asa?"

Asa's small eyes flashed. "Yon be the *Bon Ami,*" he said. "Captain Gayton's rich prize."

And I knew then that, within the law or without it, the men of New England would give as good as they got, and the war from now on would be a bitter one.

6: Adventure by Night

In the days that followed my eyes rested often on the *Bon Ami,* riding at anchor in the harbor. She made me feel that we were indeed a match for any Frenchman. Though a good ship, excelling in luxury anything we might build in the yards of Bostontown, she was not, in her main lines or in the speed she was capable of, the equal of our own ships of the same size; in this all the master builders agreed.

I scanned everything French these days with eager eyes, for at home my brother Aaron was avid for all kinds of information concerning our enemy, and his great fortress at Louisbourg.

There had been in the past much commerce between Louisbourg and Bostontown. There had also been much work there connected with the fortifications. Many a Boston and Maine man had labored there. But it was from Captain O'Hara, quite inadvertently, I learned the quaint name the French applied to all New Englanders. They called us the *Bastonnais.*

Now it happened that sometimes Feathertale John saw fit to take time off from his sailmaking. Frequently I was his companion. Mayhap it was necessary to inspect a suit of sails late fitted to some ship in the stream. Then on the way back, if it was summer, we would stop for a swim. He liked nothing better than to instruct me in the intricacies of that art. He taught me to dive, to float on my back and on my face, and all manner of strokes. Especially did we practice long periods of swimming under water. It was the one thing in which I ever outdistanced him.

In winter, on certain rare occasions, I would be asked to sup with him in his shop in the sail loft. These were special times indeed, for he customarily did not eat there, and I was not like ever to forget them. Feathertale would arrange a grill over the glowing forge coals and toast some game bird. There was often a shellfish broiled in its shell with luscious bacon toasting on top and home-made bannocks near by. And although Mistress Merrie frowned much on the adventure, she had never yet forbid me to go. Man though I was in my seventeen years, she still managed to exercise authority over me.

It was on such an occasion that I sought out Feathertale's one night. When I climbed up the long stair, Feathertale was occupied with his ledgers. I slipped to one side, and patiently waited. He muttered as he painfully made his entries. "Two score ratlines to be spliced and ready for the *Bessie Bell*, sailing on the fifth. Two moonrakers and a skysail for the *Lively*, due on the fifteenth."

Not wishing to disturb him, I curled quietly up on an old sail by the forge. It had been a heavy day at the countinghouse. I felt drowsy and, being aware of a draft from one of the windows, I pulled an old bag over me and was soon fast asleep.

When I at last awakened the place was completely dark and I was most hungry. I was at great loss to know why I was not in my own bed. A dying coal exploded and showed me the sailmaker's loft. I started up, much disturbed. It was evident that Feathertale had decided I was not coming and had locked up the shop and gone home to bed. The thought that I was indeed locked in from the outside, and could not leave, was like to throw me into a panic.

Strange creaking noises now came to disturb me. I could have sworn the old figurehead herself was walking about. A dim patch of lighter darkness located for me the great window. I sincerely hoped I should soon see it grow rosy with the dawn and know that day was at hand.

Now to anyone who has listened, it must be apparent that noises at night have distinct personalities of their own. It appeared to me that these were most uncommon stealthy. Then my teeth fairly chattered aloud when for one moment the big window was blotted out, and it was apparent that some large object had passed between me and it.

When at last a sharp whisper cut the stillness, I could have cried out in my relief. The creepings had at least human origin.

" *Voilà!* " a French voice exclaimed. " It is dark as the Bastille. Give us a light."

A guarded whisper answered, " Yo' sure, massa, yo' wantin' of a light? "

" Stir up the forge, fool," came the answer. " If any chance to see it, they will but think it has blown itself up."

Now while the second voice had been unmistakably that of a Negro, the voice of the other had spoken the French of the court. This was no common seaman. I pondered deep what he could be doing here in the heart of Bostontown.

Nevertheless, I had forethought enough to draw myself deeper under the old bag, and a fortunate thing too that I did, for in a moment a red glow illuminated the place.

By their voices I judged them to be but two, but something in the sounds suggested there might be another to the party. A wild thought went through my head that they were after the doubloons Feathertale was supposed to keep hidden in his shop. There was sound of further rummaging. And it was then it came to me that Feathertale's great ledgers were indeed a record of the comings and goings of many ships. Had I at last hit on the Frenchmen's source of information?

The rummaging continued. I had a feeling of two separate bits of business afoot, for while two were certainly concerned with the forge, a third was undoubtedly searching for something.

The light cast by the pumping of the bellows grew apace. Then my ears caught the rattle of pails. A little later an aromatic, piny odor filled the shop. It mystified me afresh. They were melting something over the forge, and I was like to give away my presence by my frantic desire to sneeze.

" Seems like it's all ready, massa. Sho' is boilin' hot."

My blood was like to have congealed in my veins. For the voice of authority responded harshly: " Fill the eyes and harden the knots with it. See there are no shrieks, fool."

My thoughts shivered back to the tale of a seaman in this very shop. 'Twas said the French pirates blinded their victims with boiling pitch.

Was their prisoner Feathertale John?

Some thought of flying to his rescue possessed me. But the voice spoke again. " Where is the key? "

" Here, massa! "

" Give it me. Feathertale desires the shop locked when we depart."

The victim was not Feathertale. Instead he seemed a party to what was going on. Feathertale, a villain! No emotion that I had yet experienced was as great as this sudden fear of facing the perfidy of an old friend.

Then my ears caught the sound of footsteps, new ones. They were coming stealthily up the stair. There were more in this thing then. By the creaking of the old timbers, the muttered exclamations, I followed the action. A pail of pitch was lifted — the grunt of the handler picking up the load was unmistakable — and was carried to the stairhead. The fourth man took it and carried it down.

An instant's selfish relief came to me. The torture was not to be in this very room.

Now muffled sounds from the front of the shop came to my straining ears. Was the big Frenchman, whose shadow I had seen between me and the great window, even now poring over Feathertale's ledger? What else could attract the French to Feathertale's shop? Was their victim the night watchman of the Winan Yards? Poor wretch! He had often been kind to me.

More cautious comings and goings. I could not understand it, but pail after pail was going down that stair. Once I heard a stifled shriek and all but cried out myself. Craven that I was, I could not bring myself to rush to the rescue. What could I do but share the victim's fate? I argued. I must keep my skin whole in order to give information.

Then I had new cause of fright. The big man, whom I judged was the leader, moved over in my direction. Suddenly he sat down, so nearly on top of me that I was at great pains not to cry out. I could hear his labored breathing above me, and there was about him a faint smell not altogether unpleasant. It was the odor of a rum of the Indies which Master Pepperrell was accustomed to import for the better trade of Bostontown and was much affected by the gallants.

Now the villain sitting so painfully close to me demanded a look into the bucket. A candle was lighted and candle and bucket brought near. I was like to die of fear that some of it should splatter on my thin covering and cause me to cry out; also the acrid odor, which did not seem to bother them at all, was terrible tickling to my nostrils.

At last to my great relief the figure removed itself from my vicinity. All three of them seemed moving toward the stair. Was the place empty? I must take my chance. What Mistress Merrie thought of my absence, if she were aware of it, was also troubling me.

It came to me that I had better douse the fire, dimming the light in the place, and that having a bucket of the stuff in my hand might be a good thing. I could pass it to one of them returning, if I got caught.

It was well I knew Feathertale's shop as my own home. Otherwise I would surely have injured myself most grievously with the scalding pitch. Even then, I was too late. Someone was coming up the stair. All thoughts of a ruse fled from my head. I crouched cravenly by the stair well, my hand over its edge.

I am not like to forget the next moment. Without warning a hand came down on mine in the darkness. In a moment the long fingers would close over it. I was lost. Some thought of jumping up and chancing a grapple with the invader was in my mind, when to my amazement, the hand, still open, was quietly removed. The figure continued up the stair, muttering something at its steepness. Fortunately, I kept my head enough to abandon my pail, swing over into the stair behind him, and race down and out. Once among the lumber stacks I knew I could play " hide-and-seek " for hours with any chance pursuer.

It was there in a pause for breath that realization came to me. There was only one hand which could possibly touch mine and be unconscious of the impact — a wooden hand, the hand of Captain O'Hara!

My thought turned furiously to the poor wretch they were tor-turing. The slow shriek was nearer now, accompanied by a soft creak. I had heard it before! I knew it for what it really was. Mounted on rollers, the mast trees were frequently turned to pre-vent them from gathering dampness in any one spot. Frequently, the turning was accompanied by this odd sound, not unlike a dis-tant shriek. The eyes they had spoken of, and the knots, were the eyes and knots of the mast trees!

But why was Captain O'Hara turning them at dead of night? What was he doing with hot pitch at this time? I made sure it was a bad business, but I did not see what I could do about it, alone, and at such an hour.

Somehow I found my direction through the dark maze of lanes to my own humble dwelling. At one point I just missed the night watchman. His cry seemed oddly pertinent, rising as it did from the void of the night. " One of the clock. And a storm brewing! "

When I arrived home, Mistress Merrie was most fortunately still sound asleep. I crept up the stair softly so as not to waken Aaron, but he heard me and whispered I should come to him. Glad of a listener, I related excitedly in low murmurs my strange adventure. He, no more than I, could surmise what it was all about. But on one point he was insistent. There was some mistake somewhere. Feathertale was not concerned in the matter, and he advised me to lay it all before him at the earliest opportunity.

Early next morning I sought Feathertale's shop. It was locked tight. I was moving away beset by new doubts when I heard voices above me.

" It is time, Dogood, I was on my way."

" Time or no time," Dogood's voice answered, " I am resolved to wait until her topsails pass Castle William."

Climbing up the stack of sweet-smelling lumber, I demanded, " What is it, Dogood? "

Little Paul raised a startled face. " It is the young man of the shoe buckles! " he announced.

Dogood frowned at me crossly. " The *Rollicking Lass*," she said, " has but just gone down the tide, taking the last of the mast trees with her." I glanced down at the sheds and saw with dismay that they were indeed empty. I was filled with anxiety.

" Is your uncle away from home, Dogood? " I demanded.

" He is. He is at this moment aboard the sloop *Tartar*, and has been since last night. She has need of a new mainsail."

Now, Paul having slipped away, somewhat foolishly no doubt I related a little of my experience of the night before, in the hope that Dogood might understand and explain to me what Captain O'Hara was up to. " Do you know what it is all about? " I asked.

Her face darkened until her frown was black indeed. " I know all about it. It is a very grave matter. But at the moment I must be off to my duties. I bid you good day." She slid off the stack and was gone before I could stop her. I was more than put out over her abrupt departure and wished I had not so thoughtlessly confided in her.

All day I worried over the matter. It was late afternoon before I found occasion to return to Feathertale's shop. I was much relieved on coming into the yard to see by the light of the forge glowing in the windows that he was at home again. I cannot say that on climbing the ladderlike stair I was much pleased to find Dogood ahead of me, and relating my tale for me.

There was none save these two in the shop that I could see, and Dogood's voice rang out as I entered.

" They were pouring hot pitch into the logs, uncle. Eben saw it. My father told me long ago it was a trick to make rotten trees seem whole. And Captain O'Hara was mixed up in it. They are rotten logs, uncle, though they appear whole," she repeated excitedly, " and the English men-of-war when they come to fight the French off our coast will go down before them. It is sheer murder of the king's ships, uncle."

Now Feathertale John had been about to turn up the ship's lantern by which he worked when the light failed. With the door still open, he had stopped and was regarding her fixedly. His unmoving hands, illumined by the light of the candle he had just ignited, struck me with strange import. I had never seen Feathertale's hands idle before.

At first I judged his stiffness signified indignation — then I wondered. Was it fear? Was Feathertale concerned in this business after all?

Then it came to me that the gathering shadows in the old shop held something of menace. Even Dogood seemed to sense it, for her voice wavered and dropped away at the end. She turned quickly as if conscious of something behind her. Then in the moving shadows features took shape, and suddenly I made out the hand of Captain O'Hara waving like the hand of fate over Dogood's golden head. The red gleam of an exploding coal showed him moving evilly out of the shadows. I am glad to remember always that although Dogood's face went the color of the sail upon which Feathertale had only now been working, she moved no whit out of Captain O'Hara's path.

" So the son of the Huguenot renegade has been at his spying again! " Captain O'Hara said coolly.

Feathertale's voice boomed out with a volume I did not know he possessed. " Is what Dogood says true, Captain O'Hara? "

" To the last word of it," he answered nonchalantly. Was he really, as he boasted, a man without fear?

" And was it for this that you borrowed my keys and not for the sharpening of your ship's tools as you instructed me last night? "

" A fine sharpening it has turned out to be! " There was something cryptic in his manner of saying it. " I had meant to share the sum with you, Feathertale."

" Share with me! " Feathertale's voice broke in fury. " I want none of your murderer's money. The governor shall know of this. The king's navy shall not go down to its death in rotten-masted ships."

" I'm afraid it won't! " Captain O'Hara's tones for some reason sounded faintly amused. " For belike the *Rollicking Lass* is at this moment in French hands, prize of the great Morpain. Would it not be a fine thing if it were the Frenchman's ships that were rotten-masted? How say you, would I then be a murderer? "

Feathertale sank back on his bench. Then he looked up defiantly. " It's a dirty trick to play on friend or foe — if it be true — and it's

60

the last time you get leave to use my shop for any reason at all, Captain O'Hara."

Captain O'Hara continued to smile. " And who is to say I did not know the *Rollicking Lass* was to be taken and the mast trees find their way into French ships? 'Tis a hero you should call me."

There was, of course, no argument to return him.

Nevertheless, I cried out, " There is not a word of truth in it, Captain O'Hara."

The man smiled back at me. " Maybe there isn't," he drawled coolly. " Such a wise lad! He must know."

But Feathertale was not through. " Dogood mentioned there were four of you. Who was the leader, Captain O'Hara? "

" Now that," said Captain O'Hara, looking very pointedly at me so that I felt momentarily guilty myself, " that would surprise you mightily."

Then I asked myself if he was trying to suggest it was someone known to me. I do not know why my thoughts should have skipped over all I knew and come to rest on Asa, unless it was because on the night I had run into Captain O'Hara on the warehouse wharf he had said he had business with Asa. But this Asa had been at some pains to deny. Then I recalled that it was Asa who first suggested the one giving information to the enemy might be this same Captain O'Hara. I frowned over my thoughts. Something made me glance again at that black, offending countenance, and I was quick to see him still looking at me, his face replete with satisfaction. Suddenly I had a new idea. Had he thrown doubt on someone else in an effort to direct my suspicions away from himself?

But now he turned his attention elsewhere. " I suppose, Feathertale, you will be returning to me the money I paid you for the rent of your shop, not wishing to take it for the purpose I made use of it in your absence? "

" Aye. I want no blood money." Feathertale started up, but seemed to think better of it. Did I imagine it or had Feathertale been about to approach the figurehead? Certainly his eyes had wandered in that direction. I recalled the words of my father as we had stood before it. " It is not the only secret the old body holds."

61

"I'll have it for you tomorrow," Feathertale ended somewhat weakly, I thought.

"Well, as for tomorrow," the Captain continued, "I am somewhat pushed for time and mayhap will return sooner."

Captain O'Hara moved toward the stair well, and I hoped he did not see the look that crossed Feathertale's face. I could scarce believe it, but for the space of one second Feathertale had looked afraid.

With his black head level with the floor Captain O'Hara turned. I would not soon forget the strange bodiless effect of that black head protruding above the floor edge under the great hand with its giant shadow waving octopuslike above it.

His eyes sought mine. "We meet again," he said coldly, and he disappeared out of sight. But his simple words filled me with new fear. Quietly Dogood closed the door of the lantern which Feathertale, in his preoccupation, had left open.

I began to wonder. If Captain O'Hara was master of a ship, as he said he was, where was it, and how was it we never saw any of his crew?

I returned home thoughtfully and found Aaron with no very warm welcome. For once I could tell him nothing of the great fortress, and I thought it wise to keep silent on all that which had occurred, for in truth it seemed most of it must be in my own head. How could Captain O'Hara know what had happened to the mast trees? He must have thought it up to annoy us and cover his own guilt.

And then Aaron's words turned my mind in another direction. "Watch out, Eben! From now on I must have every single little bit of information you can gather anent Louisbourg. Mistress Antoinette has sent me a package of colors requesting that I draw the map in more than one shade."

Now I do not know why, but the thought of Mistress Antoinette sending a communication to my brother of which he had not thought fit to inform me made me feel strangely cast down. I knew that I dreaded that moment when Aaron and she would meet. For some reason I decided there and then that I too would play the flute and felt some shame when Aaron welcomed the idea of teaching me.

When next I saw Mistress Antoinette I reported all my strange adventure. She said that Governor Shirley had already had word of it from Feathertale John. Whereupon he had ordered his men to bring Captain O'Hara to him, but that they had found him to be strangely absent and were forced to the opinion he had left the town somewhat suddenly. No record of the departure of his boat could be found.

I was glad that Captain O'Hara was gone, but my joy was short-lived. A packet arriving seven weeks from Glasgow brought news that she had bespoken a small fishing schooner along the coast, which gave word that the *Rollicking Lass* had indeed fallen to a French privateer two days' sail from Bostontown.

Was it just coincidence that Captain O'Hara's seemingly idle words should come so true? Or had he suspected her probable fate and loaded her up with the rotten trees as a way of balancing the debt against the French who had snatched many a valuable fishing cargo from us off the coast of Newfoundland? Or was it his way of playing his part in a war that was going on though still undeclared in Bostontown? And then I recalled that one of the voices that night the trees had been doctored — the voice seemingly in command — had spoken the French of the court. What was Captain O'Hara doing, taking orders from a Frenchman? I felt utterly confused by the whole matter.

My thoughts too turned to Asa. Was he concerned in this dishonest matter of doctoring the mast trees?

As for His Excellency, Governor Shirley, I had a shrewd suspicion that he was much relieved at the outcome of the matter. The trees might well have reached England and been built into ships before word of their rottenness reached the proper authorities.

I strongly suspected too that should Captain O'Hara ever return to Bostontown his words would receive more attention than ever.

7: Bad News and What Came of It

Mistress Antoinette continued her treatments of Aaron. They consisted of rides in the fresh air, and, when that same air had sharpened his usually wan appetite, plenty of good simple food. He was surely benefiting by it all. As for Mistress Merrie, I think she was both proud and troubled by our growing intimacy with the governor's household.

My Lady Shirley had surely good report of what my father and mother had been, for it seemed she could not see too much of me. She encouraged me whenever possible to accompany Mistress Antoinette on her wanderings abroad. A more venturesome piece of baggage than Mistress Antoinette I had not ever seen; nor one more quick to change her mind until she had you all peaceable, whereupon she would up-anchor and swing off on her own tack so swift it would take one of the king's frigates to overtake her.

Now I was quick to notice that Mistress Antoinette's thoughts were much on my brother Aaron, and I marveled that one as interested as she could so contain her curiosity, for, although she sent the carriage for him quite frequently, she herself did not again accompany it. She had not yet met Aaron. But her questions concerning him, on the occasions when she and I met, followed hard one upon another.

What did he look like? Would she know him if she met him unawares?

I assured her that but for the fact that my eyes were blue and his brown like my mother's we were as much alike as two ships of the same class, being both of us blond, but that in disposition no two members of any family could be more wide apart.

At that she nodded her head wisely and said, " I thought such would be the case." Then, having sighed, she added: " There could not be another like you, Eben. It were not possible." She looked at me slyly and laughed so I knew not whether I made a brave figure in her eyes or exactly the reverse.

Then she must know all about the map of Louisbourg that Aaron was making. How large was it? Had he the names of the streets properly printed on it? Did he know that the Home of the Good Sisters of the Congregation was on the Rue d'Orléans, for that she had found out from a most reliable source. I told her that I did not know whether Aaron already had the information or not, but that I was very sure he would like to have it confirmed if he already knew it. And so we talked hours on end.

There was no question that Aaron was greatly improved in body. Of his temper I cannot say so much. But since he had begun to eat I had great hopes of his recovery. It was Antoinette's delight to sit on the doorstep and hear his sweet pipings on the flute, and I could not refuse to sit beside her, although not a word would she let me speak during his playing. I was conscious at such times of a strange hurt inside, which I did not altogether understand.

It was about this time too that I came as near to quarreling with Mistress Antoinette as I was ever to do. She had been particularly tantalizing that afternoon with her continual interest in Aaron's progress, and the filching from me of certain information concerning Louisbourg " to write to Aaron," the which I would have liked very well to give him myself.

At last she said with sudden extra sweetness: " Eben, the governor has provided for me a tutor in the form of Master Skipworth. Would it not be a fine thing if you were to join me in study? He is a most learned man, much versed in the Latin roots."

Now I, suspecting some teasing, cried out angrily that I was at that moment acquiring more knowledge than Master Skipworth had in his whole head. And I did not see what good a little more knowledge of the Latin roots would do me in the matter of making note of the loading and unloading of cargo in the great ledgers of Master William Pepperrell.

Mistress Antoinette nodded her head in unexpected accord. " It is so, Eben. But Aaron now. It would be different with him. Do you not think that some occupation would be beneficial now, when he is gaining his strength and not knowing how to use it? "

" Indeed," I said, not seeing whither I was being led, " I think it would be a fine thing for him."

" Thank you, Eben," said Mistress Antoinette. " I had great wish to ask him, but did not like to do so without your consent."

It was not a day later that Aaron told me with great excitement of the arrangement that Mistress Antoinette had made with the governor, whereby he was to go there each morning and master the intricacies of knowledge along with her.

Now I suddenly flared up in a way which surprised even myself. For I had known of the matter, and had agreed it would be a fine thing. " Very well," I said, " if you find amusement in conning of the Latin roots. It would seem indeed great waste of time to me for a man of your years."

Now I surely expected that Aaron would make an angry answer. Instead he only smiled at me in a superior way and said lightly: " The Latin roots, is it? To be sure we begin with them, but know you not that Master Skipworth is a master gunner and very keen to discourse on the subject? Ah, no, it is not with the Latin roots that we will end." Aaron turned to his map again.

Then was I filled with envy. Scarce a ship of our fleet but now carried a gun and some a whole battery of them. To know aught of gunnery was to have great knowledge whether as captain or sergeant at arms, and I felt strangely cheated. Yet what time I could have had to put on it I was at a loss to know myself. It came to me I was but a dog in the manger, and a very old dog at that. I told myself that I should only rejoice that Aaron was fit to undertake such a study at last, that it was all part of Mistress Antoinette's great wisdom in seeking for him new interest at a moment when old interests had become irksome and strength had not yet come to him to take up a man's work. All the way to the warehouse I waged stiff battle with myself. There I found Dogood inquiring for me.

" My uncle," she said in her abrupt way, " is this afternoon trying out the sails of the *Hawke*, a privateer which he is refitting. He would be pleased to have you make a trip down the harbor with him. He would wish also to have Aaron and Mistress Antoinette of the party if it is possible for them to get there."

Now my heart sang at thought of such an adventure, but I was mindful of my duties and hastened to Asa. Asa informed me that there was no chance of working that afternoon. The ships expected had not made port. I was by all means to accept the invitation. It was much better to go than to sit around the warehouse worrying about the fate of our ships now a day overdue. Indeed he was eager for me to be gone, so much so that a little question entered my mind. The suspicion that Captain O'Hara, without saying a word, had seemed to implant in my mind was hard to root out. Did Asa for some purpose of his own wish me out of his way that afternoon? I put the idea hastily from me. It was indeed small of me to distrust his generous instinct to see me have a little pleasure. I had always, I reminded myself, found him a kindly, thoughtful man.

I returned to Dogood, happier than I had been for many a day. The fact that the ship we were to board was a famous privateer added to the romance of the trip. For although privateering was unlawful, war not having yet been officially declared, it was well known that the *Hawke* had been at it for some time, and her success had been remarkable.

" Is small Paul to be of the party? " I inquired. I liked the young lad somehow.

Dogood drew her eyebrows together, and I noticed that in spite of her fair hair they were dark and finely marked with a beauty I had been slow to take note of. " I do not see how I can well leave him out," she said seriously. " He is too old to fall overboard, and he knows a ship as I know my father's warehouse. Besides he has but just joined the bell ringers of the new Christ Church and feels himself a man. You are to be at the Long Wharf at the stroke of two on the Old South clock. If you are late, you will remain behind."

Dogood's seriousness was always a matter of wonderment to me. All the way home I pondered on its effect on mischievous Mistress Antoinette. I was the bearer of large news for Aaron, and I hoped that Mistress Merrie would not be of a mind to place obstacles in the way of his going. I often thought it was on account of his illness that we were so dependent on her. We were both at an age to make decisions for ourselves.

Mistress Merrie, as I suspected, frowned on the adventure instantly but on second thought did not see her way clear to prevent it. Mistress Antoinette, having been asked, would need chaperonage if she accepted. She ordered me at once to the governor's house.

As for Aaron, his face lighted and shadowed when I told him. " And how am I to get there? " he demanded fiercely. Even yet it was difficult for him to walk far.

" Why there is a fine wheelbarrow behind the house," I made reply, " and, if Mistress Antoinette does not see her way to arrange it, I will get you there myself."

Aaron smiled wanly. " You are good, Eben, but, oh! it is so wearisome to be tied to the house like some small calf when I would be up and doing."

" But you are much better, Aaron," I said.

" Aye," Aaron said, " when the time comes to take the great fortress of Louisbourg, make no mistake, I will be there to avenge my father's death."

And suddenly it came to me that men might plan a thing like that even though 'twas said the fortress was untakable by any means whatever.

Then I remembered that already we had lost some fine ships to the privateers of that same fortress, that 'twas rumored a large East Indiaman was already sheltered there under the great guns of the fortress. And I wondered if we were not rather to be slowly starved by the French in our own territory. For although ships like the *Hawke* had accounted for many French vessels, still even they were no match for the great men-of-war France was rumored to be getting ready to base there. And I thought again, Little good an English fleet stationed in Barbados is like to do us in Boston-town!

I had no need to approach Mistress Antoinette on the subject of how Aaron was to get there. The moment I mentioned he was to be of the party, she cried: " We must have a carriage. I shall ask His Excellency at once."

She was gone but a moment. " It is quite all right," she said. " I shall call for you both at two of the clock."

Then I told her of Mistress Merrie's reluctance, and that I hoped she would not change her mind about going as in that case Mistress Merrie would have ample reason for keeping Aaron home.

Mistress Antoinette solemnly promised that nothing should interfere. " But I am glad you told me, Eben," she said, " for should anything come up I am provided with an argument for going which even the governor would not wish to override. It would be too cruel."

I returned to my chores and was in the kitchen with Mistress Merrie an hour before the appointed time when there came a gentle rap at the kitchen door. I hastened to open it, thinking some neighbor had come to borrow, and could scarce believe it when Mistress Antoinette herself was there. But of a sudden my heart sank. She had surely come to tell us she could not go.

Now Mistress Antoinette had not yet met Mistress Merrie, and I was very fearful of the effect of her rich costume of a moss-colored grenadine on such a sober Puritan as Mistress Merrie. Mistress Antoinette paused meekly on the doorsill as I introduced them. Then Mistress Merrie, who had been caught stirring a pot and was somewhat embarrassed to be thus encountered, bid her coldly to enter and be seated.

This my little maid did, giving a small shiver, whereupon Mistress Merrie drew a chair closer to the fire and indicated she sit there, saying, " It is cold for this time of year, mistress."

Mistress Antoinette answered with a sweet smile: " But it is warm inside here and so cosy. The great pot hath a truly delicious odor."

Now Mistress Merrie was famed far and wide for her stews, and my little maid had hit on the one thing that would please her.

Mistress Merrie made haste to assure her: " 'Tis in great demand in cases of sickness among my neighbors. 'Tis said my stews make the sick well."

" I can well believe it," Mistress Antoinette made answer. " Yet does it make me fair homesick." Her laughing face was for once sober. " For off such a mess did I dine often on the heather hills

69

of Scotland and not off things on silver platters which have no more taste than a bit of boiled leather, being made, as they are, of salt and lamb and never a bit of love in the world."

I made sure that Mistress Merrie would frown on this, for although I loved such talk I thought she would look upon it as monstrous frivolity. Instead she seemed strangely pleased, and did a thing I would not have imagined her doing. She drew a bowl of broth and presented it to our guest, saying she hoped she would be so kind as to share it with us. Mistress Antoinette replied that she would think it great privilege, and fell upon it with a right hearty appetite.

Then it devolved that Mistress Antoinette had come early that she might take us all for a short ride first. Especially did she hope Mistress Merrie would honor her by coming. I could see our good guardian hesitating long between her desire to be seen in an equipage of the governor's and her Puritan conscience which forbade her to take such pride in pomp. But I am afraid the former won, for go she did and very proud she was of it afterward.

I had been much worried as to the meeting of Mistress Antoinette and Aaron but after all it did not seem as momentous as I had supposed it would. Mistress Antoinette turned her back while Aaron was helped down. He needed to be carried no longer. When he was all settled, she swung around and said graciously: " Master Aaron, it is great pleasure that you should deign to drive with me. I trust these trips are doing you no harm." Aaron at once fell captive under her smile — as who did not? And all during the drive I was conscious of a strange loneliness, for it seemed they two had so much to talk about concerning their coming studies together.

We dropped Mistress Merrie at the house and proceeded to the Long Wharf. One other meeting had yet to be gotten through. Dogood and Mistress Antoinette had not met.

I sought Dogood where I felt sure she would be found, at the extreme end of the Long Wharf. She was not one to stop at anything halfway. It was there we came upon her. She had hooped herself up on an old stanchion at the extreme water's edge, and I thought her bold features and streaming flaxen hair outlined against the blue of the sea were like some frigate figurehead.

With some trepidation I made the two known to each other. Mistress Antoinette curtsied low with a quaint grace. But Dogood, with that funny pucker between her eyes, made no move. " I bid you a very good day, Mistress Antoinette," she said loftily. Then her eyes sought mine reproachfully. " I was not told you were so beautiful."

Mistress Antoinette's gay laughter bubbled out, " Mayhap it is a discovery made only by yourself, Dogood."

" I wish it were so, but I doubt it is not."

I had some bewilderment as to what Dogood might mean, but Mistress Antoinette, to my infinite relief, seemed to understand perfectly and to be vastly amused thereby. " 'Twould seem, I take it, Dogood," she made ready answer, " that to you beauty of face would not always indicate goodness of heart. Maybe you are right," she sighed mischievously.

Whereupon Dogood said with great dignity, " I am but recalling the warnings of good Master Coleman in the meetinghouse."

" Faith," answered Mistress Antoinette promptly, " it must have been your own countenance which inspired that Puritan remark."

I could see that Dogood was vastly pleased, and they were by way of becoming fast friends, for which I was both surprised and thankful.

As for Aaron and Dogood, if I had hoped that he would divide his interest I was doomed to disappointment. He had known her before his sickness and contented himself with wishing her a good day and thanking her politely for the pleasure of the expected voyage. After that it was as if she were not there.

I was consumed with impatience for a closer view of the famous *Hawke*. We looked eagerly for her great sails and racing lines. But we looked in vain. Feathertale emerged from the doorway of a warehouse. We moved to greet him.

He returned the greeting gravely. " There will be no trip today," he announced. " The *Hawke* has already sailed."

Dogood's face grew thunderous, and I made sure she had made some mistake in the time. " A promise is a promise," she stormed, " and my father shall be informed of this right smartly."

" Your father, Dogood, will do nothing about it." Feathertale's voice was stern. " The *Swallow* is but just docked. She brought news which sent the *Hawke* flying out of the harbor."

" What news? " We scarce breathed for excitement.

" Canso is fallen! "

" Fallen! " We echoed it weakly.

" Aye! " said Feathertale. " To the French."

" To the Frenchies! " confirmed the captain of a near-by sloop as he joined us. " It's been sacked and burned by order of the governor of the great fortress at Louisbourg. Its garrison are even now prisoners of war. The Louisbourg forces are planning to march on Annapolis Royal with a great fleet from the French king across the water."

I think we were all too stunned to answer. Then Feathertale's voice sounded: " Aye! The first bite is Canso; the second is Annapolis Royal; the third is Bostontown."

We looked at one another. We were familiar enough with the taking of our ships at sea. But this was a land transaction. Canso was, to be sure, a barren place with only a small blockhouse and a handful of inhabitants. But it was English territory, and it was on the route from Louisbourg to Bostontown!

Aaron was first to recover.

" We must take the great fortress at Louisbourg," he cried.

I think there was not one of us who did not feel that this great fortress was the root of the matter. We could not be safe with such a bastion at our gates!

8: The Secret Society of the Red Hats

The fall of Canso was little in itself, for the place consisted of a single blockhouse and a handful of inhabitants. But that Captain Du Vivier should dash out of Louisbourg and annex English territory presaged a coming policy which struck home to every New Englander. Annapolis Royal was always in our minds. How soon would that weakened fortress fall? And what would happen to our shipping if France established a second base, as strong as Louisbourg, at our very gates?

On the heels of the dread announcement of the capture of Canso came a great storm, so that it seemed that even the elements were against us. We trembled anew for our ships at sea.

The wind howled down our little lane. The rain fell in great sheets, so that Mistress Merrie must take me from my Sabbath study of the psalms to batten down our doors and windows. For full three days I saw nought of the Province House or of Mistress Antoinette but took my part with every able-bodied man tying down our shipping. Grueling work it was too.

All day long the great ships in the harbor rode drunkenly on the pitching waves, straining at anchor as if eager to be gone, and ever and again in those moments when I could rest from my labors, I took great joy of the excitement. No ship could load or unload in such weather. Master Pepperrell's countinghouse was a strangely silent place.

Now some great ship, straining at her anchor ropes, would have her way and swing madly out into the stream, intent on her own purposes. Then, above the roar of the wind, would come a great shouting of men, and much scurrying about on the docks and aboard of her, and a hoisting of small sail and much turning of the rudder, a furious rowing of small boats which rose and disappeared on the surges like cockleshells seemingly more impotent than useful, until the mad lass would be brought under control again and ridden safely back to a new anchorage in the troubled waters. It came to me that we, as colonists, were chafing against the inaction imposed by the English crown even as these great ships. And always, as I saw them brought back, there was melancholy for me in their dropped sails, for freedom is a marvelous great thing and it is terrible to spend time in bondage. This I knew from my brother Aaron. For all through the storm his lamentations were loud that he might not take his part like a man and share in my labors, or even attend his studies at the Province House.

Then on the heels of the storm came a great change in the weather. Warm summer days, which Mistress Antoinette thought would be so good for Aaron, came at last. And with them Captain O'Hara, with news of the declaration of war. I was surprised to see he had reappeared in the town. I marveled that he went so openly abroad after the scandal of the mast trees, but possibly the knowledge that they had never reached England accounted for his freedom from arrest. His presence never failed to make me uneasy.

"Know ye all," he announced grandiloquently, "that His Britannic Majesty, King George the Second, has been pleased to inform his English colonies *and* — he added satirically — the Province of the Massachusetts Bay that a state of war exists between herself and the people of France."

It was nothing we had not suspected for some time, and at first we took it merely for another rumor. However, the very next day Antoinette confirmed it, and again we made note of the fact that Captain O'Hara had known of it in advance. What manner of man was this fellow that he should know ahead of even our governor?

At one of the clock, the very next day, Captain Jeff in His Majesty's Ship *Swallow* came ashore in great haste and sped with express to the governor. By five of the clock we all knew something untoward was afoot, for the governor had ordered the Regiment of Boston to assemble at the Dock Square. The declaration of war was then read to the troops and received with lusty cheers from the men. It was followed by the proclamation for the encouragement of His Majesty's ships of war and private ships of war. Whereupon the troops fired three volleys and paraded off to the martial piping of the fife and drum.

All our spirits lifted immediately. We felt sure now that His Majesty, having recognized the necessity of informing us, must also have recognized our need, and would surely now order some of the great men-of-war from their rich raiding around St. Kitts and Antigua into the waters of the Massachusetts Bay for our protection.

But the declaration of war meant more to us than that. It meant that now our privateersmen could go out with a clear conscience and "annoy" the enemy. To us New Englanders that was matter for great inner satisfaction.

And now all about us was a fever of fitting up of ships. Men were busy signing up on all sides. In the warehouse was nothing but talk of the rich prizes they were to bring in; of the monies already earned by ships like the *Hawke,* the *Young Eagle,* the *Boston Packet,* over whose exploits the government had been pleased to close its eyes.

Aaron was all for signing up on a privateersman at once. But Mistress Merrie did not have to worry about him long. Aaron had a rather severe relapse, bringing great fear to all of us but Antoinette. She told him in no uncertain terms that he must be content to make haste slowly, that for every hour he exerted himself he must see to it there was an equal hour of rest. I was surprised how meekly he took her scolding, how aptly he applied it, and how soon his strength returned.

It was during these long summer days that Aaron, Mistress Antoinette, Dogood, small Paul when he could, and I began to play a strange game. We would take the map we had made of the great fortress, and try to find our way about the streets of the town, describing what we saw. It was surprising how much knowledge of the place we had accumulated, even to a description of the strange sundial in the garden of the Good Sisters of the Congregation.

We went easily from the West Gate across the Esplanade up the Rue Toulouse to the Citadel steps. We climbed the King's Bastion, and sighted out across the morass. The Place d'Armes intrigued us for its view of the sea. We lingered in the governor's garden, held by the perfume and the strange rich riot of color there. We went often across the little bridge over the pond near the Maurepas Gate, for the fishermen told us that many a wild bird winging north rested here during its long flight.

When fall came it seemed that Aaron applied himself more assiduously than ever to his studies each day, and I soon came to realize that what he had predicted had come true. I saw more often mathematical calculations than Latin roots on the slate which he used to work on at home and could only surmise that lectures in gunnery were indeed replacing his study of the classics. I made inquiry one day how such things could interest a lass like Mistress Antoinette and received in reply the retort from Aaron that, though it could not have much interest for her, she never missed a lesson hour, wherefore Aaron himself thought she was there for pleasure of his company. That his surmise was probably true, I did not doubt. However, the thought did not raise my spirits.

While new reports of the fortress further emphasized its strength and impregnability, there came tales as the winter progressed that food was extremely low there, and toward Christmas we heard that the Swiss mercenary troops had openly mutinied.

But not all the news that came to our ears was heartening. Part of the tale told at Feathertale John's was so disquieting he took it to the governor's ears. It was said that five great merchantmen on their way to France had been met en route, informed of the declaration of war, and ordered into Louisbourg to pick up reinforcements and armament there. All five carried rich cargoes: one was loaded with tea and porcelain from China; two others carried piece goods and coffee; while some had " all manner of provisions." After this strengthening the *Mars* and the *Baleine* were said to mount upwards of fifty guns, and each had a crew of three hundred and fifty men. The *Fullavie, Philibert, Argonaute,* and the *Duc d'Anjou* mounted thirty guns tended by a crew of one hundred and fifty men. This was a formidable force indeed and should it remain there and be joined by a squadron of French men-of-war might well be sufficient to attack Bostontown.

Dogood's remarks were strangely pertinent. " Now, perchance," she snapped, " we shall hear from the English men-of-war. The East Indiamen are their special prizes and if they elude them by means of the shelter afforded by Louisbourg, the English may think it behooves them to take the great fortress. If England herself is to suffer, maybe she will do something about this great bastion at our very gates." As usual I felt that Dogood had hit the matter very squarely upon the head.

Many a night during that dark winter Aaron and I wakened and hied us to the window, fearful that the great beacon on the hill was ablaze — signal that the French were upon us. Wherefore ever after we referred to it as Beacon Hill. After each such occasion I noted that Aaron took up his work on gunnery under Master Skipworth with renewed enthusiasm.

Two things in that winter I am not like ever to forget. One was the trip we all made with Mistress Antoinette to the Church of the Episcopates. It seemed to me the sweet-smelling greens and the gay bells made of it a warm and friendly place, and I did not see why the Lord's house should not have the cosiness of Feathertale John's shop. The other was a day I spent with Mistress Antoinette at His Excellency's estate at Roxbury. It was a frosty morning, clear and bracing. My little maid had on a cloak of red woolly material and a red bonnet edged with beaver. I could have envied the rich fur which cuddled her white throat, and to which she had pinned a bunch of red berries late sent her from Londontown. Holly, she said it was.

Mistress Antoinette had been more than ordinarily mischievous. Perhaps to show my superior knowledge, being no match for her at a game of teasing, I had begun to draw for her in the snow a figure of a great G, which was the outline of the terrain around the fortress of Louisbourg.

I marked the fortress on the heavy leg of the G. Across the opening on the other side I noted the Point of the Lantern where was, I assured her, a most marvelous thing — a lighthouse which could not be burned by fire. Then, in between, solidly across the entrance to the harbor, I placed the island on which was situated the Island Battery. On the inner side of the harbor just opposite the island, I indicated the Royal Battery, which might silence any ship's guns which successfully passed or demolished the Island Battery.

Behind the fortress I marked the great morass and the long line of harborless shore on either side of the harbor opening, a shore so wave-ridden that none might attempt a landing there. Then outside I drew the great Gabarus Bay, a fine anchorage, it was said, in spite of the hostile shores.

" Would you not think," I said to Mistress Antoinette, " that France with a base like that in the New World would send over a great fleet and sufficient troops to conquer Bostontown? "

" It would seem a chance the French would not overlook," Mistress Antoinette agreed.

I moved away from the map, seeking a stick with which to build up the snow into the King's Bastion, and some small twigs for the guns of the salient. When I came back Mistress Antoinette was still by the pine, but there was a light of mischief in her face which made me glance hastily at my map. There I saw, in the Gabarus Bay, a quaint design of red berries.

" What may this be? " I demanded puzzled, yet delighting in the merriment which crinkled her small face. Her silvery laughter rang out at once. " This, monsieur, an' it pleasure you, is the Chapeau Rouge."

Now I saw that the red berries from her bouquet were in the shape of a little witch's hat. I gazed at it, greatly amused and struck with the fact that although Aaron and I had been familiar with the French language from childhood neither of us had made the quaint connection. For while the maps of the period all called it the Gabarus Bay, the New England fishermen were in habit of referring to it as the Chapeau Rouge.

I thought much on the matter of Chapeau Rouge meaning " Red Hat." I told Aaron and Dogood and Paul about it. I found them equally intrigued. It gave us all great joy to consider ourselves members of a secret society, the Red Hats, who would render untold aid to the Province of the Massachusetts Bay in time of war. Paul, one day, drew a little red hat on the map, and we took as our motto the motto of the flute, " *J'y suis, j'y reste,*" " Here I am, here I stay." It meant for us that we would never let the French drive us from Bostontown. Aaron added the motto also to the map, only contracting it for greater secrecy to two large *J's*. We believed it signified there that we would take the great fortress for England once and forever. Dogood, on her part, procured some bright-red flannel from which she cut some miniature hats, which we wore on occasion upon our sleeves. To us it signified we had dedicated ourselves to a high purpose. We cherished them jealously.

It was perhaps a childish idea, more becoming to Paul's age than to great lads and lasses of seventeen and nineteen, but it served to link us together and saved us from dwelling on the menace which we of the younger generation felt drawing ever nearer with the opening of the icebound St. Lawrence and the Louisbourg harbor. We began to fear the possibility of a French armada's gathering on our shores. Word of shipbuilding going on on the St. Lawrence and in Cape Breton strengthened these tales.

One item of interest about the great fortress we never entered on the map of the Red Hats.

We were all gathered in Feathertale's shop one winter day. Even Mistress Antoinette had joined us, and her eyes shone with interest in the place. Feathertale had made a place for her on the rude bench beside him — a rare honor. I thought the two of them made a strange picture in that setting so replete with shadows and long shafts of light. Of all the customary crowd, Thundercloud alone squatted in his usual place. Others there might be in the shadows about the forge, but they were not in evidence. It was a warm, sunny winter day and most of the men were busy mending ratlines broken by the storms, and drying out their sails. Aaron had brought the map of the great fortress to the shop to show Feathertale. We had spread it on the floor before the bench and were all intent on it. Even Thundercloud had drawn closer. Never having heard anything but a grunt from him, it was a shock to us to find him muttering syllables in a soft, guttural tone, his eyes gleaming excitedly.

Now Thundercloud was of the Micmac, an Abenaki tribe whose language Feathertale had acquired. The moment the old Indian began to talk, I saw Feathertale's own face show unusual interest, even excitement, and I was consumed with curiosity as to what it was all about.

Feathertale drew a long finger across the map, ending in the harbor below the Maurepas Gate, and seemed to be asking a question. The Indian grunted. With his own hand he traced a line from the King's Bastion, down through the Princess Bastion, to the point near the shore where Feathertale's finger had started. I was sorry I could not identify the exact spot Feathertale's hand covered, Mistress Antoinette having moved forward at the moment. But the Indian, having resumed his customary silence, returned to his usual seat and seemed sunk in meditation. His movement appeared to break some spell that bound us to silence.

"What is it?" demanded Aaron impatiently. "What does he say?" While Dogood cried imperiously, "Tell us at once, Uncle John."

Only Antoinette kept silence, but I thought her touch on his arm and the pleading way her dark eyes sought his were more eloquent than any of our voices.

Feathertale's own voice was always low. It seemed to me now that it sank almost to a whisper, which sent strange thrills down my own spine and made us all draw closer together.

"He said," Feathertale continued to eye the map thoughtfully, "that he helped to build the great fortress, and that there is a secret passage, running from the Princess Bastion down through the Maurepas Gate to the harbor, but that it is not on any map, as even the designer did not wish it to be known to anyone." Feathertale stopped. Then he continued: "It may well be. It is an old custom of France in the châteaux. Scarce one but has its walled stair and secret panel."

"A secret passage in the great fortress!" Dogood's voice rang out. "But why should they not put it on the map?"

Now I do not know whether the thought in my mind was that being a secret thing, it should be kept secret, or whether, as I afterward seemed to recall, there came at this moment a sharper grunt from Thundercloud. Certain it is I moved swiftly round and encountered the gaze of Captain O'Hara, who was just coming up the stair. His face startled me by its sudden foxlike look. He said lightly: " A secret passage is it in the great fortress? A fine tale without a word of truth in it." Then I saw him deliberately bend his gaze upon Dogood, and was instantly aware of a certain hypnotic quality in it.

" There is too," Dogood made instant answer. " Thundercloud says it starts — "

Feathertale John cut in sternly: " Thundercloud was relating some superstitions of his tribe concerning the fortress. 'Tis but an old Indian tale of no consequence."

I glanced quickly at Thundercloud, sure he would resent Feathertale's tone. Instead it seemed to me his grunt was filled with approval.

Whereupon Dogood sided promptly with Feathertale John, saying sharply, " Since it is not true, I will not repeat it, Captain O'Hara."

I thought if Captain O'Hara was seeking information, for once he was not likely to be satisfied. It surprised me not a little that he should let the matter drop there, but let it drop he did, going immediately to the business with Feathertale which he said had brought him in. But I bethought me I was beginning to find something a little mysterious in the comings and goings of Captain O'Hara. His presence had a way of continually surprising us.

As for the rest of us, we took our cue from Feathertale and managed to remain silent until, having taken our departure, we were on our way home. Then in guarded tones we discussed it excitely. How big was the opening? Could it be used to admit troops to the fortress? It fascinated us to think of slipping in and out of enemy territory, and no one of them the wiser.

However, the incident of the secret passage was not quite closed. A few days later Asa surprised me by saying, " This secret passage, Eben, that Thundercloud mentioned, where now might it be? "

Now I had, of course, every reason to gratify Asa's curiosity. It was a small matter, but somewhat to my own surprise I found myself reluctant to answer. I could not remember that Asa had been present that day, and strongly suspected that Captain O'Hara had been listening much longer than we had appreciated. If he were trading with the enemy, no doubt a way of secret ingress and egress to the fortress would come in mighty handy. So I told Asa I was not sure, as indeed I was not, just where it started. I added also that Feathertale had been at some pains to discredit the matter as merely an Indian tale. But I found my suspicions of Asa in no way allayed.

It was about this time that Mistress Merrie was taken with a fit of spring-cleaning and Aaron, fearing the map of the Red Hats might suffer sudden extinction under her vigorous foraging, decided it would be safer elsewhere.

It was then I recalled the hiding place in the figurehead, introduced to me by my father, the Captain St. Jean de Gervais. It became our secret hiding place for the map of the Red Hats.

And now the air all around us was filled with strange whispering. Rumors fluttered by us like falling leaves. Yet they were rumors which filled us with excitement and delight, although the news seemed to us scarce believable. It was being noised abroad that the Province of the Massachusetts Bay with the other colonies was planning an expedition against the great fortress, to silence once and forever its menace to our trade and our property. Was our dream of taking the great fortress about to come true? As for Mistress Antoinette, she would neither confirm nor deny the rumors, but her very reticence was confirmation, we felt, that the rumors themselves had foundation in His Excellency's, the Governor's, house.

Immediately our game on the map of the Red Hats took fiercer form of sport. Aaron planned a mighty attack by sea, moving all His Majesty's great men-of-war hither and thither at will over the surface of the Gabarus Bay, our Chapeau Rouge.

When Dogood objected, " But, Aaron, the English men-of-war are not here, we must plan this attack on land," small Paul would insist: " But, Dogood, we couldn't attack the fortress without the English men-of-war. It is only by ships the place can be taken."

Then I would hear Antoinette's quiet voice, " Be assured, Dogood, the English ships will come when they are needed, even from the bottom of the sea."

If, by chance, there was a pause in the operations, Paul would cry out eagerly: " Now, what shall we do next? We must do something quickly." Instantly the mischievous glint would sparkle in Antoinette's eyes and she would cry: " Let us fire a salvo! That is always a good safe thing to do! "

" But I like not killing people, Mistress Antoinette," Paul would object.

" Then let us fire it into the hills where there is nobody," Antoinette would cheerfully agree. " I doubt not it would be as effective as some of our shots, our gunners not being overly expert in the matter of hitting a target as yet." And her eyes would seek Aaron's frowning face and compel him to smile at her teasing.

But literal Dogood would see none of it except as hard, sober fact. " It is most wasteful use of good ammunition," she would announce sternly. " Hit something, Aaron! Level the King's Bastion! Silence the bells of St. Louis, St. Jean, and St. Antoine-Marie! "

As for my brother Aaron, he contented himself with saying little, but it seemed to me he looked at the map, as at a game of chess, seeing strategies far in advance of any of us.

So the war game would go on until our great ship's thirty-eight-pounders would have successfully leveled the salients and silenced the Island Battery and even the Royal Battery within the harbor, and we would sail in — an imposing spectacle — and occupy the town, flying our own colors from its proud citadel.

But in spite of many happy hours together when we all played the war game on our map of the Red Hats, I had much sadness on my own account. For in the times between Aaron brought me constant news of my little maid. I could see that studying together had shown to them the many tastes they had in common. It had created an intimacy far greater than my own with the little maid. I knew I stood little chance with her when compared with my brilliant brother.

9: Of the Terrible Trouble That Befell Me

Canso had fallen in the early summer of 1744. All that year rumors of an expedition continued. The colonies grew more and more impatient at the menace to our trade. As talk of an expedition grew stronger, Paul took his age very sorely.

One day, walking among the wharf alleys, Mistress Antoinette and I came past some slats used for the drying of codfish, and here we found Paul stretched on one of the drying racks, his feet hooked over the end, his hands, which could scarce reach, stretching over the pole at the other end, so that Mistress Antoinette cried out terrifiedly, " It is a rack! " Paul whipped over and sat up.

" Why, Paul! " I cried. " What is it that you are up to now? "

" O Eben," he cried, " it is that I am so little. I am trying to stretch myself. If I were but tall I could enlist."

" 'Tis impossible: he is but nine years old," murmured Antoinette.

As for Paul, he kicked off his clogs and, bounding up, stood himself against a door. " How high am I now? " he demanded.

Now Mistress Antoinette laughed away her fright and set her hand just above his head on the doorframe. Paul moved away, and whether by stretching or natural growth — I would not say that Mistress Antoinette had raised her hand ever so slightly as he faced about, although her eyes of a sudden danced mischievously — it would seem he had grown an inch from where the mark was a month ago.

" O Eben, see! " Paul cried. " If I could grow that much in a month, think you I would be tall enough in a twelvemonth? "

" Why of a surety! " laughed Mistress Antoinette. " An inch a month is twelve inches a year, and twelve inches a year is two feet in two years, and at the age of fourteen I would think you would be nine feet tall, and would that be enough, or would you wish to be twelve feet tall? And how would you get into doorways or down to your bench? Never would your head know what your hands were doing at all."

Little Paul's face sobered comically. " I would not do anything," he said, " whereby I should injure my ability to be a great silversmith." Whereat we all laughed heartily and Paul joined in. " You were but teasing me," he said relievedly, which amused us the more. But I could not but admire his unfailing good nature.

Frequently Aaron joined us in our explorations around the dock, Mistress Antoinette asserting it was good for him to use his new strength moderately. Sometimes a captain would invite us aboard, and, perched in the lee of the deckhouse, Aaron would take out his flute and play a few airs, passing sweet, remarking that it was for the entertainment of any of the crew. On such occasions I noted that Mistress Antoinette sat, a rapt figure, seeming to have wandered into some realm beyond human ken, and I was conscious of feeling alone and shut out.

Now I had grown so used to Mistress Antoinette's company, with or without the others, that it seemed I had no single thought separate from her. Aaron lately had found himself work. It was not of the sea which he loved, his strength being even yet insufficient for the heavy tasks of the lower decks. One of Paul's uncles was the owner of some fine horses. At times they needed exercising beyond what he was able to give them, and he had seen fit to hire Aaron for the work. I often thought that all of Aaron's recklessness was in his thoughts. He was most careful in all his actions and seemed in this matter to have the patience to ride them sufficiently but not to excess, wherefore the good Mr. Hitchbourn seemed well pleased. It served to keep Aaron in the open the sunny part of each day and was doing amazing things to his spirits.

It was one of those winter days when the summer seems to have returned again, and I was feeling not a little irked that I must help Mistress Merrie by watching a bit of pork roasting on the spit for the day's dinner. My flute was my only company. I was trying out some strange new airs I had wish to master, fast-tripping little jigs I had heard piped on a horn in the Bunch of Grapes when I had gone there on some errand for Master William. I was quite sure that Mistress Merrie would most heartily disapprove of them and was glad to practice them when she was not about, thinking to surprise Aaron. The door was open to the sunshine, for I had a great fire going on the hearth and the room was cosy as a ship's deckhouse. I was succeeding rather well, I thought, and was admiring the golden patch which the sun had flung in the open doorway, when suddenly I thought I must surely be dreaming. It seemed that the notes had indeed taken the form of a dancing figure. There was a wild grace in the twisting, turning, pirouetting little form. It was a moment or two before I could grasp the fact that it was in truth Mistress Antoinette.

I stopped abruptly, and the dancing figure came to rest in a little curtsy at my feet, while a sweet voice demanded of me, " Why look you so, Eben? "

" It seems you are not real," I made answer.

" And is it so glad you are to see me that you think you see me in your dreams? " she would know.

" That must be the truth of it," I answered boldly.

She hung her head with sudden wilting as one from whom the strength has flowed away. " Come out into the full sunlight," she said quickly. " I like not to be confined when I am sad."

" But why should you be sad? Is it evil news from France? "

" Tell me, Eben, would it sadden you overmuch to think I would not come here again? "

" Antoinette," I cried, forgetful in my great fear to " mistress " her. " Has the governor forbid your coming? Has — "

" No! No! No! " she made hasty answer, and for the first time I saw her lips quiver. " I am sailing on the tide this day two days for Londontown, and O Eben, I know not when I shall ever return."

I sat myself down on the narrow doorsill, forgetful of the time of year, as one turned to stone.

" Why is it? " I managed to gasp at last.

" I know not," she whispered. " My father has been recalled. I am to return with him."

Suddenly she was gone.

Now I had been too young to remember my mother, but my father's loss was still upon me. It seemed I was losing him anew. It fell upon me as a great calamity. So hurt was I, I could not eat my evening meal. Mistress Merrie must scold me severely for my waste of the food the Lord had provided, and no one knowing how soon the invasion would be upon us when we might well be in dire want. I know not why I could not eat. And although Aaron looked at me strangely, it was morning before ever I could tell him the sad news.

Aaron was strangely thoughtful when he knew. I marveled that he was not more cast down. Had he perhaps had hint of it before? The thought hurt me anew.

It was Aaron who told Paul and Dogood. Dogood's answer, in spite of my dreariness, amused me greatly.

" I could go to England too," she announced instantly. " 'Tis my father's ship she sails on, and he has many relatives there, besides having more money than His Excellency, the Governor, himself. 'Tis not such a great thing, this traveling to England."

I decided it was all in line with Dogood's queerness and promptly forgot the matter.

The hours fled all too swiftly. We stood on the Long Wharf to say good-by. Strange I thought it to see Mistress Antoinette so sad. Now I had never met Mistress Antoinette's father. The tall man with the lean, bony face and the long, sensitive nose was unknown to me, but I realized from their greeting that he and Aaron had met before. It gave me a sense of being shut out, and then I heard Antoinette murmuring, " And this is Eben, father, Aaron's brother. I would have you know him too."

Turning, I saw a man clad in the bonnie kilt of the Stuarts. A womanish rig some consider it, but I thought then, and I think now, it is uncommon handsome on a great man.

The Stuart, for one long moment, bent his full attention upon me. And I never saw a stranger combination, for there was in the stern contours of his countenance the strength of his native crags, but there was too a sensitiveness of nostril, a sweetness of expression, which minded me of a brook-watered dell in one of our own forests. His gaze seemed to play over me like a great light baring my soul. For some reason it was for me a moment of great anxiety. Then it seemed to me a soft, happy sigh escaped my little maid. The Stuart thrust out a lean, muscular hand, and a clear ringing voice announced above me, " I like ye fine, laddie." Instantly pride filled me. For some reason I had a sense of an uncommon honor having been conferred upon me, and I knew then that, were I Antoinette, I would follow the Stuart to the end of the earth.

At the last moment, Paul came clopping in on one of his uncle's nags. And I thought how much he had grown since the day we had stood before the Proclamation. He had brought a gift for each of us. He had persuaded Dogood to cut him some new red-flannel hats, and his father had allowed him some small silver shavings. With these he had hammered a border of silver binding around each red hat. And, concealed in the tracing with which he had been at some pains to decorate the lower side, was a set of initials, identifying each one. He was particularly proud of his S. I felt sure the lad was like to be what he wished most, a great silversmith. As he pointed out, they could be sewed to our sleeves, or on our caps, a secret insigne.

" It is a beautiful gift, dear," Antoinette told him. " I shall keep it always, Paul."

Then Aaron, flinging his arm about Antoinette, openly kissed her, and a sharp pang went through me, so that I moved hurriedly away and stood in a corner of the wharf, sheltered from all observers by a great stack of hogsheads.

All in a moment I found Antoinette beside me. " Do not forget me," she cried, and buried her face in my sleeve. " O Eben! Do not forget me, ever."

Then by some strange chance — I know not how I dared — I found her in my arms, and I too kissed her. And the wonder of it was that suddenly all sadness left me. It was as if I had come upon a stream of clear, bubbling water and, jaded and weary, I had drunk of its waters and been renewed. My spirits soared to exaltation.

It was well that something occurred almost immediately that turned our attention from ourselves. Aaron summoned me hastily, for there down the Long Wharf, accompanied by numerous relatives and a wheelbarrow of bundles, came Dogood.

I could scarce believe my eyes. Was Dogood also embarking on a voyage?

" But Dogood," Paul remonstrated, standing squarely in her pathway, " you are my neighbor and you did not tell me you were going away." Then he added quaintly and I thought it explained their odd companionship, " You are not one who should travel alone, being too impulsive."

" I am not in mood to be argued with," said Dogood sharply. " I am traveling in company with Mistress Antoinette and her father to Londontown, and it is high time I should be off."

Then Paul presented her with her red hat, and I thought she looked uncommon pleased at receiving it.

As the boat carried them to their ship, I was pleased to see them clinging together, but it seemed to me that Dogood's face was the whiter of the two. Possibly at last her quick-tempered nature, strange mixture of practicality and utter waywardness, had ridden her into a greater adventure than she had bargained for.

As for Mistress Antoinette, her eyes remained upon us as the small boat pulled away, and swift as a cold chill the thought came to me, Are they resting on Aaron longer than on me?

Presently the Stuart and the two maids climbed aboard the large vessel, which almost immediately weighed anchor. As I heard the rattle of the long chain going aboard, I thought that the chains that had been freed of holding the ship had indeed fallen upon me, binding me to Antoinette. Paul clattered away. I turned back with Aaron, and of a sudden was filled with a gnawing ache which I could not assuage. Nor did I assuage it in the weeks which followed. The *Flying Fortune*, bearing Antoinette and Dogood and the brave Stuart away, had taken a bit of my heart with it.

Then I glanced at Aaron, momentarily stricken, and I knew that he shared my desolation, but it was no consolation to me. Rather it deepened my loss. For the first time we had something we could not share.

It was well for me that within a few weeks I heard news of such import that, for the moment, I was like to push my loss into the back of my mind.

At Master Pepperrell's I learned, albeit secretly, that agitation was abroad in the Assembly to equip an expedition against the French in Cape Breton. It was said His Excellency, Governor Shirley, was greatly in favor of it. Aaron, when I confided in him, was much overjoyed. Was our dream of storming the great fortress about to come true?

From Feathertale I learned that, while the merchants were all for it, the farmers were against it. We were a peaceful people who had left old wars behind with the Old World, we thought, and the farmers saw in it but a continuance of the old rivalries. But to Aaron and me it was a fight for life and freedom to carry on our trade in the New World. It was bitter disappointment then to us when we learned that the Assembly had voted against the whole matter.

Only Feathertale remained undisturbed. " His Excellency, Governor Shirley," he assured us, " is not a man to retreat lightly from an advanced position. He has great energy and uncommon stubbornness in the pursuit of an idea. The matter is not done with by any means."

We soon found that Feathertale, as usual, had prophesied well.

Great was our joy when the matter was again brought to vote in the General Assembly, this time to be carried, albeit by the slim margin of a single vote. It was said that one of the Assemblymen, a member of the opposition, had broken his leg on the way to the meeting and had been unable to vote.

In the spring then, as soon as the ice around Louisbourg made navigation possible, we were to send an expedition against the French in Cape Breton.

We, the men of New England, were to storm the impregnable

fortress of Louisbourg. It was an inspiring thought! We had no trained troops! We had no heavy ordnance and few small arms — not enough to equip properly the men we had sent to the relief of Annapolis Royal. We had no men-of-war! But we had an indomitable courage. England, when she saw our spirit, would surely send some men-of-war! She would see what free men could do and take pride in her young colony.

Neither Aaron nor I doubted our ability to accomplish it triumphantly.

The weeks that followed Mistress Antoinette's departure were weeks teeming with excitement!

10 : To Arms! To Arms!

Now on all sides came the cry, " To arms! To arms! "

The streets thrilled with the martial clamor of the drums, summoning old and young to the recruiting places. The pulpits rang with the war cry. Even good Master Coleman was exhorting his people: " Down with the papists." It seemed strange to me that the expedition against the great fortress, which we were undoubtedly undertaking to save our own skins and coffers, should suddenly have taken on the spirit of a crusade. However, it must be admitted that in Protestant Bostontown this gave great impetus to the recruiting.

The first requisite was a leader. My joy was large when good Master William Pepperrell was made commander in chief.

His news was continuous. New Hampshire was sending us men. Connecticut too promised some companies. Maine, his own part of the country, would send her quota. New York promised a train of artillery. Rhode Island could contribute a sloop, the *Tartar*. Pennsylvania could not square it with her conscience to send men, but she promised to send a goodly quota of pounds, shillings, and pence.

When I remarked to Aaron that I thought it much better that we go out and take the great fortress than to sit at home and await the French invasion, he laughed aloud. " O Eben," he cried, " 'tis not fear of invasion is driving them to war. Do you not know that the merchants wish it because the French are seriously interfering with their trade? And the fishermen wish it, because they are being driven from the fishing grounds? And the Churchmen wish it, because they consider the French nothing but heathens? The French will never invade Bostontown, although," he added soberly, " they might make living here very difficult."

Then I told him that he sounded just like Dogood, and he replied, unabashed, " 'Twas Dogood gave me the idea."

Now under all the excitement my thoughts ran often to Mistress Antoinette and Dogood. I could not but see that my brother, Aaron, was much changed for their going. The change gave me vague uneasiness. He seemed to have become a man. I asked myself, Is it because he has won Mistress Antoinette?

One place the change was especially marked was in his attitude to the flute. He could not any longer bear to play it. I could understand this a little, for it was for both of us replete with memories of her. Only I courted the pain it brought. And I rejoiced now that he no longer used it, because I might take it to the warehouse continually. But, if I enjoyed the flute, there was one thing connected with her that I could not bring myself to regard again — I dared not look at the map of the Red Hats.

Both from choice and necessity I spent much more of my time at the warehouse than formerly. From choice, because by virtue of the master's position as commander in chief the warehouse had become the very hub of all the news. From necessity, because the coming and going of a ship was now shrouded in mystery. Often a ship would conceal her identity by false flags, refusing to speak to friend or foe, so that our first warning of her approach was seeing her riding up the stream. We must keep a sharp lookout at all times, that the unloading crew might be on the dock as soon as she dropped anchor in the stream, for time was often a factor in eluding a raider.

I was sitting in the warehouse one day, keeping watch and playing my flute, when word was brought to me that the master had wish to see me to ask me some question concerning my ledgers. I hastened to put the flute away and comply with his wishes. It was our custom to close the door of the warehouse if we were leaving it alone. But on this occasion I knew that Asa was but just beyond the wharf aboard a big vessel and likely to return at any minute. I myself, I knew, would not be long. I left the doors open.

When I returned Asa had not come back, although he did so almost immediately. He informed me then that the *Goodson*, a boat we expected, was in the offing, according to a packet which had just made port from New York, and would come in as soon as it was dark. The waters near the mouth of the harbor were especially dangerous. Asa said I might as well go home, for there would be nothing doing before the morrow. I begged him to let me stay, for I was eager to practice a little longer, something it was impossible to do at home, since Aaron did not wish to hear a sound of it.

Asa said since I was wishful of staying he would return to the boat and finish his task before locking up.

I played over a rollicking song or two and then bethought me of the bird song I had heard on two or three occasions, the musical trillip. I tried it out on the flute. And then a mysterious thing occurred. Glancing up, I could have sworn that I saw the face of my father, Captain St. Jean de Gervais, etched upon the shadow. It was there for only a moment's duration, but so real it was that I jumped to my feet and started toward it. The next moment the face which I had seen but dimly was gone, vanished into the darkness. I had an instant feeling it was but an illusion. Nevertheless, I made earnest search. I recalled my desire to avenge his death and I brought myself severely to task for having let my thoughts run so much to Mistress Antoinette. Then I heard a high cackle, and I knew that Captain O'Hara had entered the warehouse, although how he had come, I could not tell. I had not seen him enter.

" Ah," he taunted, " and hast thou met Morpain yet and exterminated the French of Louisbourg? "

I told him sourly that I would most surely face Morpain yet, whereat he smiled evilly and said: " I thought you had done it already! I shall be expecting news of it any minute, Master Eben, son of the Captain St. Jean de Gervais."

There was a concealed sneer in the way he pronounced my father's name, but I could not at the moment think of a suitable rejoinder. Instead, I replied hotly that I was like to be very busy otherwise for some time to come — and then bethought me of the information I was giving away; for to be busy in the warehouse meant but one thing — the coming or going of a ship.

He was not dull. His sharp glance told me to my dismay that he had understood what I meant. I was seeking frantically for a way in which to rectify my mistake when a packet came full sail up to the dock. A man leaped ashore and made for the warehouse. He was carrying dispatches. Then I saw Asa and a handful of sailors from the other ship waylay him.

" Any news? " they cried.

" 'Tis Annapolis Royal," he cried.

" The French have it! " someone shouted. We waited, chilled by a sense of coming disaster.

" No," cried the messenger. " The French thought our relieving force a party of friends. They dashed to the shore to welcome us. Learning their mistake, they were thrown into great confusion and retired precipitantly. They ran back not only to their own camp but beyond it. Indeed, I would not wonder they were still going and had almost reached Louisbourg by now."

" But why bring a besieging force to Annapolis Royal at all, if not to take it? " Asa voiced the wonder that was in all of us.

" Maybe they came but to spy," Captain O'Hara's high voice entered the conversation with ear-cutting distinctness, and his eyes sought mine in a way that none could miss. " I am not surprised, having known a Frenchman or two."

At that I blazed out at him, " My father was an honest New Englander, though born in France."

" Aye? " Captain O'Hara's tone was slow and questioning. " But

I was thinking of his son." Now a laugh went up at my very evident discomfiture. It rankled deep within me.

Then Asa, thinking it had gone far enough, said: " Cease your bickering, Captain O'Hara. It might behoove you to go more carefully, the governor not being quite through with you in the matter of the mast trees."

I did not like the look that Captain O'Hara threw me. There was a cold hate in it, which chilled me. I had a feeling we had a score to settle, and the desire was not all on my side.

On the morrow the matter of Captain O'Hara was brought to my attention anew. For word came up the stream that three of our ships had been chased by a French privateer. And although the *Goodson* got in, the other two did not. Was I in any way responsible?

Sore-distressed, I approached Master William, now become General William Pepperrell, but I found it difficult as ever to give him his title. He promptly laughed away my fears. " 'Tis but the chances of war, Eben. As for Captain O'Hara, I do not like his looks — he always impresses me as one with something to conceal — but that is a personal prejudice. He is a good seaman, I hear, in spite of his deformity. As for the mast trees, even if they had reached England, I am afraid a great many New Englanders do not think it cheating to cheat the crown."

I tried hard to accept his rating of Captain O'Hara, but I could not bring myself to cease my distrust.

Now, sitting alone in Feathertale's shop not long after this, I bethought me of the map of the Red Hats. Surely, in view of what was planned, it would be of some service to His Excellency and Master William. I jumped up and, crossing the room, touched the spring in the figurehead, snatching out the roll which lay inside. I was very careful to reclose the aperture, that none might know of its existence.

Then such a longing for a sight of Antoinette's dear writing overcame me that I, perforce, must open it. I unrolled and unrolled — came to the end. There was nothing inside. Our map of the Red Hats was gone!

Snatching up the roll, I dashed away. A thought had come to me. Paul in his cleverness might have discovered the spring and taken the map to work on. Although so much younger, he was much the best draughtsman of us all, his fingers having a unique cunning in such matters.

I found young Paul at work in his father's shop and told him my idea. Paul's eyes opened wide. " But, Eben," he cried, " you never showed me the secret of the hiding place. I would not have gone looking for it myself."

I knew instantly this was so.

I would have apologized, but a sudden new idea showed itself distressingly in Paul's face. " Eben," he cried, " if a Frenchman should get hold of our map, do you think it would do harm? "

Now this was a new idea. However, there was still Aaron who might have it.

I left Paul hurriedly and raced home, but along the way Paul's idea struck me in a new light. The names of the British ships, their number of guns, method of disposal, though expounded by Aaron, had been, I felt sure, Antoinette's ideas. Could it be that she had picked up the information at the governor's house and was inadvertently giving away advance plans of the proposed attack? It filled me with new uneasiness and speeded my feet toward Aaron.

" Aaron! " I fairly shouted it, as I climbed the stair to his room. " Aaron! The map of the Red Hats is gone! Did you take it? "

Aaron looked up absently from his work and scowled at me in a way reminiscent of Dogood. " What are you shouting, Eben? " I repeated my statement trying to control my exasperation. Aaron looked hard at me. " What are you talking about, Eben? I saw it myself but recently." I had early imparted the secret of the figurehead to Aaron, feeling that our father had meant the information for us both.

" You saw but the wrapper," I told him. But he would not believe it was gone, saying someone had consulted it and not put it back, or it had fallen out, the spring coming open. We sought Feathertale's again and made diligent search. It was to both of us like losing Antoinette.

Then Feathertale John too voiced the thought that had been torturing me: " Think you, Aaron, the map could do harm, were it to fall into French hands? The figurehead is an old piece. It has stood there many years. I know not how many have had its secret." I could see the loss of the map troubled him greatly and I felt more uneasiness myself.

" Yes." Aaron was taking the matter seriously at last. " Yes, it was a plan of attack and possibly mirrored more than we knew of what is about to happen. Probably Mistress Antoinette's information was drawn from matters she had heard discussed at the Province House. You must go to the governor at once, Eben! I will stay here and see if I cannot find further trace of it."

I turned my steps now to the Province House, much concerned about it all. It seemed to me we had been monstrous careless to have let the map get away from us.

I had, as usual, little difficulty in reaching Governor Shirley, though he was at the moment, I was glad to see, speeding the departure of my master, now General Pepperrell.

" Your Excellency," I said, " I would speak with you as soon as possible concerning a matter of grave importance, I fear."

For once the governor shook his head. " I am sorry, Eben, General Pepperrell has been to see me with matters of importance which I must attend to at once."

But here Master William put in kindly: " I think they can wait a moment, Your Excellency. The lad seems in some distress. Let us hear what he has to tell us."

" Very well, then, Eben, if you will speak quickly." Now this I was more than glad to do.

I had not said half a dozen words when the faces of both men sobered. I answered question after question, thrown at me in quick succession. How large was the map? Had we specified the mode of attack? Had we accurately computed the approaches? I answered all and volunteered more, only I said nought of the Red Hats itself, or of Mistress Antoinette's part in it then. Presently I drew for them the map from memory. Crude as my drawing was it showed the different waters and the different gates and bastions. I drew for a third time the huge *G* which had come to have for me a great fascination.

Then Master Pepperrell asked, " What say these men, Eben, of the morass? "

" They say indeed it is impassable, sir, for any great body of men or munitions. You will notice we made our attack by sea."

It all grew more terrible as I watched their sober faces. Then Master Pepperrell continued, " Tell me, Eben, how many men-of-war had you assembled for the attack? "

I recalled the map a moment, then answered surely, " I would say close on a hundred, sir."

Governor Shirley and Master Pepperrell looked amazed. " Why, Eben, I doubt even in the English navy there are that many available in these waters."

" Maybe not," I said, and then added unguardedly, " but Mistress Antoinette was ever a thorough one and would have a most tremendous fleet." And then an amazing thing happened. Master Pepperrell threw back his head and laughed. " I am not sure," he said shrewdly, " that after all this is a matter of regret. Such a plan of attack may give the French the idea that a great fleet of English men-of-war are with us. It may well paralyze them."

And then it came to me that in all our games we had planned on having the English navy with us. Of a sudden the full purport of what we had undertaken rushed over me afresh.

I started to go. The governor laid a kindly hand on my shoulder. " Do not worry, Eben. It may be that this incident will further our plans, rather than retard them. I doubt if there is aught to worry about. Rather, it may be a matter of congratulation."

I hastened back to tell Aaron, much relieved that we had not jeopardized the entire expedition. I could not find him in the house. Nor was he at Feathertale John's, nor had Master Skipworth, to whom I finally resorted, seen aught of him since early morning. Supper came and went. Midnight! Morning! Like the map, my brother, Aaron, had completely disappeared!

11: I Get a Great Fright

At once I sought the governor's aid. His Excellency listened most patiently. Then he said: " I think, Eben, that Aaron, being overzealous to get the map back, has followed a clue aboard some ship and it has sailed away with him. You will hear of him betimes."

Nevertheless, such was my distress that he sent a company of men to search the lumberyard and to examine the wharves. It was great relief to all of us when Aaron's dead body was not brought to light.

As for Mistress Merrie, Aaron's disappearance seemed to age her. I came to see that in spite of her disciplined emotions Mistress Merrie had had great fondness for him and was racked with anxiety and sorrow over his disappearance.

My thoughts, frantic at times, turned often to Captain O'Hara. What part had he played in this? I knew him for an astute man. If he had wished to punish me for my spying, he could not have done it more acutely than by hitting at someone I loved. Nothing he could have done to me would have hurt so much. I even demanded of Asa where he was. Asa said quietly: " Captain O'Hara's whereabouts, Eben, are largely problematical. His boat is but a disreputable old hulk and lies far out in the stream when he is in port. Rarely if ever does he come up to the dock."

I soon identified the craft and made note that Captain O'Hara's crew disposed of a considerable number of kentals of fish in Bostontown; it was rumored he was a man of some substance. This was confirmed for me when one day, perusing the ledgers of the warehouse, I saw where Master Pepperrell had bought from Captain O'Hara a sizeable shipment of cod, and the latter had accepted in exchange some share in one of our big merchantmen. The incident explained his intimacy with Asa. After some difficulty I located a member of his crew and accosted him, but he seemed unnaturally dumb and could give me no account of his master's whereabouts.

Now new terror was upon me. There arrived a day when we all had to face the fact that Antoinette's boat, the *Flying Fortune,* was long overdue. More than one boat had crossed and returned since her going, but not a single one had sighted the *Flying Fortune.* Even the dubious hope that she might have fallen prey to a French privateer was denied to us, for it did not seem possible that this could have occurred without our hearing of it. We had had two exchanges of prisoners between Bostontown and Louisbourg. We knew much of what went on there.

To my continued importuning, the governor at last replied: " I am slowly coming to the opinion, Eben, that she must have sunk with all hands on the Sable Shoals. I grieve deeply for little Mistress Antoinette, and for the Stuart himself, a fine gentleman." Then, seeing my distress, he added quickly: " But I do not think such a fate has overtaken Aaron. You will hear from him, I am sure."

As the expedition began to fill every mind, there was great fear in my heart that I might not be able to join it. When I approached General Pepperrell, he was somewhat dubious and insisted I secure Mistress Merrie's consent first. That I did obtain it was due to a strange circumstance.

One afternoon, while making up the day's unloadings for Master Pepperrell, who was sitting beside me awaiting my figures, a military figure strode in upon us, his sword clanking mightily.

" William," he cried, " what this expedition needs is a motto. There is nothing more binding on a common group than a common purpose."

General Pepperrell looked thoughtful. " Let us have Master Whitefield, the minister, seek one for us." I perceived his desire to ensure the motto's being of Holy Writ.

At the general's dictation I penned an epistle to the Rev. Mr. Whitefield. His answer was immediate. " *Nil desperandum Christo Duce,"* he wrote back — " Do not despair: the Lord is leading."

It must be admitted that on publication of the motto recruiting sped apace, and even Mistress Merrie could then find no excuse to keep me at home.

Now the excitement was in my heart too. I was going abroad.

I was to face, and take, I did not doubt, the impregnable fortress of Louisbourg, of which we had so long talked. Then suddenly my heart would drop within me, and the thought of my two losses would strike me afresh. It was on one such occasion that Asa brought me word: " There is a missive for you, Eben, at the post office, advertised as needing a shilling fee. I doubt not it has connection with Aaron."

All the way there I argued the letter was from Antoinette. Antoinette must be alive.

But Asa was right. It was from Aaron and read: " Dear brother, I am of His Majesty's navy. Already I have found Master Skipworth's training of great advantage to me. There is large prize money in the navy, and I would have my share for Antoinette.

" We have captured a Spanish ship and are at the moment overhauling a French East Indiaman. They be rich ships, Eben. Tell Mistress Merrie that Aaron St. Jean de Gervais is still taking care of her." There was enclosed a matter of nine pounds. It was signed: " Your loving brother, Aaron St. Jean de Gervais. Aboard His Majesty's Ship *Mermaid*, St. Kitts, the 7th of March, 1745, but I do not think I will be here overlong."

Aaron was alive! I reflected it was like him merely to announce the fact and leave me consumed with curiosity as to how it had come about. Aaron was alive! In the king's navy! I told it to myself over and over again. It was like a miracle.

Mistress Merrie, poor woman, on hearing the news, sank immediately to her knees to render thanks to heaven for his safety.

I ran to inform Feathertale, who rejoiced with me, and then I hied me to the general. " We will meet at Louisbourg," I told him confidently after relating my news.

I thought he hesitated. Then: " I hope so, Eben. I do hope so," he said. But at the moment I was too excited to question what that hesitancy might mean.

Old Master Skipworth's pleasure was good to see. " He was an apt pupil," he said with ill-concealed pride. " But I trained him well."

Now later, as I reread the epistle in a more sober mood, I was aware of something in it I had not taken note of in my first excitement at receiving it. Aaron had said, " There is large prize money in the navy, and I would have my share for Antoinette." I asked myself fiercely, Is Antoinette already his? Even if she were dead, it did not seem I could bear the thought. Then I chid myself. Aaron was alive! That was thought enough.

A little later Mistress Merrie had a visit from Adam Peddling, now become master of a privateer. He explained that some leagues out he had bespoken the Rhode Island sloop *Tartar* convoying a French prize. On board the prize, bound and gagged, they had found a New England man, and the *Tartar* wished to send him aboard Captain Peddling's craft, then en route to Virginia, where he might the sooner find succor. The prisoner had turned out to be Aaron. Captain Peddling assured us his trouble had been mostly lack of good food. He had improved immediately on being rescued. And on reaching the cape and being apprised of the need of gunners in the king's navy had signed on immediately. Aaron had informed him that he had been leaving Feathertale John's when he had been seized from behind, bound, and gagged. His capturers had spoken the French tongue and had said something about his being the spy the master had wanted taken. Wherefore, Aaron thought he had been taken in mistake.

Instantly, I made sure that Captain O'Hara was at the back of the incident. Aaron might have been taken in mistake, but, if he had been, it had undoubtedly been in place of me.

I could not help agreeing with Mistress Merrie that Providence had been most kind in the matter. After all, Aaron was alive and well and happy. I knew how easily the matter might have turned out quite differently if Aaron's succor had been long delayed.

My rage at Captain O'Hara seemed to blot out my personal fear of the man, and in the days that followed I sought him far and wide along the water front, but for some reason his disreputable old boat came no more to Bostontown. But the incident, in some way, tended to restore my faith in Asa. And I was glad when I heard that he was to be our cook on the expedition.

At last I stood with the other men of Bostontown, awaiting my turn to board the *Shirley Galley*, flagship of General Pepperrell's forces. Mistress Merrie and small Paul had come to see me off. Feathertale John was going with us.

"I may not be of much use at the fighting," Feathertale had said, "but my thread and my needle will see service enough, I do not doubt."

Now, as I stood there it came to me that I was, after all, going into great danger and might well not return. Aaron also was in a precarious position. I would like my silver shoe buckles to go to someone who would truly prize them. I decided to leave them with young Paul.

"Here, Paul," I said as my turn to enter the small boat arrived. "This is my parting gift." I thrust them into his hand.

His hand had no sooner closed on them than he knew what they were. His face shone. "O Eben!" he cried, his eyes going down to them. "Be assured I will treasure them always. The chasing is most truly beautiful." In those last moments his gaze was more often for them than for me, which was as well, I thought.

From the sloop's deck I could see ninety sets of white sails. A fairer fleet I had not yet seen in Boston Harbor. There was the *Prince of Orange*, riding pridefully, and beyond her the great *Bon Ami*, requisitioned to our use and straining to be gone, the *Tartar*, and the *Piscataqua* — an armada indeed!

In and out of the great ships plied the little boats, deep loaded with men and equipment. And mingled with the musical creak of the stays, the rippling wash of water against our bows, the gay shouts of the men saying their farewells, came the distant, rhythmic beat of the drums on the shore. And all seemed to pant in my ears like a refrain: "Aaron is alive! Aaron is alive!" I could not help thinking that as Aaron had been returned to us from the dead, as it were, so we might soon have word of Mistress Antoinette.

And now Asa came rushing aboard. "Eben," he cried, "where is the governor? Is he with Master Pepperrell? Take this epistle to him at once. It is but just arrived by packet from England and undoubtedly concerns our going."

I snatched the heavily sealed packet and with grave misgivings climbed to the bridge. Governor Shirley and General Pepperrell were conferring with the captain of the *Galley*. The governor ripped it open. His face sobered.

"What is it, Will?" I heard the general ask quickly, for once forgetful of formality.

Governor Shirley raised somber eyes. "The English men-of-war are not joining us."

The ensuing silence was ominous. It seemed to me I could hear Dogood saying fiercely: "We have been taxed and governed and left to fight our own battles. 'Tis fine protection the crown accords us." A thought struck me. We would never start now: Our fine expedition was over.

The governor looked at General Pepperrell. There was an unspoken question in his eyes.

General Pepperrell squared his great shoulders. He was become a man on parade, facing the order to charge. "*Nil desperandum Christo Duce.*" Our motto echoed in my head. Then the general spoke. "We will go, Your Excellency, and, please God, we will show the English crown it has as good fighting men in the colonies as at home."

"If you go in that spirit, general," the governor replied, "you cannot fail to win. I wish you Godspeed!" The governor wheeled and left, and I seemed to hear a voice repeating deep down within me a phrase I had heard in the meetinghouse: "As is your day, so shall your strength be."

Then General Pepperrell turned to me. "Say nought of this, Eben, below. It would be something of a blow to their enthusiasm."

"Aye, sir," I replied, knowing only too well it would be a blow indeed.

I returned to the lower deck and gazed on that busy scene. We were embarking three thousand men to do the impossible, for every man to whom I had talked had agreed that a land assault would never succeed. As for our own ships the range of their guns was in no wise equal to the range of the forty-two-pounders in the batteries and bastions of the great fortress. We would be annihilated before we could fire an effective shot. Of a sudden, fierce doubt assailed me on all sides. I recalled Captain O'Hara's prophecy that Louisbourg would never be taken. It was impregnable from all sides. And I recalled too a certain afternoon in Feathertale John's shop when young Franklin had brought in a letter from his brother in Philadelphia. In it Benjamin had written, " Fortified towns are hard nuts to crack and your teeth are not accustomed to it, but some seem to think that forts are as easy taken as snuff." It had seemed to us something to smile over at the time, but now I wondered. Was there not more truth in it than we had surmised?

I told myself that our one hope lay in our all arriving safe and sound and so formidable in appearance that the French would follow their tactics at Annapolis Royal and abandon the mighty fortress at sight of us! Then a thought came stabbing over me. Such a result depended on the element of surprise. If the map of the Red Hats had fallen into French hands, then even that advantage was denied us.

Melancholy must at that moment have laid deep hold upon me, for I recall that I faced the fact of annihilation with equanimity — thinking perhaps it would but mean for me a reunion with Antoinette.

Toward sunset came the sounds I had long awaited. The rattle of anchor chains being hauled in, the rumble and creek of canvas under full sail. But in them for me now was only sadness. I would not meet Aaron in Louisbourgtown.

It was about this time I became aware I had a neighbor. He was a fine-looking lad, tall and slim like Aaron, with a lean, eager face and eyes that in their ability to sparkle and laugh on occasion made me think of Mistress Antoinette.

" Hurrah! " he cried triumphantly. " When we sail into Boston-town again, we shall have swept the Frenchies from the colonies. Louisbourg will be ours! Then, perhaps, His Majesty, King George of England, will see what the blood of the men of New England can accomplish. My name is Billy Tufts. What is yours? "

I made haste to tell him. We were friends at once, he being a very likable fellow and I much in need of comradship. Knowing what I knew, I had a heavy heart indeed.

The wind freshened. There was much talk among the seasoned sailors as to how much ice we should encounter. It seemed when we were but a few hours out the wind was bitter enough to have swept across the great Arctic ice floes. But I soon found I was there to do other than just think.

My duties aboard were mostly concerned with Asa, who was our cook. I must fill the cook's kettle from the huge water casks and pipe the men to meals. Asa's stove stood in the center of the deck below the gun galley, and here from a great black iron pot he ladled out a tin mug of soup and gave to each one a piece of hardtack.

That evening I found Billy examining my flute. He had suffered much from homesickness and when he cried out: " A tune, Eben! Let us have a tune to make us forget," I could not deny him. Besides, the cry was instantly caught up by the men.

A couple of Irish sailors volunteered a strange dance. There was not much space between the guns and the stair wells and the stores with which we were deep loaded. But they managed to find sufficient room for their antics and did amuse us all mightily.

With Feathertale John sitting there in our midst, his hands even then busy weaving a net with which to catch fish for all of us at the first stop, I was carried back to the sailmaker's shop in Bostontown. I felt great longing for Mistress Antoinette and Aaron and Dogood and young Paul. Now and then I looked somewhat uneasily into the shadows, fearful of discerning there the evil face of Captain O'Hara. Glad I was not to find him there. But I did see someone else equally familiar, and the sight of him lifted my spirits considerably. For Thundercloud had ensconced himself at the base of a gun. It was the first I knew of his presence with us, and it gave me new courage to feel his watchful, silent regard.

Then in the midst of our merriment who should charge down upon us but good Master Moody, the preacher, who was accompanying us. Thundering at us above the roar of the seas and the rattle of the ship's timbers, he exhorted us not to occupy our minds with temptations of the Devil. There and then he preached a mighty sermon on the text, " The righteous man is more excellent than his neighbor."

I was not soon to forget the dark confines of the galley, with the men sprawled all over the kegs of powder and barrels of flour, the swinging lanterns giving but feeble light, and the shadowy grotesqueries playing across the ceiling so low that they seemed like hobgoblins about to pounce down upon us.

At last Master Moody retired to his hammock. The lanterns were turned low. The men flung themselves down where they were. Before I realized where I was, I was sitting up in the dark, marveling what terrible thing had happened to me, for in my ears was a sharp retort as of guns, and the vessel seemed to be turning upside down. The smell was such as I had never smelled before, and in my ears was a frightful sound as of a dog in great pain.

My first thought was that we had met up with Morpain and were in the midst of an engagement with the great pirate. " Are we under fire? " I managed to ask of the darkness.

" Aye! " shouted a voice I did not recognize. " But it is not the Frenchies. It is the sea training her guns on our timbers."

" Will we weather it? " I demanded fearfully.

" Aye," the voice grumbled. " 'Tis only a gun or a crag can sink a Massachusetts ship. We'll not meet either this trip. For the Frenchies do not know we are coming, and the wind is offshore where the sea has no crags."

I started up much comforted, and made for the deck, but the hatches were securely battened down, and there was nothing I could do but lie and suffer.

My thoughts turned as ever to Antoinette. For even such as this and worse had she passed through. I wondered too about Aaron. Was all as right with him as his letter seemed to suggest?

It was the longest night ever I spent. Glad was I when a gray day broke at last and the word came that the general had need of me to draft a letter or two in the captain's cabin, Master Greene being ill.

It was then I learned we were to rendezvous at Canso. The French had been at some pains to capture it, but having burned it to the ground had immediately departed, leaving no force behind.

On the third day of April we sighted Nova Scotia and on the fourth Canso Harbor. Eagerly we watched for ice and for our own fleet of sails. I knew the general was much worried over the fate of our ships in the great storm. There was also the danger of an encounter with the French.

As the weather cleared, we looked eagerly about us. Of all the great armada with which we had started only a few sails could now be seen. The general's face had grown leaner. Even Billy stopped his cheery comments. It was not until we had reached the coast and rounded a point that our fears were allayed. The New Hampshire men had reached port ahead of us, and had made anchor. Instantly our ship rang with cheers. Disembarkation began at once. All that day belated members of our fleet continued to gather. With each newly arrived sail a cheer went up.

As I felt the good hard land again under my feet, I was reminded of one of the first remarks Antoinette had made to me. " Ships! " she had cried. " I wish I might never see another! "

Soon the whole hill rang with activity. General Pepperrell had brought the framework for a new blockhouse. Carpenters among us began their hammering. At dusk fires gleamed all over the hill-side. Men brought up fish from the sea. They roasted game from the near-by thickets.

Eager to strengthen our legs, Billy and I made a tour of the camp. I found myself telling him much of my history, including our game of the Red Hats and the mystery concerning the flute. He listened most intently.

When we returned we found Feathertale John unsheathing his needle and unpacking his thread. It was strange indeed to see him plying his old trade, mending the damage the storm had cost us by the light of a flaming torch in the shadow of a spruce shelter.

" I have news for you, Eben," he said unexpectedly. " One here is but late from Londontown. He passed on the way out the great privateer Morpain and was chased by him. Morpain was using a

Massachusetts ship. Her name still gleamed on her prow — the *Flying Fortune.*

My heart took a sudden leap. I ran singing out into the night. If the *Flying Fortune* had not gone down on the shoals but had been taken by the French, then Antoinette might still be alive. At that point I stopped. Antoinette captive of Morpain! I did not sleep that night.

Some days later excitement in the camp brought Billy and me out of the general's tent into the sunshine. Shouting was all about us, and each man's eyes were on the sea. Moving down upon us in a stately fashion could be seen a great ship of war.

" The French! The French! To arms! " the cry went up. I felt sudden calamity in the air. Had we survived the storm to perish on a strange shore under the guns of a French man-of-war? Would our armada be wiped out, before it had come in sight of Louisbourg-town and the great fortress?

PART TWO

Louisbourgtown

12: Louisbourg at Last!

We watched the great ship swooping down upon us. It was all that we could do. Our guns were impotent against her. The New York train of artillery being still on the way, we had none of sufficient range to reach her.

" Think you, we should make cover, Billy? " I asked anxiously.

It was Asa who answered, a great soup ladle in his hand. " It is as like the Frenchies to miss what they aim at as hit it," he said. " They will aim for us, having seen our shelters long since."

We watched and waited, the sick crawling to the shelter doors, all business of the camp suspended.

Hither and yon the great ship tacked. " A craft new released from Louisbourg slips," one cried. My nerves tingled. Each moment we expected a smashing shot to tear into our midst.

Then a flutter of activity around her mainmast. Breathless waiting. A wild huzza from the men beside us. The British ensign floated from the ship's mainmast. I recalled Antoinette's remark, " The ships of England, Eben, will come when they are needed, even from the bottom of the sea."

" 'Tis the *Eltham!* " one shouted behind me. The crowd took it up. " The *Eltham!* The *Eltham!* " The *Eltham* was familiar to us. She had been used to escort the mast ships across the water.

Then I heard Asa's cry: " The *Eltham* is a ship of Admiral Warren's squadron! The admiral himself must be on the way. Now we will do things! "

Then Master Moody's voice boomed over the hillside: " Thy people shall be willing in the day of Thy power."

I could well believe that to Master Moody and the instigators of the expedition, the arrival of the English fleet, after we had given it up, was indeed guarantee that Providence was on our side. And I thought how General Pepperrell had been justified in his gallant start, when it seemed as if we were to stand alone.

By dawn the *Eltham* was joined by three others.

"The *Superb!* The *Launceton!* The *Mermaid!*" The men identified them excitedly. The *Mermaid!* I stood transfixed. Aaron's ship. Was he even now straining his eyes to see me? I could scarcely believe it that he should be so near.

Fresh confidence poured about us. The storm was forgotten. We were once more a host set on conquering the great fortress and assured of victory. A small boat could be seen coming ashore.

The admiral's message was brief. Admiral Warren begged to inform General Pepperrell that on receiving orders to proceed to the relief of the Massachusetts expedition, he had set sail at once for Bostontown, but learning offshore that the expedition had already sailed he had lost no time in docking in Bostontown. Instead he had sent an express to Governor Shirley informing him of his intentions, and had set out at once for the rendezvous. He was now proceeding to Louisbourg to begin a blockade the while he covered our landing.

I took pride that the Admiral Peter Warren was a man after my own heart, prompt to make a decision, and wasting no time in the carrying out of it.

As the great ships tacked into the wind and sailed away, I found myself standing near the general. Of all the surrounding throng, I alone knew that the coming of the English ships was a piece of unexpected good fortune for us. The general, looking down, espied me. He smiled happily. " Ah, Eben," he said, " I have always found that fortune favors a man of daring. It was, indeed, a daring adventure to undertake alone, and one might think a somewhat desperate one, but now am I greatly confirmed in our ultimate success."

Whereupon I heard a murmur near by: " The Lord is truly with us."

We soon had further confirmation of our good fortune in having

114

the English ships of war along. Our scout ships brought in word that Louisbourg Harbor and the Gabarus Bay were locked in ice and unapproachable. We would have to delay our arrival. It filled us with uneasiness. If the French ships were on the way, and we were delayed in Canso, they might well arrive ahead of us and oppose our landing.

There was other reason too for our uneasiness. We were all well aware that a large force of French and Indians sent to attack Annapolis Royal had most mysteriously disappeared from before the gates of that fort. It was thought they had been ordered to Louisbourg. Whether they had already passed the straits to Cape Breton Island we did not know, but Captain Cutter, with a few small ships, was ordered to patrol the waters between Canso and Cape Breton and let no enemy craft through.

It was the feeling of all our officers that the success of our venture depended upon our getting into the fortress before this great addition to its strength by sea and by land arrived. We were frantic to get started. But the days passed. We did not move.

Then there came a morning when from the sea an ominous sound reached our ears. We hugged the water front, and listened. It was the distant boom of heavy firing. Somewhere offshore an attack was going on. Was it a running engagement between Admiral Warren's ships and the new French fleet? Were the French winning or were we?

Eighteen long hours passed before we knew. I was helping Asa when Billy raced in with the news. A scout ship had returned.

" We have met the enemy," Billy boasted.

" Did we take him? " Asa demanded shrewdly.

Billy sobered a bit. " No, we did not. It was a running fight and though she was a great frigate, heavily manned and named the *Renommée,* we were too much for her — she turned tail and ran."

" That is a likely story! " Asa was openly skeptical.

"But it is true," Billy insisted. Later we found it was. Most amazingly the ship had fled back to Louisbourg and finding it ice-locked had headed toward France. Whether she had seen our fleet or not, we did not know, but we suspected she had. If the French king was not aware of our expedition, he would know of it now, we were sure.

New eagerness to be up and away possessed us. But the waiting began again.

We filled the weary hours with drilling — our officers trying with great labor to weld something useful out of our undisciplined ranks.

Three weeks passed. At last the dispatch arrived. Admiral Warren begged lief to inform us the ice was gone. The Chapeau Rouge was clear. Once again I watched a white fleet dotting the waters.

We left at Canso only the sick, a handful of able-bodied men to guard them, some of the carpenters to continue the work on the blockhouse, and Captain Cutter's small company to patrol the Straits of Canso and cut off any relief which might be coming to Louisbourg by land or sea from Quebec or Annapolis Royal.

In the late afternoon we passed through Admiral Warren's lines. Cheer after cheer greeted us. Flags dipped!

We fired no gun. Such an act was foolish waste of good powder, with which we were not any too well supplied.

As we glided past His Majesty's Ship *Mermaid*, I strained my eyes, but, if Aaron were on deck, I did not pick him out. At that early hour of the day it was not easy to distinguish small objects at any great distance.

Now, on leaving Bostontown, Governor Shirley had been at some pains to provide us with a complete plan of attack as well as other necessary equipment. We were to arrive by night, embark immediately, and storm the fortress forthwith. The enemy was to be taken completely by surprise.

I do not doubt that Admiral Warren realized the futility of an attack without any reconnoitering, especially on unfamiliar terrain. However that may be, we arrived in daylight, having encountered a calm on the way and having been forced to lay to for several hours. The enemy, therefore, was not surprised, and I heard no more of Governor Shirley's elaborate plan either that day or on any succeeding day during the siege. We found the situation quite other than he imagined it would be.

It was sunrise when at last we came to rest at our anchorage in the Chapeau Rouge Bay. The waters were rose gold. It was a place of wide entrance and great shelter. As the pilots took us to our places, a sudden silence fell over our anchoring fleet. The sails ceased their straining, the masts their uneasy creaking. I turned my eager gaze upon that great fortress of which I had heard so much, and which of a sudden I hoped might be sheltering the person of Mistress Antoinette.

On our immediate left was a black rock line of coast against which the sea dashed unceasingly. Beyond that was a strip of low, marshy ground, which I did not need to be told was the morass. Some distance back it stopped abruptly, and the land rose sharply into spruce-clad hills.

Immediately in front of us, flung out on the high part of a point, lay the fortress! My eyes scanned it eagerly — a mass of masonry rising out of greensward bristling with guns. It suggested to me a guardian mastiff, high of haunch and lower of shoulder, crouching on the eminence, eyes guarding the lower reaches where the waves crashed against the black shore.

Now I had heard much of its twin spires, but nothing that had been told me quite prepared me for what I saw — two steeples infinitely graceful, whose slender shafts caught the light of the opening day and became rapiers of gold pointed upwards into the glory of the morning sky. And then, even as I looked, across the waters came the sweet sound of silver bells, chiming musically, to me a strange phenomenon in that great wilderness of barren hills and wild morass and spindrift sea. I had thought of the moment long and in detail, but the effect of that great sleeping fortress upon me when I at last saw it was profoundly stirring.

" The bells of St. Louis, St. Jean, and St. Antoine-Marie," murmured Asa, " in the citadel of the King's Bastion and the hospital. I have seen them."

And I bethought me that whether raised by papists or not, those delicate twin spires were things of strange beauty, and it was great sacrilege that our ragged army should turn on them the villainy of our guns. Then I reflected on the damage the French had done us, of their league with the Indians, the fact that Antoinette was even now probably a prisoner among them, and I knew that we had but come to do our duty as we saw it, but in the doing of it undoubtedly many good things would be swept away.

All night, although out of range of the fort guns, we kept steady vigil. When Billy and I demanded of Asa of what the general was afraid, he answered: " Fire ships! Three or four blazing hulks driven down amongst us by the wind would do us great damage."

Such a horror had not occurred to me. Perhaps for the first time I realized what war was.

However, we were unmolested, and the day was scarce started when the disembarkation began.

Now I knew that the place selected for our encampment had been about four miles on the left of the fortress, where we had been assured there was a good brook and higher ground in the midst of the morass. Billy and I, watching the disembarkation, were therefore greatly surprised when we saw that the first boats drew off toward the fortress and started disembarking almost under the nose of it.

" There is some terrible mistake! " cried Billy. " And see, Eben, what is that? "

I looked where he pointed. My heart stood still. A party of French had issued from the fortress and were marching across the morass to that point where the troops must land. The attack had begun. We had defeated our purpose of a surprise attack by arriving at sunrise instead of after sunset, and here were the French ready and able to oppose our landing.

With conflict actually upon us, the men were hard to hold. They tumbled into the small boats. Many shallops left scarce filled, so eager were the oarsmen to be off. Billy was as mad as the rest and insisted on being among the first of his company.

" Good-by, Eben! " he cried hoarsely. " I'll bring you a Frenchman's hat for supper. Good-by! " And I heard the password being murmured on every hand: " King George forever! "

Now, watching Billy's boat draw away, I noted that it was making for the original point of landing, planned some miles below.

And the wisdom of thus deploying the first few boats in the opposite direction nearer the fortress was instantly seen. For the French company was already committed to its rendezvous, and under cover of that small engagement we were busily landing a horde of troops much farther away.

Impatient to be gone with the rest, I yet had to wait for orders, and I enjoyed not a little the idea of Billy's chagrin. I discovered Asa much excited by the fighting and in great haste to get away. He was having trouble with his pots and pans, and to my great delight I received permission to help him.

When at last we pushed off, several flung themselves into our boat and we were like to have capsized, and for many strokes of the oars I could not distinguish the men from the pots and kettles and skillets among which they had flung themselves.

It was plain too that Asa, under orders only to land, had selected his own dock. We were heading for the engagement!

As we neared the great rocks with the waters smashing over them, I was sure we would be dashed to pieces and sunk. But Asa, I was to find, was also an excellent seaman. He selected his place carefully, heading us apparently straight for the rocks until I made out a narrow opening of a few feet where the ledges had been worn away and cut apart. As we neared it, two of the seamen leaped onto the rocks, lightening the boat. They landed waist high and scrambled through the shallows to the top of the ledge where they dropped exhausted. Meanwhile, Asa shot us through the opening on the breast of a swell. We found ourselves in a deep puddle sheltered from the sea by a knub of rock, where, except for the rise and fall of the swells, we were fairly still. So deep cushioned in seaweed were the surrounding rocks that I could see the boat would come to little harm. Stopping only to hurl the painter over a knub of rock, Asa, armed with a cutlass, sprang ashore. The others followed.

In the excitement of landing, and the clouds of spray through which we had passed, I had lost sight of the Frenchmen. I now saw there was fierce fighting back on the morass and I too snatched up a cutlass and followed.

I cannot say that for all my youth and natural agility I kept fair pace with them, for they were men trained in the experience of slippery decks and icy shrouds, and made remarkable speed over a terrain which I verily believe is the worst in the world. For either one was like to sink to one's waist in marshy swamp or else one sprawled drunkenly over the slippery seaweed, ending with a crash on one's belly on the jagged rocks with which the morass was strangely ribbed at intervals.

Suddenly the air was split by an explosion, and I was flung down on my face and covered with mud. I felt sure my last hour had come. When I gained my senses again I saw that a great shot had ploughed into the morass just ahead of me and my escape had indeed been narrow. One of our seamen was nursing his arm on the other side of it.

"Art hurt?" he shouted. I jumped up to show him that I was not, whereupon he turned at once and followed the engagement where it was retreating up into the green slopes which ringed the morass. I had to make a big detour to gain the hill, and probably took myself out of range of the big gun, for although it fired two or three more times, the shots did not reach me.

It was great relief to me to gain the woods, and I dashed into them in search of my comrades. They were nowhere in sight, and I penetrated some distance before the stillness startled me and I realized that in my impetuosity I had completely lost myself.

Panic seized me that I should be thus alone in a foreign wood and not like to be missed in the hurry and scurry of disembarking. Was that a dark skin beyond yonder tree? That shining thing between the branches — was it a Frenchman's musket? I held myself sternly in hand and came at last to a little glade which harbored a high rock. I made haste to climb it in the hope of getting from it some glimpse of the sea. I had gained the top when a deep groan from below startled me considerably.

To my surprise, I espied there on the lower ledges a recumbent figure. It was a Frenchman, and by his rich surcoat and silken scarf I made no doubt he was a man of some importance among them. Lying there below me, stretched to his full length, he seemed a man of extraordinary height. His face, though white and drawn, was smiling up at me, as if amused at my startlement.

"Good morrow, Pop Eyes!" he said in English. "And wouldst mind handing me a goblet of pure water? Indeed, I am fair dying of thirst."

"Shurily," I made answer, using a word I had caught from Mistress Antoinette's quaint vocabulary, "if such a thing be in these wild parts." I busied myself climbing down the ledges.

"I would not stick at the goblet," he made a wry face, "if I had but its contents. There is nought, I'll be bound, in your water bottle. 'Tis plain you were in such haste to meet the wicked papistical Frenchman, you gave no thought to such greedy necessities."

Now, although his remark was shrewdly true, there was that of mockery in his manner as would seem to belittle our good New England armament, so I told him, somewhat brusquely, he was my prisoner.

"Indeed," he said, mopping the sweat from his face, and my heart went out to him for his gallantry, for I made sure that he was all the while in great pain. "Of a truth I am your prisoner, and what are you going to do about it?" It was a pertinent question.

I knew I could do nothing, for indeed I was so lost that I did not know in what quarter to seek the encampment unless he should direct me, which he seemed to understand perfectly and secretly enjoy.

Of a sudden his face contracted with new pain. "I am perishing for water," he muttered. "Wouldst not go to yonder brook? I assure you I am almost beyond endurance of my pain."

Now maybe he was my enemy, but I could not gainsay his plea. "If you will but show me the way," I said, "I will get it for you." I was well aware it might be a trap, but still I could not bring myself to refuse aid to one in such a plight.

"I can promise you one thing," he said, and it seemed to me he spoke with a good deal more difficulty, "whether you believe it or not — these woods — are barren of life. Except, maybe some boys and girls of your own age — late arrived — in the New England expedition."

I was well aware that even in his agony, he was making a mock of me, but I closed my ears to his pleasantries and listened carefully to his directions. I should follow an old rock wall to a pine tree. Continue across an open pasture to a grove of birch inside which was a little brook. As I turned to go, I heard an odd sound and turning saw his eyes and hand pointing and questioning what I had on my back. Now it was but my knapsack from which protruded my flute, and I had told him and turned away when chance took a hand in the game, for as I straightened myself up a branch of spruce ripped both from my back. Did I imagine it? Did the hand that reached out for the flute grasp it as something familiar? Was this man, with his white face and agonized eyes, its owner? Was it his voice I had heard in Bostontown?

I was on the point of questioning him concerning it when his face contracted anew, reminding me of his urgent need. Leaving both where they had fallen, I sped away, accompanied only by my good cutlass, which I held ready under my hand.

I found all just as he said. Kneeling at the base of a rock out of which issued the little brook, I filled my bottle. A snapping twig brought me suddenly to my feet. I swung around and was just in time to see a figure slip behind a tall boulder half shrouded in bushes a few feet away. A cold shiver ran through me. Was it a Frenchman or, worse still, the vanguard of a company of Indians, scalping knives ready? Out of the lichen of the rock a liquid black eye was regarding me.

"Come out in the king's name!" I ordered in my very best French.

To my surprise the figure obeyed, and a shabby form stepped forward. My amazement was extreme when I recognized in him the Negro who had taken Antoinette's money.

I am pretty sure that he recognized me also, so uneasy was his manner. Or perhaps it was just that he saw in me one of the newly arrived enemies. My French tongue, it was apparent, had momentarily deceived him. Now it was evident he was about to spring upon me. Just then, however, the curious trillip I had heard in Bostontown was flung down the wind from some place not far distant. Of a sudden I knew that the song had been the notes of a flute. A look of amazement crossed the face of the Negro. And then with a leap like a denizen of the wild he cleared the brook, plunged into the birches, and disappeared over the wall.

There was nothing for me to do but to return to my prisoner. As I hastened back I recalled that the gay trillip had sounded only once. Was it my prisoner who had piped it? Were the woods filled with Frenchmen, after all, whom he was summoning to his aid? Was I in great danger, and, if not, how was I to get my prisoner to camp? And what was become of Asa and the rest of our men? All these thoughts and more poured through my head as I made my way back.

But when I reached the ledge again my prisoner was gone. Lying where he had been was my knapsack and the flute. I scanned the woods on every hand, convinced that in his wounded condition he could not have gone far. I listened carefully, sure that I would hear again his unexpected, mocking speech. I did not find or hear him.

Then it came to me that I was lost. Panic seized me. I was like to have gone to pieces entirely, but shortly I remembered a saying of one of the seamen to whom I had talked in the shop of Feathertale John: " It is a strange thing, known to only a few, but most assuredly true as I have good reason to know, in Nova Scotia the tops of the trees point north. It is good as a compass to one who finds himself lost."

By this means I found my way back to the edge of the woods overlooking the fortress and the morass.

It was great relief to me to see again the busy scene below me. Far out on the horizon the sail of Admiral Warren's four great ships kept guarded watch. I wondered if Aaron was really aboard one of them. General Pepperrell had promised me he would question the admiral concerning him. Then I remembered that Aaron did not know that Antoinette's ship had never reached England.

Closer in shore almost a hundred sail of transports and provincial ships debarked an unceasing horde. The land below me, solid morass to the sea, rose to a small knoll on the right at the water's edge. It was cut almost in two by a small stream of water. On this knoll was continual movement and an ever-increasing throng. From the Coromandière, or Freshwater Cove as it was called, a steady stream of straggling figures was wending its way shoreward. Now and then the line massed in a scarlet blot as some company in brilliant red uniforms marched in military formation, but for the most part it was a straggling mob clad in somber gray or in the blue of the sea. Many had come garbed in the honest linsey-woolsey of the home looms. Then strange emotion welled within me. Our flag rose over the encampment and spread its streamer to the breeze.

Now and then a puff of smoke from the Massachusetts sloops or the great men-of-war heralded a roar like distant thunder. A shower of dirt from the morass showed the determination of our ships' captains to discourage any further sallies from the fortress.

I noted too that in all the confusion of the landing the big guns of the fortress had been for the most part silent. It was then I realized that so great had been their dependence on the impassability of the morass that the bulk of the fortress defenses commanded the harbor mouth. The place we had chosen for our encampment was just beyond the range of their guns.

Now down the air came the sudden clamor of the bells of St. Louis, St. Jean, and St. Anto ne-Marie, as if the hand that rang them were unsteadied by frantic fear. I could see, from my high position, across the fortress into the harbor of Louisbourg. It was dotted with numerous small boats converging upon the fortress from various directions. I knew then that the ringing of the bells was an alarm, summoning the people of the settlements to the asylum of the fortress.

The town was hidden by the eminence of the citadel, but I was filled with wonder over the neat precision of the peaked salient of the King's Bastion, extending out over the morass.

Then I perceived another thing. On the trail across the neck of land which led to the fortress something was moving. A small, cumbersome object seemed to be making its way laboriously across. Then I perceived that the Dauphin Gate was being opened. A couple of French guards now dashed out with a litter. Something in the shape and color of the moving object which they seemed desirous of rescuing reminded me of my prisoner.

The cumbersome object resolved itself into two figures, one of which was carefully placed upon the litter. Then I perceived in the other the shabby outlines of my opponent at the well. It seemed safe to assume that the Negro had been my prisoner's servant: summoned to him by the trillip of the flute, he had borne his master back on his shoulders. My surmise that my prisoner was a man of importance within the French fortress was abundantly justified. And certainly he had been in Bostontown.

The party reached the walls in safety. The massive gates closed behind it.

I turned my attention with some trepidation to my own plight.

13: I Am of Some Service to the General

I had to admit that my position was somewhat desperate. Whether the woods behind me were as free of the enemy as the Frenchman had said I had no means of telling.

Leaving the shelter of the spruce I entered the open and plunged down the hill. Almost at once I floundered into the morass. Glad indeed was I for the psalms with which Mistress Merrie had so plentifully supplied me. "'The Lord is my refuge and my strength,'" I chanted as I struggled across, "'a very present help in time of trouble.'" By this means I held myself steadfast and gained the knoll upon which we were building our camp.

My first concern was for Asa and his crew. I found him setting up his kitchen in a shelter mainly composed of the cases which had contained his supplies. He was plainly pleased with his own ingenuity. He stopped his work long enough to scold me roundly for having lost the party. It was a miracle I had returned.

As for Asa himself, it would seem that having reached the woods, he and his party had promptly given up the chase. When I inquired about his kettles and pans, I found that he had sent the most necessary by another boat which had reached the Coromandière Cove without mishap. As soon as it was dark he planned to retrieve the shallop in which we had come ashore. Finally, and a bit belatedly I thought, he was pleased to inform me that the general was seeking me and seemed much put about over my defection. Indeed, according to Asa, I might well be already listed as a deserter.

Much concerned over my own conduct, and still very wet from the morass and the landing, I sought the general's quarters.

He and several of his staff were conferring about a rude board set up on barrel tops under the open sky.

" Ah! " General Pepperrell espied me. " Here is the lad of whom I was speaking. Come, Eben, where have you been? "

I related my experiences. At once Colonel Vaughan spoke up. " The lad is the very one to go with us! "

Now I did not know what the escapade that was afoot might be, but sure I was that if Colonel Vaughan was of it, it would be exciting. My ardor, however, was instantly damped by the grave countenance of the general. " He is very young to send on such an adventure," he demurred.

Colonel Vaughan replied impatiently: " It is not a time for consideration of such a matter. He could be of great value to me, being able to understand this strange tongue and being in a manner familiar with the general layout of the terrain."

Still the general hesitated. " I doubt not he is overventuresome, having already been outside our lines, and we not properly landed yet."

" I am sorry, sir," I made haste to answer, " but it could not well be avoided."

Whereat their sober faces relaxed, many smiled, and Colonel Vaughan remarked dryly, " I'll be bound, it could not."

" Why not let the lad decide for himself? " one of the other officers spoke up. " We are about to reconnoiter the woods and the surrounding settlements. What say, lad, wouldst be of the party? "

" I would ask nothing better! " I cried.

" Bravo! " cried Colonel Vaughan. " Give me willing followers." And, though still seemingly doubtful of the wisdom of the matter, General Pepperrell gave his consent.

" Then that is settled," Colonel Vaughan concluded. " We start at sunset. See that you be on hand."

I raced back to Asa's fire with my news. There was a bitter chill in the air and the fire felt unusually good. Here I found Billy. He was as much excited as I over my plans.

" I must be of this expedition too, Eben. I shall seek Colonel Vaughan at once."

Billy departed, and Asa being in better mood toward me provided a dry coat, for which I was very grateful.

Toward midafternoon a cold mist rolled in from the sea, obliterating the ships, and though monstrous uncomfortable it was good for our purpose, serving to conceal our movements from the enemy.

Without so much as a bugle call Colonel Vaughan, with four hundred of us, slipped up through the low bushes on the banks of the stream which divided our encampment into two parts, and, skirting the morass, plunged into the woods of the hills surrounding it. I cannot say that Billy and I were exactly the hindmost. It cheered me greatly to see that Thundercloud was of the party.

A little later one whispered that we were passing the Royal Battery. I looked down curiously on the wall of gray mist, and saw the tesselated embattlements of two round towers mushrooming eerily up out of the fog.

Toward dusk we reached the head of the harbor. Here was a small settlement.

I could not myself take part in the fierce exultation of the New England troops as they applied the flaming torch, and house after house went up in flames. I found myself inwardly weeping. The simple French peasants stood so quietly, the red fires revealing on their faces a stoic tragedy.

All evening in a rude shelter, Colonel Vaughan interrogated them. They seemed a gentle kind of folk like ourselves and I recalled a remark of Dogood's that, left alone, we of the New World could have gotten along finely. But I did note that the Indians present viewed us with dark suspicion.

The tale of the inhabitants was invariably the same. There was, they insisted, a large force of French and red men on the way from upper Canada, coming by sea and land. There was also a huge fleet together with some supply ships expected hourly from France.

The idea of a big enemy force, well-equipped, pouring down the hills which commanded our encampment alarmed us all.

It was a strange scene. Above were the crude rafters from which still hung a couple of hams and a rasher of bacon. Below in the feeble light stood rank on rank of keen-faced men of New England. In the center the French inhabitants faced their judges with countenances pitifully fearful, while in one corner a handful of savages in full war paint stood still as carven images. Only their eyes were alive, and the light in them mirrored no good will as they rested on us. I wondered how safe we were.

Some newcomers now arriving, I marked an Indian in elaborate headdress who of a sudden took strange interest in me. He even left his group and, coming close to me, began to jabber excitedly and point to my sleeve. I found to my amazement his interest was in my red hat.

Had he news of Dogood and Antoinette? I turned to Thundercloud and demanded he interpret for me. He seemed reluctant to do it, and I knew by his manner when he faced the stranger that he accounted him no ordinary individual. I had great but fearful hopes of what we might learn. Then of a sudden my heart went cold within me. The sachem — for that he undoubtedly was in his own tribe — pointed to my little red hat and swung himself around. He displayed a like emblem on his armlet! I peered down to decipher the initials. *A. C. S.* It was Antoinette's!

Then I forced myself to look at what I had been trying to avoid seeing for several seconds, something it was easy to omit in that uncertain light — the scalps that depended from his belt. Horror seized me anew. Matted and dirty, two long thick locks were suspended there. Women's scalps! One golden! One raven black! Dogood's and Antoinette's!

As I realized the full significance of it, the rude place whirled around me. Deep, engulfing horror washed over me as the seas enveloped the rocks of that hostile shore. I recalled that Antoinette's boat, the *Flying Fortune,* had fallen prey to Morpain! Had he abandoned the womenfolk to a band of red men of Nova Scotia, savages like this Algonquin?

Proudly the sachem held up the scalp locks for all to see. Thundercloud, bending over, fingered them with scowling face and emitted a series of hoarse gutturals. I could feel the mounting excitement of the throng, red men and New Englanders. The former were edging nearer, while an angrily murmured cry for vengeance was rising from the latter. With difficulty Colonel Vaughan got hold of the situation. He ordered them all to stand back, and Thundercloud to explain.

Of a sudden Thundercloud refused to interpret further. My suspicions were confirmed. I poured question after question over him with ever-sickening heart. It was no use. He was grown stubborn, and I could well guess why. He dared not tell these white men what his own race had done to two white girls, one of them ward of Governor Shirley himself. Colonel Vaughan had no better success. He settled the matter by clapping the strange sachem into custody.

I slept little that night. It was not the damp cold which kept me awake. It was a nightmare which would not depart, a vision of a murderous knife in a savage hand, flourishing around Antoinette's dark head. I heard her pitiful screams and awoke to find camp breaking up. I sought out the sachem, determined to discover the worst. He was gone, escaped. It was easy to understand, in view of the weariness of our guard. Nevertheless, I had a strong suspicion that Thundercloud had had some hand in the matter. Did he condone the deed? Once again I was to have my faith in an old friend severely shaken.

Next day the march continued. Coming to a long log hut, Colonel Vaughan, fearful of a trap, ordered it fired at once. A moment later, the air was split by a terrific explosion which rocked us off our feet. When we came to, great clouds of smoke were drifting over the harbor toward the fortress in a long banner of black. As I picked myself up I caught a whispered remark from an officer. " Pity we had not known these Frenchmen would run at our coming. We might have saved all those supplies."

The second officer, I now saw, was none other than Colonel Vaughan. " It is not to be regretted perhaps," he answered shrewdly. " If the French think it is heavy ordnance, they may judge us stronger than we are and offer to surrender the sooner."

I thought there was something in it, for the French could hardly conceive of us willfully wasting good powder.

It was our plan to continue our march around the harbor to the Point of the Lantern on the other side of the mouth, but that occurred which brought us to a swift halt. A low, dull, terrifying rumble from our rear smote our ears. It seemed to come from the hills behind us and was to all who knew the sound of mortars.

" The French! The Acadian forces have arrived! " someone cried out. " They have set a trap for us, waiting until we landed to attack. We are lost! "

As we all waited for the sound to be repeated, I wondered. Was this my last day on earth?

14: The Grand Battery Causes Us Great Anxiety

It was a tense moment for all of us. Scouts were sent back. We waited, hands on muskets. Curiously enough the sound was not repeated.

At the end of two hours our scouts returned. They had found no explanation for the discharge. The woods were still empty. Colonel Vaughan, however, thought it wise to order an immediate return. He shrewdly divided his men. The main force was to move swiftly back to the encampment. Colonel Vaughan with a smaller party would follow and fan out, making a thorough search along the route. Needless to say Billy and I managed to be of the smaller company. As we came out on the Greene Hill Colonel Vaughan with a mere handful of us moved cautiously down the incline.

Now all the morning I had marched in a kind of daze. I felt sure that if Mistress Antoinette had suffered this ordeal she would never survive it. I felt she was most truly lost to me forever, and was ready to fling myself upon the Royal Battery singlehanded. But Colonel Vaughan was very insistent that we were to make only a trip of reconnaissance.

The fog had departed with the night, and the day was extremely clear.

From the green-clad hills we looked down upon the Royal Battery, a long line of barracks ending on either side in a circular tower with parapets. The French engineers, I reflected, had planned well. Should any ships elude the Island Battery and the shoals which surrounded it, they would have to face the Royal Battery as they came in.

Billy was beside me. " Look, Eben," he cried, " is it not queer? There is no smoke rising from the chimneys of the barracks."

I do not think the idea would have occurred to me, but I saw that the colonel was considering it.

" And the flag is gone too," Billy cried excitedly.

In the morning light the battery had a wrecked appearance, and I perceived that the expedition had caught them in the act of repairing the outer wall. Much of it was down.

Colonel Vaughan turned to Thundercloud. " Think you this is a trap laid for us, Thundercloud? "

It seemed to me I had been suspecting traps ever since I had landed, and the French had continually belied their reputation.

Whether Thundercloud was sullen from the night before or

just being cautious I could not tell. He did not reply, and after a while I discovered that the Indian had slipped away. I brooded over this fact with dark suspicion until, some moments later, Billy caught my arm.

Staggering out of the forest toward the morass just below us was a familiar figure.

" Thundercloud! " I exclaimed.

" He is drunk! " Billy whispered. " He will be shot! "

I wondered. Had he drunk himself into forgetfulness of what the sachem had told him concerning Mistress Antoinette's fate?

But, doubting him as I did, I yet could not see him butchered, and started to his assistance when Billy held me back.

" Wait! " he cautioned. " It is a ruse! "

Now I noticed that Thundercloud, although he was reeling very realistically, was aiming at the battery and drawing nearer every moment. We waited breathlessly. Every minute we expected to see that little flash, that white breath of smoke with its accompanying sharp pop which would spell his end. It did not come. Thundercloud continued to roll. He even fell down once or twice. He staggered up and swayed out in a great zigzag. Were they waiting until he had reached the wall, hoping in this way to induce the rest of us to venture into their trap?

Billy's eyes never left Thundercloud. " The Indian is wily," he said. " He is not seeking the breach in the wall, but one of the casements in the tower."

I made no doubt that Thundercloud's keen eyes were raking the battery from end to end.

His last roll brought him under an embrasure. We saw him stagger and clutch the wall wildly.

" I wonder! " Billy murmured. " Does he hear something? "

Before he had finished speaking, Thundercloud had flung an arm over the sloping ledge and with the swift action which indicated he was working with all his faculties alert he slipped over the sill and disappeared.

Now everything was forgotten in our excitement. What a thing to tell the general! And Governor Shirley! But could it be true?

Could we without firing a single shot capture the Royal Battery? Its guns reached both the fortress and the Island Battery. Were we intrenched in it, we could sink any ship that might slip through the blockade in the fog of that bleak shore.

It seemed years before we were reassured. Then Billy was the first to understand. He leaped up and cheered wildly. " Hurrah! " he shouted. " Hurrah! "

Standing on the parapet, executing a wild war dance, Thundercloud was telling us in sign language that the battery had been evacuated!

" Forward, men! " Colonel Vaughan's sharp order rang out. I am much afraid it echoed far behind Billy and me.

In an incredibly short time we were down the hill and slipping through the morass. It seemed indeed a grim business when a muffled roar came from the fortress and a shot plunged into the shore on the other side of the battery. The shot had widely missed its mark, but it told us that the French were aware of our conquest of what they had abandoned, and would contest it bitterly.

As we reached the gate, Thundercloud swung it open. His face was beaming. I did not doubt that he felt now he had made up for the seeming sullenness of his refusal to interpret the night before. And in a way he had.

I had heard much of the alabaster whiteness of the Normandy stone with which the fortress was faced, but what I saw before me surpassed in beauty all my imaginings.

That the evacuation had been precipitous we soon discovered. The storeroom still contained some quantities of supplies. The torn paper about made me think that some selection had been made. To our great joy there was considerable powder. And best of all, on the ramparts and in the embrasures of the towers, were twenty-eight forty-two-pounders! They had been spiked, but we found, on investigation, the job had been so clumsily managed that a little work by our gunners would put them back into condition in a few hours. All the trunnions were intact.

Our great need had been heavy ordnance. Here it was ready mounted to our use. And I thought how shrewd our leaders had been, for, although we had no forty-two-pounders ourselves, we had come supplied with shot for the same! It had been thought we would do what we did—capture the guns from the French.

" Eben! " Billy announced. " We must hold this battery at all costs."

I readily agreed with him. But could we? Doubt filled me! I could not understand why the enemy had abandoned it.

There was even loot of a sort, mute testimony to the speed of the evacuation. Down in the officers' quarters we discovered pewter tankards of a beauty that would have held young Paul spellbound.

One door that Billy and I cautiously opened gave entrance to a tiny chapel. Even Billy, stanch Puritan that he was, doffed his cap in reverence. I gazed at the white altar with its silver candlesticks. The gentle face of the Virgin and Child reminded me of Antoinette in her least mocking mood, and I thought that for all the tales I had heard of papacy as an evil thing there was something gentle in this worship of a Mother and her Child, and something devout in a race who raised a chapel under the guns of their ramparts.

We found no prisoners to take. The place had been completely evacuated. Again we wondered why. Our sense of some mystery was tinged with fear.

On the platform of the great salient between the towers Colonel Vaughan summoned us together. He announced: " The Royal Battery is ours. We have taken it by the grace of God in the name of His Most Gracious Majesty, King George the Second. I shall send immediately for reinforcements and a flag. See that you acquit yourselves like men, and by that same grace of God we will hold the place till succor come."

Here a shout from Billy Tufts drew all eyes toward him. He had stripped off the red coat he was wearing and was climbing the mast coatless in the bitter wind.

" Colonel Vaughan! " he cried breathlessly as he ascended. " We do not need a flag! Will not this do? "

The men started to cheer, but were instantly stopped by the

colonel. I saw then what was in his mind in restraining it. Billy, his red coat over one arm, was fair target for the guns of the fortress. We could only watch and pray silently that he be spared.

Now either the French in the great fortress were fearfully short of shot and shell, or else they were completely paralyzed by our audacity: they fired no shot. Billy reached the top and secured the flag and slid down again unharmed.

Later when he was able to replace his own garment with an officer's coat of bright blue and scarlet of the Karrer Regiment that had manned the battery, his happiness amused us all. He made me teach him a few French words. His linguistic defects did much to lighten the uneasiness of the next few hours. Whatever had caused the French to abandon the battery, it was reasonable to suppose that on later consideration they would repent of their rashness and reattack. And we were but a handful of men and young lads.

From the ramparts the town was clearly visible. It was like a bright jewel set amid the green terraces of the fortifications. I could not but admire the neat precision of its thirteen streets spread like a map up the hill to the high citadel. I could clearly distinguish dark forms moving in the streets. Was one of them Morpain? I had regarded him always as the murderer of my father. I now added to his score the death of Antoinette. If the occasion ever arrived that he was in my power, I vowed to spare him no mercy. I hoped now that that day was not far off.

My moment of reflection was broken into by a request from Colonel Vaughan that I report to him below. Billy was ordered to keep watch on the parapet and give instant warning of any attempt by the French to return.

I found the colonel in a room I believed to be that of the French commandant.

Snatching up a great quill and dipping it into a silver inkpot, bright and shining from recent care, he handed it to me, saying, " I could wish they had been so thoughtful in the matter of a piece of paper."

Instantly my thought flew to the storeroom. Telling him I knew where I could secure it, I hastened down there. The piece I finally selected was not so big as I could have wished, but the colonel was nonetheless grateful. However, he was at some pains not to over-fill it.

Then did I write, I thought, the strangest document, both in its shape and in its content, man had ever seen. For so short were we of paper that we did not dare trim it, but I must bend my writing to its strange contours:

" Royal Battery at Louisbourg, May 2, 1745. May it please your Honor to be informed yet with ye Grace of God and ye Courage of about thirteen men, I entered this place about nine o'clock and am waiting here for a reinforcement and flag."

The colonel stopped as the sound of running steps in the corridor reached us. Dread seized me.

It was Billy!

" Colonel Vaughan! " he panted. " A landing party is gathering even now at the Point of the Lantern. And small boats are setting out toward us from the fortress. We are about to be attacked! "

The colonel answered calmly. " Return, boy. Inform me when they are arrived within musket shot."

Even the general himself, I was sure, could not have been more cool. It seemed to me if the French had had more of this same quality, they would not now be fighting to regain that which they had so recently abandoned.

Billy, his French coat flapping behind him, rushed off.

Colonel Vaughan calmly finished his letter. And with the Frenchman's quill he signed it, and with the Frenchman's wax we sealed it up. " I think," Colonel Vaughan commanded, " you will have to take it, Eben. I cannot spare any of the men."

I could scarce believe that I was to be the bearer of such large news.

Colonel Vaughan caught up his musket. " Go quickly, Eben! And God grant that you get through! "

Concealing the letter on my person, I dashed out of the barracks and through the breach in the outer wall. A rattle of musket fire rippled out behind me as I floundered out over the

morass, which here, fortunately, was a narrow strip. I prayed that
the fire was coming from our own men and that they had landed
a well-aimed shot at the boats coming to besiege them. I did not
dare look back. Was the victory I was about to announce an empty
one? Would the gallant little band of twelve stanch hearts I had
left behind in the Royal Battery be overwhelmed and shot to
pieces before I could make the general's encampment and get aid?

More firing winged my feet.

I plunged into the woods, dashed between the dark trunks of
pines and scrubby spruce, and burst into the first clearing.

15: I Have Doubts for My Dear One

" Jerusha! " muttered a voice. " 'Tis Master William's
ledger lad! "

It was a company of Vaughan's own men, helping to erect a battery on the Greene Hill. Breathlessly I told them. " The Royal
Battery is taken! It is being attacked! Colonel Vaughan is besieged there! "

" Hurrah! " they shouted recklessly as if the war were over.
Instantly they were gone. Only one remained long enough to inform me that a battery was building lower down on the hill, opposite the Dauphin or West Gate of the town. It was designed to
play upon the outer wall of the fortress and create a breach.

I sped on my way with my precious letter. At the new earthworks I delayed long enough to retail my news. The joy of the
men was unbounded. Cheers, which the inhabitants of the fortress
could scarce fail to hear, rose gaily.

I looked with curiosity upon the fortress and now discovered a
strange thing. The day had started off crystal clear, but already had
become overcast. And I saw long streamers of fog again obscur-
ing it.

Once past the fortress, I could see the white tents of our own encampment. Some had already been erected. But between them and me was the morass over which a slow miasmatic mist was creeping and bringing with it an icy breath which seemed to chill my very marrow.

In the raw dampness I could dimly see our men struggling vainly to bring the heavy guns across the terrible terrain. Fear clutched my heart. The first gun was sunk to its carriage in the mire. As the men pulled themselves clear they sank weakly on the wet rock ledges. It looked a hopeless task. Were the French engineers right after all? Was a land attack impossible because of the difficulty of landing the heavy ordnance?

My heart dropped from its great elation. I went doggedly on.

When I reached the encampment and had given the old countersign, " King George forever! " I found the general in speech with Richard Gridley, the engineer, and several of his officers. They were a sober crowd. I gathered that this matter of landing guns on the morass was greatly concerning them.

The general perused my letter intently. Then, with greatly relieved face, he announced it to his officers. Instantly their countenances lightened.

" This is indeed good news, Eben! " said the general. " Gridley, what about armorers for the spiked guns? "

Gridley replied with enthusiasm. " There is Pomeroy, sir, an excellent man."

" Good," the general turned to his secretary, Richard Greene. " Write an order that Pomeroy and such men as he shall select proceed at once to the Royal Battery. Inform Admiral Warren of our success. Order Colonel Waldo's regiment to relieve Vaughan. And, Moulton, announce the news to the men. It will put new heart into them. Gentlemen, that is all. How many guns, Eben, did you say there were? "

" An' it please you, sir," I found myself unconsciously mimicking Antoinette, " there are twenty-eight forty-two-pounders, two eighteen-pounders and several hundred shells, some cannon and a deal of good powder."

A few of the officers stayed their departure to listen. I saw deeper satisfaction illumine each face. We were terribly short of ammunition and heavy ordnance.

"It is well," said the general. "We will bring one of the forty-two's to the new battery building on the hill, that it may batter down the wall at the Dauphin Gate. Colonel Vaughan gained more than he wasted when he blew up the French supply store. I do not doubt that the men of the Royal Battery thought the noise was made by recently arrived guns, and fled precipitately."

The general would hear all I knew concerning the Royal Battery. I described it again as fully as I could, even to the little chapel, which seemed to interest him mightily. "Ah, Eben," he said, " I sometimes wonder what does it matter how we worship so long as we worship something higher than ourselves?"

When I related my adventure with the Indian and my fears for Mistress Antoinette, his face grew stern.

"Pray God, Eben, it be not so!"

I pleaded to be sent out with Colonel Vaughan to the Royal Battery and allowed to accompany Colonel Waldo in his scouting, but the general shook his head.

"No, no, Eben. It is a dangerous business, and anyway I need you here. Mr. Greene is much overloaded with his duties. The admiral has already written me some lengthy epistles " — the general sent me a sly smile — "and must be replied to." Then he added in a kindly tone, " I have yet to hear from him concerning Aaron."

I replied that I wished only to do my duty and would do as he commanded, that I wanted to scout because I had great desire to see again the Indian sachem who had had contact with Antoinette. I was of the opinion that he was likely still in the neighborhood.

General Pepperrell was doubtful. But he did say: " I will have in Thundercloud, Eben, and question him myself. He will talk for me, I am sure, and we will get to the root of the matter."

Then he continued: " I am deeply grateful for all the information you have brought in and will tell Governor Shirley so. At the moment I think I shall not inform him of this matter of Mistress Antoinette. I think, myself, that the Stuart and his party would have been transferred to some English ship in exchange for several able-bodied Frenchmen. The fortress, they tell me, is terrible short of men and the Stuart was a man of great value as a hostage. You will find that he and his daughter and Dogood are probably even now on the way to England by way of Jamaica or the Barbados. As for the matter of the Red Hat badges, it is quite possible they were stolen from them before they were exchanged."

Now this was a new idea to me and cheered me mightily, so that I put far from me the thought of Mistress Antoinette's torture and death. Then I reflected that in the Barbados or in England Antoinette was equally far removed from me, which plunged me into despair again.

" Morpain is an exceedingly shrewd man," the general concluded. " I know he would consider the hostage angle. However, I will inform Colonel Waldo's company to be on the lookout for news of two English-speaking girls and for the Stuart himself, in case they were landed here. Of course, if Morpain sent them to the fortress, we may not get word of them until it is taken."

The knowledge that the general did entertain the thought that Antoinete might still be alive sent my heart soaring. But a moment later I reflected sadly that Thundercloud's information, when fully disclosed, might be final indeed.

Fog obscured me the moment I left the general's quarters. I was glad to seek the warmth and shelter of Asa's fire. I was roasting a duck egg which he had given me when Billy sprang at us out of the mist. I had great fright, thinking that the Royal Battery had been retaken by our enemies.

Billy's laugh reassured me. " Do not look so troubled," he cried. " I am but come with good news: we drove the Frenchies back, sinking their boats with our shellfire, even before the relief you sent had arrived! What news is there here? "

I told him of the general's promise to write the admiral concerning Aaron. Also of the trouble we were having in landing the heavy ordnance and of the remedy suggested by Colonel Mesharvey.

" Let us go at once and see how it is progressing," cried Billy.

"It is a fine idea and worthy of our New England men. 'Tis said, Eben, that what we lack in strength and guns is made up for in persistence and ingenuity. We are most certainly men of daring."

"Most certainly you appreciate yourself," Asa made tart remark. But I think he was pleased too, for he produced another egg, which Billy, who was always hungry, dispatched with pleasurable speed.

At the morass good fortune seemed again to be favoring us. A neat cradle had already been fashioned out of crude lumber, and a heavy mortar slung in it, to which long hawsers had been attached. Straining at these lines, linked to them by breast yokes, even as the animals at home, two hundred of our New England men struggled forward in the icy slough of the morass. Even the streamers of fog were aiding in concealing our movements from the enemy. And the gun was moving, although by inches. I thought that what men could do, we men of New England would.

Thundercloud arrived from the Royal Battery that same night. General Pepperrell sent for me to be present when he interviewed him. When Thundercloud complained that English was difficult for him, the general had in Feathertale to interpret. Thundercloud seemed much pleased at that, and I rather thought he shrewdly imagined that in talking through Feathertale he was putting the burden of his disclosures on the latter.

Thundercloud then conversed in deep gutturals for some time, his eyes now shining luminously, now growing dark and sullen as with secret anger. My fears mounted momentarily and my patience was all but exhausted when Feathertale at last began. He spoke slowly, as if aware of the gravity of what he was disclosing, his eyes ever on Thundercloud. The latter grunted his approval at intervals.

I wondered how much Feathertale would be willing to retell us.

"Morpain," he began, "pressed with other sea business, landed the two girls and the Englishman he had captured on the shores of Nova Scotia in the vicinity of Minas, where a considerable force of French and Indians sent from Quebec for an attack on Annapolis Royal were wintering. He handed the prisoners over to the sachem and a small band of followers with instructions to escort them

141

safely to the big wigwam. I take it this was the fortress at Louisbourg?" Feathertale looked inquiringly at Thundercloud, who nodded vigorously.

"The sachem and his company started out, but on the way incurred in some manner the displeasure of the native tribes. There was a fight." Feathertale definitely slowed his speech here. "Stuart was killed, or at least the man we suppose was Stuart. One of the girls was slightly wounded, as was the sachem. As soon as the girls were able to travel, the native group picked up the girl prisoners and made off. The sachem's wounds were slow in healing, but he did recover and started with his band in pursuit. They picked up the trail and followed to the Strait of Canso. Here they were slowed up again by the moving ice and the necessity of procuring some means of crossing. By the time they got across, the native tribes had undoubtedly reached the fortress. Indeed the sachem had secured word from the villagers as he journeyed that the English girls were ahead of them. The sachem was on his way into the fortress when intercepted by our men. The sachem has good assurances the English squaws reached the fortress in safety."

Feathertale stopped speaking. I thought myself that if the wily sachem had had wish to concoct a tale to cover his own evil-doing, he had done a good job of it. As for me, I did not believe a word of it. He was wearing that at his belt which belied his words.

"Is that all?" General Pepperrell demanded, sharp as a pistol shot. I noted his face was whiter than usual.

To my great disappointment, Feathertale nodded.

"But the sachem was wearing white women's scalps," I cried in scorn. "What does he say to that?"

Feathertale looked uneasy. His gaze toward Thundercloud was plainly troubled.

Thundercloud himself made answer. "Sachem," he said slowly with stormy eyes, "not have white squaw scalps!"

I looked at him in amazement.

"But, Thundercloud," I cried, "you touched them yourself."

Thundercloud bent his gaze upon me and the strange thing was it seemed not so much in anger as in mesmeric determination.

142

" Sachem," he repeated, " not have white squaw scalps." We could wring no more from him but that persistent reiteration.

It was not the smallest part of the whole tragic incident that my faith in Thundercloud was lost. I knew that many of the Indians lied with the unconscious abandon of an imaginative child. But Thundercloud had always seemed to me, in his heart, a white man.

All that night I pondered the circumstances. If the tale of the sachem, and Thundercloud's interpretation of it, had been correct, then two white women had been taken as prisoners into the fortress, both of them captives of Morpain, and one of them had worn Antoinette's red hat! Could they be other than Antoinette and Dogood? But what proof had we that they had ever reached it? I shuddered when I recalled the reference to the wounding. Had this referred to the scalping? Had they survived it? Was Feathertale, or even Thundercloud, telling us the whole story? I could not sleep that night for thinking of the horror of it.

It was well that the very next day matters of import occurred to distract my attention. At a council of war, Admiral Warren attending, it was decided to send into the fortress a summons of surrender.

I could not myself think that the French, entrenched as they were, would pay much attention to it, but as Billy pointed out, while we had landed the bulk of our troops and supplies, the enemy could not possibly know that it was our all. On a clear day they could plainly discern the hundred sail in which we had arrived, flanked by the great ships of the men-of-war squadron. They might well think our strength was overwhelming. I knew that Billy could be right. Both Admiral Warren and General Pepperrell were at some pains to see that no small boats from the harbor got out on a tour of reconnaissance.

And so the guns ceased firing, and we waited patiently with high hopes that long day until our white flag should return to us.

Master Greene was at some pains to show me a copy of the document of which he was no little proud, having assisted in the composing of it, and I could not but admit it had a right valiant sound to it. How swiftly our trouble would be over if it so impressed the

French! How soon my doubts and fears for Antoinette would be relieved!

Happening to make a trip to the Royal Battery, on errand of the general during the morning, I was much struck by the quiet of the green hills around the fortress, for now that the guns were silent I could hear all manner of sweet living sounds — trees murmuring, and wooing birds, and the rhythmic roar of the surf beating a quiet accompaniment. When I arrived at the hill battery, the men there were at pains to point out to me the ramparts of the fortress, alive with color as the women and children, secure in the temporary armistice which silenced our guns, assembled for air and to assuage their natural curiosity concerning us. And I thought again how sad it was that people so like us should be at war with us over a matter of the Old World which was really none of our business. I made no doubt that what troubles we had in the New World could have been quite easily smoothed out had we been the only ones concerned in the matter.

We had not long to wait. Before five o'clock our emissary was returned to us — the French had refused to surrender, the guns had taken up again their mission of destruction, and the women and children had returned to the dreary solitude of the casemates of which I had had such gloomy description. Like us the French proposed to be loyal to the master under whom they served. It seemed to me that was matter for admiration even in an enemy.

The war was on. All our talk now was of the grand assault we must make very soon. Indeed, the assembly gathering one morning decided to make it that very night, but, after talk with their men and some sober thinking within themselves, they changed their minds before night. It was General Pepperrell's own opinion that to make the assault before we had breached a hole in the walls through which to pour our men and equipment was to court certain defeat, and I could see he was much relieved at their decision. I was like to agree with him most heartily and glad was I when it came to my ears that the matter had been postponed.

The next few weeks I was employed as runner between the Royal Battery and the encampment.

We had ascertained that the woods were free of both French and Indians. We did know, however, that one of the fortress captains, Beaubassin by name, was at large with a small force of Indians and French, on the Point of the Lantern, opposite the town. Should his forces become augmented by the French and Indians daily expected from Minas, we might at any moment find the woods all around the encampment anything but safe.

I made the trips somewhat fearfully, it must be confessed, and always when I came back Billy welcomed me as one returned from the dead until he persuaded the general that, in case of attack, two emissaries were better than one. Thereafter, to his great joy and mine also, Billy always accompanied me.

Most of the letters I brought from the Royal Battery to the general consisted of requests for more powder or shot and shell. The orders that were sent back by the general always contained sharp admonition to expend the ammunition carefully.

As the days passed, and we advanced our batteries nearer and nearer to the West Gate in the Dauphin Bastion, the effect of the barrage was visible. In spite of frantic patching on the part of the French, every night we were effecting a considerable breach in the fortress wall. The day of assault was drawing nearer.

On their part, the French returned the barrage, but either they were most shocking bad shots, or else in that uncertain weather the guns were hard to sight. Their shells, while they did considerable damage, killing and wounding our men, more often fell wide of the mark than upon it. Indeed, some of them never exploded at all. And nothing pleased our New England troops better than to dash out of cover, collect the unexploded shells, and send them back from our own guns. Now and then one of our guns overshot the gate and exploded in the town. My heart trembled for the safety of Antoinette. There was a recklessness about the hill batteries and their frantic firing evident even to Billy and me. They had already overheated a mortar and blown it up with the loss of some of their men and the total loss of the gun itself. They were dependent on General Waldo in the Royal Battery for their ammunition, and he continually complained they were a wasteful lot.

Billy and I had a secret feeling that the expedition was in more danger from the undisciplined quality of our own troops than from the shot of the enemy. The loss of the mortar was no small thing. Had we had sufficient guns to spare a few to send against Beaubassin on the Point of the Lantern, we might have established a battery there to play on the Island Battery. Until it was silenced Admiral Warren could not come near enough to play his great guns on the town.

Frequently when we returned to General Pepperrell he would be deep in a lengthy epistle from Admiral Warren. On one occasion the little admiral had burst out, " For the love of reason let us do something! "

I looked down from the knoll on the morass. Our men were still toiling waist-deep in the icy mire all day, and sinking at night, still wet, upon hard beds under rude shelters of spruce or sailcloth. They were determined not to give up until the last gun was landed. I felt sudden anger at the admiral, sitting snug in his comfortable ship able to up and maneuver out of the way if attack came. But the reply of the general, though firm, was in no way discourteous. And again I thought the crown did not provide us with rulers who were any greater men, or who could excel in wisdom and patience and good manners our own New England men.

Some of the admiral's own predicament appeared in his next letter brought us by small boat across the sea: " Ten sail of men-of-war (French) are gone to the West Indies which may possibly bend their course this way."

It filled us too with uneasiness, but it did not deflect the general from his set course. He was determined to land all his ordnance and batter a large hole in the outer wall near the Dauphin's Bastion before he made his land attack. He saw the futility of attempting to charge up the open glacis — the greensward slopes which rolled up to the top of the eighty-foot moat under the raking fire from the great guns of the King's Bastion.

16: I Learn More of the Secret of the Fortress

And now there was good news from the fleet to cheer us.

The general made public a dispatch newly arrived from Admiral Peter Warren. It seemed they had sighted and engaged a French brig, the *St. Jean de Luz*. After a stiff fight she had fallen to their guns and was found to be laden with brandy and provisions for the fortress. The admiral wrote, " Captain Fones will give you an account of what was in the prize and will spare you and the rest of the gentlemen anything you want out of her."

Now I was frequently of use to Master Greene, the general's secretary, in making copies of the letters for Governor Shirley, so it happened that I saw the full text and the general's reply thereto. Neither was exactly reassuring.

Admiral Warren continued, " We hear by her [meaning the *St. Jean de Luz*] four sail of men-of-war, one of seventy-two guns, the other three of fifty-six, and three company ships of thirty guns each may be daily expected here, which makes me impatient for the *Princess Mary* and *Hector* to put us upon a par with them."

This sounded as if the French fleet, of which we had heard persistent rumors, was indeed heading our way. It was grave news, indeed, and I could see that both the general and Master Greene so regarded it.

The admiral further showed his sense of the gravity of the approaching situation, for he continued: " As it will be necessary now we expect such a force from France to keep our ships out and together, it will be of the utmost service to order the schooners and sloops to fill our water, and bring it out to us, most of the colony cruisers being quite out of water and wood. . . . Three of the French brig's men got ashore at the easternmost part of this island, but hope they won't be able to get into Louisbourg. . . ." And finally he suggested: " Two or three of the worst of the schooners to be made into fire vessels would be of the greatest consequence if a superior force to us should arrive. If you'll please to order two or three, with a whale boat to each, I'll get them prepared for that purpose."

The general's answer was prompt. He ordered off four of the transports with wood and water, "two of which to be improved for fire ships if you think proper." He also offered to have some fire ships prepared inside the harbor at the Royal Battery. But he had to add the damaging news, "We have since my last continued our fire on the enemy from the West Gate Battery which has shattered the wall considerably, but we were so unfortunate last night as to split one of the forty-two-pounders." I could imagine the peppery little admiral's reception of that. And I thought a lesser man than Master William would have concealed it, but the general was not one to shirk the responsibilities of any deficiency in his own command. He too showed his anxiety, for he added: " I am desirous of a general consultation as soon as possible in order to determine a speedy and vigorous attack with our united force. Our men sicken apace. Great numbers are now unfit for service."

It seemed to me we had reached a very grave state of affairs indeed and were in immediate danger of complete annihilation. The admiral I knew as a shrewd, fearless man, not given to womanish qualms. If he considered himself, with the ships he now had, no match for the oncoming French fleet, then truly he was not. And if the English ships were defeated, then would we be the ones blockaded, for I did not doubt that should the fortress receive added supplies of men and food and ammunition, they would instantly sally forth to accomplish our destruction. That they had not done so before this caused us to wonder. Our camp was without walls and manned, I suspected, by very indifferent guards most of the time. We could only surmise that the reason the French did not come was that they were even more short of powder and shell than we had been led to believe, or, because of the recent mutiny of the mercenary soldiers who manned the fortress, they were none too sure of the loyalty of their troops. In this I could not but feel they were most woefully shortsighted. For whatever men trained for war might do in peacetime, I did not think it reasonable that they should forget their calling in time of war. And that the French themselves might sooner or later come to this view also, I considered quite possible.

I was completely cast down and very fearful of what lay ahead, and I could see that the officers who surrounded the general were in like mind with me.

Now it happened that there was brought in, by a later messenger, information that was of great importance to me. And I thought how fine a man the admiral was at heart that in the midst of all his anxieties he had time for a purely personal matter and that he could appreciate how much the news he was sending meant to the one for whom General Pepperrell was seeking it.

Admiral Warren was pleased to inform General Pepperrell that he had made earnest inquiry and had found there was aboard the H. M. S. *Mermaid* one by name of Aaron St. Jean de Gervais, a gunner of Bostontown, and he took time to add the further good tidings: " I have excellent report of the same."

Aaron was at Louisbourg! He was there. I would see him when we took the fortress!

" It is good news, indeed, Eben," the general broke in on my thoughts. " I am glad he has given a fine account of himself. I doubt not Aaron will be a rich man someday. Every man in the navy is to have his share of the prize money, I am told. And some of these French ships be veritable treasure houses."

I thought then, somewhat selfishly, that Mistress Antoinette, if she were alive and within the great fortress, was moving still farther from me every day. I did not think she was one to be moved by personal advantage, but I did not see how anyone could resist my brilliant brother; and Aaron, with a small fortune in his own right, would have no hesitancy in seeking Mistress Antoinette. I could not, pauper that I was, stand in his way. The fogs which so frequently invaded that coast were not heavier than my spirits at this moment.

Now the thought of Aaron and Antoinette together drew my mind of necessity to Bostontown, and I soon found myself thinking of Captain O'Hara. I had wondered often what had become of him. It had seemed to me that such an expedition would have been very much after his own heart. But I could not get word of him in any of our regiments.

I was, therefore, not entirely surprised one day when I learned from Feathertale John that one of Captain O'Hara's men had been seen coming ashore from a small boat. I made at once for the general's quarters. It occurred to me that Captain O'Hara was most likely come with his man, and for once I was eager to see him. It was possible that he might have further information concerning Antoinette. I arrived there just in time to find a rough-looking fellow, much bundled up as to cap and scarf against the cold and damp of the weather, about to accost the general. It seemed that Captain O'Hara himself was offshore with a boatload of fish which he was most eager to land and sell to the general. Now I knew we were extremely short of provision and I looked for the general to accept immediately. I could scarce believe it when I heard him refuse the offer somewhat abruptly, and follow his refusal with an order to the fellow to be off about his business instanter. As the lumbering fellow turned to go I found myself the recipient of a glance so keen and sharp as to seem utterly out of keeping with the general dumb lumpishness of the figure.

As the fellow ambled off, the general turned and discovered the amazement upon my face. He was kind enough to explain. " Captain O'Hara's boat, Eben, was intercepted by Admiral Warren's men coming in. I think the admiral must have sent for him. He wrote me by express that the man was undoubtedly a most proper scoundrel and desired I should not trade with him on any account whatever." As the general paused he heaved a sigh that seemed to me replete with disappointment. " It is great pity, Eben, for I was most sorely in need of the provender he offered. Strange that such a disability as Captain O'Hara's could prejudice a stranger against him! "

I reflected that it might have been his disability, which was certainly fearsome enough, and it might not, but the admiral and I appeared to be of the same mind concerning him. But then I thought the general's mind was undoubtedly the best mind amongst us all and was the one most like to be right. Nevertheless, I still found it difficult to agree with him in his trust of Captain O'Hara.

Later I learned from Feathertale that Captain O'Hara's crewman had done some talking while ashore. He had boasted that Captain O'Hara had been inside the fortress recently, having disguised himself during the port captain's absence as none other than Morpain himself. He hinted that Captain O'Hara had news of value to give to our side.

I found myself wondering if Admiral Warren had been quite as shrewd as we thought him, at which point I brought myself up short. To sow doubt of our ally was probably Captain O'Hara's deliberate intention. On the heels of this a wild thought came to me. I wished I had looked at the crewman more sharply. It was quite possible it had been Captain O'Hara himself in disguise, although it did seem unnatural that he should so conceal his injured member, which he was used to flourish at us.

I remembered too that as I had watched the stranger departing in his small boat I had found Thundercloud beside me, a Thundercloud in the act of making one of his rare speeches. " Him plenty bad man! " he had murmured, waving his hand in the direction of the departing crewman. I had thought him referring to the master himself, and at the moment it had been for me but the pot calling the kettle black, for I no longer trusted Thundercloud.

But now I wondered. Had Thundercloud penetrated the crewman's disguise and recognized him as Captain O'Hara? I knew that the look I had received from the crewman on parting was no ordinary glance.

Now, as ever in Bostontown, I spent much of these anxious days in Feathertale's rude shack. I was of an age to take up a needle and learn of him, and with so many ships in the Chapeau Rouge Bay, and such wild weather as we had encountered on the voyage hither, Feathertale was hard pushed to keep up with the work and in great need of my assistance.

Our talk on such occasions was still of the great fortress. It fascinated me to listen to tales about it, and then go out on the hillside and devour with my eyes its star-shaped contours. I thought much of the secret passage and at last persuaded Feathertale to inquire of Thundercloud where it was situated. For some reason Feathertale was most reluctant to do so, but at last he acceded to my continued importuning and, when Thundercloud returned from his next scouting trip, interrogated him concerning it.

I would have given much to have understood the talk which followed. It was a decidedly lengthy communication. But the slow interchange at last ended, and Feathertale deigned to interpret.

" I greatly fear, Eben," he said, " that the secret passage is an egress but not an entrance to the fortress; that is, it is easier to emerge by it than to enter, and that is as it should be, the place being a fortress. I do not understand it myself, but that seems to be what Thundercloud wishes me to understand."

I thought I understood it perfectly. Knowing the adventurous spirit of Billy and my own urge to see Mistress Antoinette, Thundercloud was fearful that if he imparted its whereabouts, Billy and I might attempt to find it.

Feathertale, however, was pleased to inform us further that, starting in the Princess Bastion, the tunnel ran down past the Maurepas Gate. In one of the prison cells there, the better for its concealment, was a second entrance, by means of a carved stone panel. By turning the tongue of one of the carven lilies, a spring was released which would open the panel. Eventually anyone following the passage thus disclosed would gain egress to the harbor between the fortress and the Island Battery.

Billy and I talked much of wandering that bleak shore at night and marking its outlet. What deterred us was the fact that the French, though woefully lax in the matter of defending a battery like the Royal, patrolled the shore most thoroughly. Billy and I could not see how it would help our cause to get ourselves shot before we had even located it.

I managed in these days to write a short note to Aaron, telling him that I had good reason to believe that Antoinette had never reached England but was taken prisoner, and was inside the fortress under care of the Sisters of the Congregation. It seemed only right to inform him. I sent the note to the *Mermaid,* by the general's own messenger. But whether it was not received, or whether it was lost, or whether Aaron's reply to me suffered that fate, I could not tell. I waited in vain for an answer.

Meanwhile Admiral Warren was growing as impatient as any of us over our continued inactivity. Finally he persuaded the general, much against his will, to order an attack on the Island Battery.

To our great chagrin the luck which had so far protected us was completely absent. The attack was a most dismal failure. Our plan was discovered. A rain of shot and shell poured down on our open shallops and whaleboats. They were swamped before ever they landed. Several of our men were killed, and many were drowned. Cheers from the fortress, so loud we could hear them, added to our mortification. Few of our men escaped.

Several days passed. The French fleet had not yet materialized, although the rumor that it was bending our way continued. Once again the admiral became insistent. The Island Battery must be taken. He promised to augment our slender forces from the fleet. It was to be a volunteer detachment. I tried hard to be of the party but was emphatically denied. Billy had better luck and was chosen. It was great grief to me that he should go without me.

Alas, for our hopes! This venture also ended in failure, a failure made the more bitter because this time our forces had actually effected a surprise landing and might have made a success of it had not someone, overly exuberant, sure that success was in our hands, started to cheer. Instantly the sleeping sentries were alerted. The guns spoke, and doomed the attack.

Billy managed to get back, but he was much upset. He had conceived the idea, rightly or wrongly, that he had been the guilty man who had first started the cheer. It was a grave doubt to carry around with one, and I was at some pains during the next few days to get his mind off it.

I learned later that some of the *Mermaid's* men had been of the party, Aaron among them. He had been wounded and taken prisoner, it was said. I could see how his impetuous tongue might have led him to volunteer. But I found myself wondering. Had he had my letter? Was he aware that Antoinette was in the fortress? It was common knowledge that the Good Sisters of the Congregation and their charges visited the sick and imprisoned. Had it been in Aaron's mind that if the attack failed and he was taken prisoner, he would at least be nearer Antoinette?

The bells of St. Louis, St. Jean, and St. Antoine-Marie never tinkled their sweet music on the evening air but my thoughts turned to my two dear ones within the fortress. I wondered if all was already lost to me with Antoinette.

After each such period, I chid myself sternly. I told myself I could have no thought of Mistress Antoinette until I had settled my score with Morpain himself for the death of my father. I grew as impatient as Admiral Warren for that moment when I should meet my enemy. I did not doubt my ability to conquer him.

But, as if fortune thought we had borne enough, that occurred which cheered us mightily. The New York train of artillery arrived aboard a sloop. It increased our store of ammunition appreciably and relieved our minds on that score, at least temporarily. Also, we had word from the fleet that Admiral Warren's expected re-enforcement of ships was close at hand. The *Princess Mary* and the *Hector* had been sighted. While not exactly a match even now for the expected French, we had a fighting chance.

But our jubilation never seemed of long duration. A great ship managed to elude Admiral Warren's watch and the provincial sloops and, running the blockade, passed the Royal Battery and came safely to anchor against the shore of the town. Shouts of joy echoed from the streets of the town, and could be plainly heard in the hill batteries.

To add to our troubles scurvy appeared among the men and the morale of our troops suffered appreciably. It was due largely to the food or lack of it, and I could see that the general was much troubled by it. Once when the admiral sent him a large box of yellow lemons, I found him gazing at them with strange intentness. " It is a bad situation, Eben, when one can be so moved by an appeal to the appetite. I grieve for the needs of our men."

That Billy and I and the few we knew were not ill at this time was possibly due to Mistress Merrie's timely thought. For I received at this time a small packet from her containing some yarbs. The letter accompanying them was written by young Paul:

" Mistress Merrie sends greetings as do I also. She would have you sup long and regular on the yarbs. They are to be brewed six hours over a slow fire. I hear no word of Mistress Antoinette. It does trouble me much. Dogood was a most venturesome lass. Mistress Merrie says God guard you. I also. I hope the siege progresses satisfactorily to our side. Your friend, Paul."

When Thundercloud, after sniffing the yarbs, grunted: " Medicine man. Good," Asa consented to brew them. It turned out to be a most bitter dose, but I do not doubt we benefited by it tremendously, for none of us were ill.

Altogether it was a most trying time, and at last I sought out the general determined to take Admiral Warren's advice and do something. As I spoke French with native ease, I thought I might gain access to the fortress as a spy. I wanted permission to try.

But before I could put my plans into effect, fate most unexpectedly played into my hands. I was soon to find myself, to my own surprise, looking at the walls of the fortress from the inside.

17: The House of the Good Sisters of the Congregation

I did not gain the general's consent to my proposal. But I did secure permission for Billy and myself to accompany a scouting party.

We left early in the morning just before dawn. Our guns were already playing havoc with the enemy's fortifications when we passed the new battery on the hill.

By working frantically at night, the men had managed to throw up a new earthwork several yards nearer the West Gate. The work had of necessity been done very hastily, and the protection it afforded was pitifully weak. As the captain pointed out to us, should the French be minded to make a sortie, it was extremely vulnerable to attack, but, as he further remarked, the French would seem to have been discouraged by the results of the sortie they had attempted at the moment of our landing. I wondered how long they would continue in their stupidity, for it was evident that, poor as the defenses were, the battery itself was giving a good account of itself.

A quite considerable hole had already been started in the outer wall to one side of the West Gate. Our gunners were much encouraged. As for the French gunners, they seemed to be having difficulty in getting the new range. Their shells continued to fall wide of their mark, though kicking up quite a dust in the vicinity, which led us to believe they would soon be doing better.

We were very glad to move on, and a little later looked down with pride on our own flag flying over the Royal Battery.

We came at last to the ashes of the village we had burned on our first night ashore, and I thought its blackened ruins cried out in shame of our deed. From there, instead of following the harbor around to the Point of the Lantern, our orders were to strike inland.

Billy was much excited. We soon found ourselves well ahead of the scouting party. Born in New Hampshire, Billy could read the woods like an Indian. I had had some trouble with a bad heel, and soon after we gained the woods it began to bother me. Billy insisted I rest while he returned to the captain for some ointment we knew he was carrying.

Only too glad to tarry at first, I soon became oppressed and uneasy at the silence, and, thinking to meet him halfway, started back in pursuit of him. Before five minutes had passed I realized I was completely lost. Panic seized me, and by the time I got over my fright all hope of finding Billy was completely gone.

I continued to wander and at last, faint and weary, came in sight of the sea and a small village. Finding myself once more among fellow men, I regained my composure. I told myself the French were folk like ourselves, and withal a merry people, so I pulled out my flute and proceeded to play it the while I drew near.

Latterly I had had some feeling that the flute on the occasions I had played it had worked me no good, but it seemed now a helpful weapon and thoroughly appropriate for a young French lad who had lost his family through raids of the enemy and was himself seeking shelter in the great fortress. This was to be my story.

Blowing blithely, I marched boldly into the village. As Feathertale and the general had both told me, he who walks boldly disarms fear.

At once doors flew open. My repertoire growing thin, I bethought me of the bird trillip I had heard in Bostontown. Was it some signal? I played it, and was instantly aware it was known. The villagers now came forth boldly.

One woman with sharp black eyes looked me over rather shrewdly. " You are the son of the captain, are you not? " she said in a voice hoarse with cold. " I had heard he was newly arrived from France."

Now I did not know to whom she might refer, but as my father was the captain of *The Golden Lily,* I thought it no more than the truth to say I was.

" I thought so," she croaked back. " There be not two such flutes in the country. Come in! "

The hut I entered was an unexpectedly cosy place. A great fire glittered below a rack of pewter and brown luster whose like I had not seen even in Bostontown. In one corner was a fine old carved escritoire. I felt sudden joy that I was no longer with my comrades and under the stern necessity of destroying such beauty.

The woman regarded me warily. I suspected she was one always certain to make extra sure of any matter. Questions began.

Did I come from across the harbor? Was it true that a great horde had appeared from New England and was besieging the fortress? To the latter I answered with the truth. They were crossing the morass. Whereupon her man who had entered, said that was very good. They would stick to their necks in the mud and perish. I did not disabuse his faith.

I felt sure it was not my French which was troubling the woman. As the son of the captain, whoever he might be, it was to be supposed that I would speak the French of the court, as indeed I did. Here luck had certainly favored me, in a way I had not foreseen.

The man — his name, I learned later, was Pelletier — now informed me he was engaged in shipbuilding. He took me outside and showed me with great pride some logs of lumber washed ashore from a ship which had been taken from the English and brought into the harbor. He pointed proudly to the great *G. R.* that stood for *Georgius Rex* and informed me it was the mark of the best lumber from New England. He planned to make a new boat of it.

Now I had been at some pains to hate Morpain and the French as a nation, but I could not see simple peasant folk so much like ourselves putting to sea in rotten-masted ships. Though fearful of arousing the woman's suspicions further, I said that I had heard there was much dissension between the English and the New Englanders, and that the New England men were in the habit of cheating the crown on occasion by shipping rotten mast trees. I suggested we saw a knot through and investigate, which we did. The treachery was immediately apparent.

Now as I pondered the matter, I felt certain that the private brand below the *G. R.* had been the brand on the lot shipped out on the ill-fated *Rollicking Lass*. Captain O'Hara's tale had been true then, as we later heard. The trees had fallen into French hands. Had Captain O'Hara known they had because he himself had engineered the matter? I distrusted him afresh.

I soon perceived that my instinct in confiding in the Frenchman had made for me a new friend. As for the man's wife, she regarded me gloomily a moment and then murmured as if talking to herself, "It is still a thing I do not understand."

I was invited to supper when I learned that the woman had been brought up by the Good Sisters of the Congregation in Louisbourg-town, had later served in a store there, and was fully cognizant of much that was going on. Her early question had been in the nature of checking up.

She told me she had been in the fortress the first few days of the siege. "And I cannot understand it," she repeated. "The phraseology referred separately to the land force and the sea force. It was like a siege conducted by two different nations, and not like that of one party subject to another."

In view of what Aaron was to get out of the siege, and what I was not to get, I decided the woman had most shrewdly appraised the situation.

Toward evening the husband showed me a small boat, heavily laden. " Tonight," he informed me, " I shall set out for the fortress and sell these fish in the town. It is food that is sorely needed."

" I have been told," I said, " that the English ships are keeping a most strict blockade. Is it possible to enter the harbor now? "

" 'Tis nothing at all to a small boat, familiar with these waters," he replied, and I stored up the knowledge for the general.

He went on to say he was much troubled because his wife, who had always accompanied him, was not able to go on account of her cold. He had great need of someone to help him in handling the boat in the currents off the harbor mouth.

I knew then that as by a miracle my chance had come.

" Could I be of help to you? " I asked.

" You could, indeed," he replied, seemingly relieved. " I do not wish to ask my neighbors, not being of a mind to tell them what I am engaged in, lest the English arriving they should inform on me. They think I take them to a ship offshore." Then he added, " But you must bear in mind that should the English take us, we should most likely be hanged at the yardarm."

I said quickly and without thought that I had heard the New Englanders treated their prisoners well.

" It is not of the same source as I have had information," he responded shortly, then added: " Of course, the son of a noted Frenchman, like yourself, educated at court, would no doubt receive honorable attention. But a poor fisherman like myself would receive short shrift. Still, if you are of a mind to come with me, you are safer within the fortress than without."

Now I had, because of the chill atmosphere, kept my cloak about me, but supper being ready, I flung it off, and looked up to find the woman gazing at me fixedly. I thought at first she was suffering from some seizure. Then I noted it was the red hat which had caught her attention. I was conscious at once of some subtle alteration in her manner, although I do not think her less astute husband was aware of it.

It ran excitedly through my mind that here in this lonely outpost she might have had contact with the sachem. Perhaps she had knowledge too of Antoinette within the fortress. I was about to interrogate her when I realized that Antoinette was a member of an enemy race, although because of her knowledge of French the people of Louisbourg might not be fully aware of it. Morpain might well have passed her off as French to save questions and trouble. But Dogood was the difficulty. By no manner of means could Dogood with her outspoken New England tongue be taken for a French girl. I decided the subject was too dangerous to approach directly. Also I was suddenly aware of a growing coldness in the woman's manner. The red hat had certainly held for her some sinister significance. I thought sadly my chances for entering the fortress were growing less and less every minute.

But to my surprise when the moment arrived the woman made no objection to my going. She even accompanied us, much muffled up, to the boat, shoving into Pelletier's pocket at the last moment a note containing a memo of some thread she needed to finish a piece of lace, which she thought the Good Sisters could send her.

I found Pelletier in no mood to talk and did not mind. I had much to think about. I did not waste much time on Billy. With his knowledge of the woods I knew nothing serious could happen to him.

Pelletier dug deep with his oars, making dip and lift with surprising quietness. Nevertheless, with each drip of the blade between strokes, I saw a phosphorescent sheen spread over the waters, and my heart feared me for the safety of our journey. We were outside in the Gabarus Bay and moving toward the entrance to the harbor.

We crept across the waters, a dark blot blending, I hoped, with the sea. I could dimly make out the dark line of the shore. There was a heavy swell, and at times the water hit our boat with a resounding thwack and then a deep gulp. I thought were I occupant of one of the colony ships we passed, I would not mistake what was happening.

Far out I espied a light which seemed to mingle with the stars. An odd thrill went through me at the thought of the English dogs of war keeping such silent watch.

"English ships," the Frenchman sneered, then rapped out an imprecation which chilled my blood. Certainly we were hated by these Frenchmen. When I thought of the villages we were burning I recalled that they had reason.

Presently he began giving me instructions. We were running toward the opening of the harbor and must pass close to the Island Battery. Not a word must be spoken, not a movement made. He would direct the boat, and the tide would wash us in. If the Island Battery took us for the enemy, we should be in a bad way. Cautiously he made me change places with him. I took the oars and held them aloft, and he took the tiller. We struck a deep swell immediately, and I thought we would give ourselves away, so loud was the report it made as it slammed down on top of us. Then some unseen current of the water seemed to snatch us up on a crest, and in an incredibly short time we were slipping past the high wall of the island fortification. As we came in the lee of the buildings I knew that the crash of the sea on the open beaches in front was drowning out all other sound.

On our right was the Point of the Lantern. I peered through the murk, fearful of the sentries. I thought Beaubassin and his group from the fort might have established themselves there. But if any guards were posted there they must have recognized us as friends. I thought anew how strategic for our purpose was the Point of the Lantern. But it was a long haul to bring our guns from the Royal Battery, and they could ill be spared. Even with the newly arrived New York train, we were not overly supplied.

Now came the worst of our journey. We were within range of the guns of the Royal Battery.

A whispered command from Pelletier ordered me to lift the oars I had been plying for a short space. I could feel by the shudder of the boat that he was raising the rudder also. The action confused me until I heard a peculiar scraping under the keel. Then I knew that I had yet another piece of news for the general. They had placed a boom across the fortress end of the harbor.

We were come among the various shipping tied up there by our blockade. Cautious challenges were flung at us out of the night from the black hulls looming above us. The French were more vigilant than our forces, I thought. At last we glided up to a long wharf and were sharply challenged.

Pelletier replied at once, " *L'ami du roi.*"

" *Passez-vous, l'ami du roi,*" came back the answer.

We tied up. I helped Pelletier to land several great tubs of fresh fish. Dark figures loomed about us in the uncertain light of a couple of lanterns. To my surprise no one looked at me. I was sure that food was already causing them grave concern, even as we had heard. We entered through a gate and came into a dimly lit enclosure, and I could see a second larger gate at the far end. The town was well guarded from the sea side.

There was now begun a shrewd bickering which convinced me the Frenchman was a merchant first and a patriot afterward. He drove a most hard bargain.

This concluded, we were allowed to pass on our journey to the House of the Good Sisters of the Congregation. Now I thought to break away here in the unlighted streets, but I found I was expected to carry one half of the load of a huge basket of fish intended for the Good Sisters, and I could not well desert my friend. Besides, I quickly decided that the House of the Sisters was exactly the place I most desired to go, since it probably harbored Antoinette.

We set out through the quaint streets. It was very dark, but I could see the silhouette of the citadel, many of its windows showing light at the edges, towering above us. I longed for the light of day, that I might consider its generous proportions. It seemed impossible to me that I was at last so near the bells of St. Louis, St. Jean, and St. Antoine-Marie.

Pelletier walked boldly up to the door under the little light and tapped lightly upon the knocker. Presently a light gleamed through a wicket in the door, and dim features regarded us from the opening. A whispered colloquy followed, in which I thought I caught some mention of the name of Morpain.

Evidently Pelletier was known, for almost at once the shutter was closed. We heard a sound of drawing bolts and the door swung open.

" *Entrez!* " a sweet young voice commanded. I perceived a young figure in an enormous wimple and gray dress.

I know not why that great hall should bring vividly back to me the thought of Mistress Merrie. She would indeed have lifted her hands in horror that I should enter a religious house of the papists. But it seemed to me a vastly pleasing place. Never had I seen higher polished woodwork and floors. They shone like mirrors. On either side were doorways and between two great carved chairs of exquisite French workmanship. Far back in the hall an ornate stairway rose regally to the second floor. In an angle of its curve stood an image of lovely blue and gold. Below was a bouquet of roses, the first I had seen in many months. It sent my mind back to the Roxbury gardens of Governor Shirley and new memories of Antoinette.

The Good Sister disappeared. Pelletier crossed himself devoutly and seemed somewhat uneasy. I crossed myself too and felt strange pleasure in the doing of it — it seemed to me a holy place. For of a sudden there was in my ears the lilt of the psalms which Mistress Merrie had been at some pains to teach me. I thought it passing strange until I realized that in the air was faraway chanting of many voices inexpressibly beautiful.

Now the portress returned, saying the Reverend Mother would be there immediately. She opened a door on the right and ushered us into a room dim lit by great wall sconces. A few chairs sat primly against the walls. But I made out at the far end a couple of kneeling figures, one in black and one in gray. It was a moment before I knew that they were kneeling at a bier and that we were in the presence of the dead.

Here too there penetrated that sound of distant chanting in perfect unison, infinitely soothing, as if after the harsh struggle of the landing, the untidiness of our living, the uncertainty of attack, I had wandered into a place of eternal peace.

It seemed a long time till the Reverend Mother came, but so still were the kneeling figures that I marveled that they were real.

With a start I found that a new personage was with us and that she was considering me shrewdly. I had heard no door open and could only think she had glided in from behind one of the curtains which broke the wall at intervals. She too was clad in a dark habit.

I received then a distinct shock. For taking no notice of the Frenchman, she held out her hand to me to salute, saying cordially: " *Morpain fils!* You are welcome! "

Morpain fils! The son of Morpain! The man who was my enemy. Whom I was there to kill! That was who they thought I was! Strange irony. My reply of acknowledgment startled me with its loudness in that quiet place.

Then Pelletier spoke up. I suspected he was a bit jealous of the attention I was receiving. " My wife, Reverend Mother, sends her compliments, and could she have a little more of the thread to make her lace. It is all written here." He handed her the slip of paper.

Now the Good Mother was a large woman of commanding mien. She was all in black save for the wimple. Though her eyes were kind, they were shrewd, and I began to feel uneasy.

She took the note he offered and unfolded it slowly. Meanwhile, she thanked him for the fish and asked if he would be good enough to clean it, the Sisters being none too skillful in such matters, besides being pushed taking care of so many wounded. Pelletier seemed proud to be of use and asked only to be taken to the kitchens.

The Mother then opened the note and began to read it. It was at once as if a glacier had come between us. I knew the meaning of Madame Pelletier's acquiescence in my coming. She had denounced me to the Reverend Mother and here was I within the walls, hidden in the heart of the Sisters of the Congregation, a New Englander and a spy! I felt my hours of life were most surely numbered.

With a stony glance she commanded Pelletier to be off. I did not think he had anything to do with the matter, so great was his surprise. He looked at me in open bewilderment as one who knew that strange things were afoot of which I was the center. She herself followed him to the door, bidding me, nay commanding me, to wait. As it closed upon her, I looked around me. My case seemed desperate indeed. Then I noted a movement on the part of the kneeling Sisters. Both rose to their feet. Two new Sisters, both in black this time, took their places. The one in black passed out at the rear. But the one in gray, turning, head bent, fingers fumbling in front of her, moved toward me. Held by a strange fascination, I could do nothing until she passed. As she reached me, she raised her head. I gazed into the dear face of Mistress Antoinette!

18: I Meet My Enemy

Once again I had need of iron control. The face so pitifully thin was doubly dear to me. Antoinette, it was evident, had known suffering of no ordinary kind. It was with difficulty I refrained from taking her into my arms.

And then Mistress Antoinette did something which made me think she had lost her wits. She caught my hand up passionately in her own. It was the end, I thought, and did not much care, so wondrous it seemed to me to feel her hands touching mine again.

But then I had sudden evidence that it was but her quick way of keeping her wits. For whispering hurriedly in French, she became suddenly busy with a great white roll which she produced from some pocket of her voluminous gray robe.

" *Le pauvre homme!* " she murmured. " He is indeed wounded. Such a time it is." As she talked the white bandage flew through her nimble fingers and went rapidly around my own. " Nobody is safe at all," she murmured. " The hordes of enemies are all around us. Yesterday our brave men were driven from the West Gate. Ten of them wounded, ten, *monsieur,* and we so short of stout fellows to defend the fortress. Ah, *monsieur,* you are indeed in good luck not to be lying there, even as he." She nodded her head in the direction of the bier with its still burden and the kneeling Sisters. " Ten wounded and five of them dead," the voice rippled on. " It was terrible. The balls landed in the heart of the King's Bastion! Ah, *monsieur,* if only the great French men-of-war would come in time. We would then make short shrift of all our enemies."

Now, so eager was I with my own questions that I scarce listened until in a flash I perceived that Mistress Antoinette was pushing home each remark with a sharp tap of my hand. Was she telling me the number of dead and wounded in their forces by yesterday's engagement? that our guns had found true mark? that a great force was even now expected from France?

" It is indeed so, Sister," I managed to answer in French, unable for the moment to think as quickly as she! I well knew that her desire for knowledge must be as eager as my own.

" Ah, *monsieur,* each day, I watch and watch. They do not come. But they will. They will, *monsieur,* from near if not from far."

A French force by sea, I took note. We expected it from France, but it might also come from the St. Lawrence where we had been told a fleet was indeed building. Was this the meaning of the delay in the arrival of the ships that had been sighted " bending our way "? Had the French decided they were not necessary, having constructed a fleet nearer the fortress? But I made note it was the same tale here within the fortress as the one outside. A French fleet was most undoubtedly in the offing. Fear possessed me anew at our delay in attacking. I sympathized with Admiral Warren's repeated pleas to do something.

Then as my hand swelled to immense proportions, I heard something else. Deep underneath, soft as fall of leaf on summer night, Antoinette was whispering in English. " You are in great danger, Eben." Did I imagine it or did her hands start toward the red hat on my sleeve and suddenly desist, after a quick look around? Maybe I had gained some height in the months since I had seen her. I guessed it was too high up for her to reach conveniently and not be seen by anyone entering the room. " Get rid of it. Quickly, Eben," she murmured. " Back of you, the curtains. There is a window, open. Count two hundred after I am gone. Pretend to faint. Roll through the curtains. The sill is low. Stop at the fifth window south."

Then her voice picked up again its soft even tenor: " There, *monsieur*, it is indeed fortunate that you came to Sister Ignace. If it is not well, come again, but I think you will not need to."

And not till then did my laggard wits begin to work. "*Merci*, Sister. You are an angel of mercy. Harm will not come to you. All will yet be well."

A swift flicker of relief crossed her still face. I had tried to convey to her that we were hopeful of the future and I thought she understood. Next moment she was gliding away.

I counted to two hundred and tried not to hurry the count. My ears seemed to leave my head in their effort to catch the faintest movement outside the room. How soon would the Reverend Mother return? Surely it was madness to wait. Yet did I obey Mistress Antoinette, although a timber of the wall creaking so alarmed me that I almost did not. It was the hardest thing ever I did. But having at last managed the count and one more for good measure, I slumped faintly against the curtains, which parted suddenly, disclosing a wide window, open on the street. The curtains dropped again behind me. I leaped out. Gaining my feet, I counted the windows as I sprinted along the Rue de Royale. At the fifth I all but fell over something. For one wild moment I thought that Mistress Antoinette herself had joined me. Then I knew that it was but an empty cloak. Fortunately my wits were quick to get her meaning. I slipped into it and pulled the cowl over my head.

I was not a moment too soon. A light came flashing out of the Rue de Dauphin and shone fully upon me.

Had my hour indeed come? My knees would scarce bear me up.

I had a thought that I should run for it, but fortunately discarded the idea as quickly as it came, for the owner of the voice greeted me pleasantly. "*Bon soir, Soeur*," he murmured.

In a feigned voice I muttered some kind of greeting. My questioner did not seem to notice its hoarseness.

Now I had thought the fellow would be content with his " good evening." I was mistaken. He swung into step beside me. And his next speech surprised me greatly.

" I know where you are going, Sister," he said, " and I will light you on your way."

It occurred to me that if he did, he knew more than I did, but there was nothing I could do but murmur, " *Merci, monsieur,*" as I judged the Sister would address him. He was evidently greatly pleased by the title and to my embarrassment seemed determined to remain with me.

Then he raised his voice into an odd singsong and cried aloud in French, " Twel-----ve of the clock! All-ll-ll's well! "

He was the night watchman!

" It is a terrible time, Sister," he chatted. " Two cannon shots fell on the King's Bastion today, wrecking one of our mortars. And *le bon Dieu* knows how many will fall tomorrow. They say there is not food enough in the town for a long siege. It was told me some fish came in tonight but I have not the rights of it. It is not a tale you have heard, Sister, is it? "

" It is not," I murmured, wary of any discussion.

But I made note of his information and also of the direction he was taking. I felt I knew the alleys of Louisbourg even as Boston-town. If only there had been more light than that of his feeble lantern. It seemed to me we were tending in the direction of the Rue de Royale and the Circular Battery near the West Gate. I cudgeled my brains to think up some way to get rid of the fellow without exciting his suspicion. My wits failed me. Billy or Mistress Antoinette, I thought, would have had a shipload of ideas.

I finally decided that when we reached our destination, wherever it was, if it turned out to be a house, I would step inside the door-way until he had passed on.

It seemed to me as we moved down the lanes the town had a most evil smell. The streets were completely deserted. The old fellow was most glad of a gossip in his lonely vigil. I could have learned much, could I have directed his conversation, but it was too risky a thing to attempt, and he very soon turned his thoughts to his own ills — the cold and the loneliness.

168

At last my conductor stopped before a tall barrack three stories high in the Rue Toulouse.

The door was ajar. I prepared to bid him adieu when he startled me by announcing, " I would be glad to light you up the stair, Sister, but it is not permitted that I leave the streets when on duty."

Assuming a voice as near to that of a woman as I could, I thanked him. At last he was off. I was slipping through the doorway to the street again when a faint light illumined the rude hall, and another voice doomed me with its proximity.

" Ah, Sister," said the new voice in peasant French, " you have come to see *monsieur le capitaine*. He is not so good tonight. 'Tis dark at the turn of the stair. I will light you up." Taking a position at the bottom, she swung her lantern aloft.

I saw nothing to do but to start my climb. An idea came to me. If the man above was sick and alone, I could slip out of my cloak, enter as a boy from the villages, and say I was but a homeless refugee. Because of my experience with Aaron, I made no doubt I could be of value in nursing him and might remain there hidden some time.

I hurried my steps as the light grew fainter on the second flight. Happening to glance down the well of the stair to see if she was still there, I could see her watching.

Then swinging away from the stair, I turned confidently toward a doorway I made out faintly at the end of the hall. But before I reached it, I found myself facing two Swiss guards. Wisely or unwisely, in the surprise of the moment, I prepared to bolt. In that single second I reached for the balustrade with the idea of leaping over it to the stair below. But the hand Antoinette had bandaged refused to take sufficient grip. I lost a few precious seconds and in them the guards were upon me, flinging my cloak from me in the scuffle and showing me up for what I was.

In the excitement one of them fired his carbine, fortunately missing me.

Then a voice oddly familiar called from the room within: " What portends, sergeant? Or is it that you are playing chess and have taken several men."

I was hustled into a great attic room. In a fine old bed I beheld a long, lean, familiar figure with a blond head. It was my prisoner of the hills!

" He was gaining admittance, Captain Morpain," my guard explained.

Morpain! I was face to face with my father's murderer at last!

The sick man frowned at me, then smiled wickedly in sudden memory. " *Mon enfant* of the hills," he mocked. " And now that you know me for who I am, *enfant,* would you still fetch me a glass of water? "

I kept unwilling silence.

A great fury possessed me that I had had this man in my power and let him go. This man who I felt was responsible for my father's death, the man who later had abandoned Antoinette to a horrible experience.

As if getting down to the business in hand, he blazed out at me in sudden anger, " Know you that Morpain is not to be interfered with! " Now this puzzled me not a little, for although I had planned to interfere with him to the best of my ability, I did not see that I had yet accomplished it. Then as quickly his face cleared a bit, and his next words held a generosity I could not but admire. " It is true," he continued, "I am somewhat beholden to you for my escape in the incident on the hills, but — " his frown returned — " I do not understand why you are here. Search him! "

The search was made with great thoroughness and none too gentle hands. But save for the red hat, which to my great sorrow they ripped from me, they found nothing. However, that would seem to have been enough. At its discovery, made somewhat late in the search, Morpain bent upon me a look of sudden, devastating hatred. And yet there was surprise in it too. I was at a loss to account for it.

But a still greater surprise was in store for me. My guard, on discovering the flute slung at my side, fairly pounced upon it. Then he held it up mutely, his eyes on Morpain. Instantly Morpain's already black face grew blacker. Flinging out a long arm, he sent it clattering to the floor. " I have had trouble enough with that! " he cried. " Let me never see it again."

The flute was Morpain's. Morpain had been in Bostontown! At last I understood. By giving the alarm in Bostontown, I had most certainly interfered with his plans! In spite of my dark plight a little ray of triumph shot through me. I might not have conquered my enemy, but most certainly I had " annoyed " him, as our saying went for a light engagement.

But my flying thoughts were brought back rudely. Morpain was smiling a cold, deadly smile. " *Mon enfant* is wounded. I hope it burns like hades, even as mine is now doing! Throw him into the dungeons of the citadel. I will rid myself of him at my leisure."

I was seized by rude hands and almost thrown down the stair.

I told myself that Morpain was suffering, but his temper was that of a person on the mend: this I knew from Aaron. I would hear from him right soon, I did not doubt, and when I did all would be over for me.

Once again I entered the lanes of Louisbourgtown, only this time I was under heavy guard. Our feet rang a strange knell on the cobbled ways. Once we went up a narrow flight of steps into a wide-open place. The parade ground, I said to myself. As if in answer a silver bell in the clock tower rang a ghostly note.

The moon was up now. The clouds had cleared away. The night was crisply clear. In spite of my terrible plight, I gazed with interest on the noble line of the citadel building with its slender spire etched blackly against the velvet blue of the night. Would my eyes ever again gaze on the gloriously spangled heavens? Fear gripped me.

More steps. A wide stone plaza. Then a high doorway. Again I was struck by the ghostly whiteness of the Normandy stone with which it was faced. It glistened in the first rays of the moon like young frost. Strange, I thought, that I should be going to my doom in such a wealth of beauty.

The Swiss guard saluted my escort and looked at me curiously. He let us go by. We entered a great hall.

Instantly my guard demanded: "A torch! Make haste there! A torch!" His voice had an ominous sound.

A torch was thrust into his hand immediately. Bearing the burning fagot high overhead, they led me down a long, steep stair. With each step the air seemed to grow colder and damper. A second's pause in a gallery. Then down and still farther down. Five flights I counted.

I began to wonder if any had ever been so far below before, and if I was to be thrust out of sight and forgotten.

Did anyone know the full extent of this great fortification?

At last, in freezing cold and bitter damp, I was thrust into a cell. With a rusty rattle the door was banged sharply to behind me.

I was alone in a great darkness. Fear such as I had never known overwhelmed me. I knew despair.

19: Under the King's Bastion

The few seconds of light, while the flaring torch had been there, had shown me a stone cell, the great walls of which dripped with moisture. A single rough bench occupied one wall.

I groped my way to it and sank down. Light and footsteps receded.

The sense of being deep down underground where I might be forgotten — left to moulder to my death — chilled me. The darkness and the loneliness and the doubt were terrible. I never afterward could bear to think of those first few hours.

At last a faint, gray light penetrated my cell. I espied a narrow slit of a window high in the wall. The discovery that I could tell day from night worked strange wonders within me. It brought new life.

I found that by dragging my bench under it, and standing upon it, I could catch a glimpse of the moat beyond. Then the cry of a bird came to me, the plaintive honk of a wild goose on the marshes. A moment later a dull rumble caught my ear and a shower of gravel rattled past the opening, some strewing itself untidily on my cell floor. I knew then the sound I had heard was the rumble of our guns finding their mark. I was still in the land of the living and our side was winning.

Then the sight of my still-bandaged hand brought my thoughts back to Antoinette. Very tenderly I undid the wrapping she had placed around it. I knew then that I greatly desired to live. I set my mind determinedly on thoughts of escape — a strangely hopeless goal, it seemed to me.

Later I caught the sound of footsteps. They grew louder, approached. Was I about to be released? I rose trembling. A faint light penetrated the partly solid door. It did not open. I perceived then it contained a small wicket down by the floor. Through this something was thrust. Light and footsteps receded. No human voice had accosted me. Suddenly I had a strange desire to weep.

I examined what had been left. A cup, a plate, and — I could scarce believe it — my flute. Why had it been returned to me? Morpain's flute! But it was strange comfort to me in that dark cell. Not the least part of its comfort was the ability it gave me to make myself heard. I seemed to have acquired a voice which would reach up through the moat to the top of the King's Bastion. I could not be forgotten.

I inspected my food. The plate and cup were of pewter rather lovely in form. They contained only water and a thin piece of bread. Still it was sustenance. I ate and drank ravenously.

And now a new sound came to me in my tomblike cell — the sound of marching feet, the heavy tread of numberless feet falling in unison, rhythmic, steady. I knew it for the martial tread of the French troops crossing the bridge over the moat to the Covered Way on the other side. I thought of our own forces, ragged, faltering, undisciplined. I marveled that we should think ourselves a match for experienced regiments, trained in the finest army in the world.

I now turned my thoughts to the events of the last night. It was evident that our map had reached French hands. The mark of the hat upon it had become for them the mark of a spy. They must have published the fact abroad too, because Pelletier's wife had recognized it and denounced me. And Antoinette's eyes had been on it as she whispered: " Get rid of it quickly, Eben. You are in great danger." And then it came to me that Antoinette's own red hat had passed to the sachem. How he had got it, I could only guess. But for this I was deeply grateful: she had arrived at the fortress without it. In their minds she had no connection with it. I wondered how Dogood had fared.

But one thing puzzled me. Why had it filled Morpain with such especial fury to find that I was a member of this supposed gang of spies?

Then I recalled the bitter way he had thrust aside the flute. Had Morpain's been the French voice I had heard on the warehouse waters that night in Bostontown? Which brought another thought swift on the heels of it. Captain O'Hara had preceded the voices with his presence on the wharf. He had gone at the signal on the flute. I put with this the visiting seaman's boast in our camp recently that Captain O'Hara had visited the fortress in Morpain's absence, and had gotten in and out by impersonating him. I did not believe the story. But I felt sure the story would never have been concocted if Morpain and Captain O'Hara had been complete strangers. I knew the truth of what I had suspected for some time. Captain O'Hara was playing both sides of the conflict. He was, as Admiral Warren suspected, " a very proper scoundrel." I had sudden new respect for this peppery little servant of the crown. Certainly he was shrewd.

But in the end I had to admit there was much about the whole matter I still could not understand.

Twice during that day I caught the clamor of the bells of St. Louis, St. Jean, and St. Antoine-Marie. They sounded surprisingly clear and sweet. Then I bethought me of Master Moody and his invocations and of the psalms which Mistress Merrie had been at such pains to teach me, and I too sought spiritual aid and was comforted.

Now as day followed day and two weeks went by, the thing that was hardest for me to bear was my utter ignorance as to the progress of the siege. I have said that I could hear the rumble of our shells landing on the King's Bastion above my head. But there came a day when they too were strangely silent. I could only ask myself, Had the enemy succeeded in silencing our batteries on the Greene Hill, or had our men again run out of powder? When there came to my ears a little later the sound of cheering from the troops in the Covered Way across the moat, I was like to have died of despair. Then I bethought me of the bells of St. Louis, St. Jean, and St. Antoine-Marie. They would surely ring out a signal victory. It was great comfort to me when they remained silent. I could only surmise it was a local victory, but how disastrous to our plans I could only faintly guess.

I turned now to the matter of my escape. Some way, I was convinced, it must be accomplished. I recalled Thundercloud's description of the entrance in the Princess Bastion, with a second opening in one of the cells of the Maurepas Gate. Of a sudden I had an idea. I would petition the governor, Clovis du Chambon, for a change of imprisonment to a place fitter for human habitation.

I reasoned that I was in truth only Pelletier's prisoner of war. I had not been properly tried and proved a spy. But when I sought about for paper and ink with which to make my plea, I realized I had none, and no pleading request for such materials brought any response from my grunting guard. I was bitterly disappointed. We had heard many tales of the disaffection of the French troops. If my guard was a sample, I realized with a sinking heart, we were not like to get much help from them.

But perhaps my worst enemy in those frightful weeks was the bitter cold. I was like to have died of it each night.

My spirits had reached the lowest ebb yet when one evening I had an unexpected visitor.

The guard who opened my door seemed to have closed it upon a shadow. For a moment I had a distinct feeling of fear, and then something in the cloaked figure gave me assurance. He was, I felt sure, a priestly visitor. I recalled that a condemned man was always given spiritual aid on his last night. Promptly a great weight descended upon me. This was the end. I was to be shot without trial. Then a voice low and clear and strangely inspiring echoed against the stone arches of my cell.

And as I listened to his courageous discourse I told myself that though he was a papist, he knew how to comfort as even our Master Moody did not. His talk was simple and manly, inspiring me to courage in the ordeal ahead and comforting me with the thought that this life is but a phase of a greater life to come, in which I would be united with my dear ones.

Now as he spoke I found myself listening so intently that when he paused, seemingly finished, it was a shock to me to realize that the sound I had been hearing for some time was the sound of my guard moving impatiently outside the door, endeavoring to indicate to both of us that my visitor's time was up. My monitor too was become aware of it. He moved restlessly. And I could dimly feel that he was making above me the sign of the cross. Whereupon I murmured softly, " I thank thee, Father." For it seemed to me that that was what one of his own flock would have said to him, and truly he had comforted me as my own father would have done had he been in the land of the living and able to comfort me in this dark hour. Something — perhaps in my phrasing — must have made him suspect that I was not of his faith, for he gave a slight start. But upon reflection I decided I must have pleased him, for he drew nearer, murmuring, " Tell me, lad, is there aught that you would have to comfort you in these last hours? "

I found his hand upon my shoulder tremendous comforting. This was then the end, I thought. Little use my petition, could I have made it! Then I thought of Antoinette. I would have given much to see her dear face just once again. But swiftly I knew I dare not involve her in my trouble. And then there came the thought: I was not dead yet. I would not give up. So I said boldly: " You are most kind, Father. I have been very desirous of petitioning the governor for a change of prison. It would be great satisfaction to me to spend my last hours in a more habitable place,

I understand there are cells in the Maurepas Gate of fair comfort. After all I am a prisoner of war."

It seemed to me a sigh escaped him. He hesitated. Then he murmured: " I will do what I can, lad. God keep you! Farewell! "

Now, in spite of the fact that I felt sure his visit foreshadowed my end probably in the early hours of the morning, I slept long and soundly that night and was much surprised to find myself still alive when light came again next morning.

On looking toward my door, I was startled to see a small object lying just inside my wicket. I hastened across and snatched it up. It was a small but beautifully bound book, a copy of the Old Testament. The smooth quality and exquisite tooling of the binding pleased me mightily in my bare prison, and I knew that its contents would be of great comfort to me. Hurrying with it to my window I held the flyleaf up to the light. I had wish to know its former owner, whom I had no doubt was my visitor of last evening. And I thought that my flute had come in like manner. Had I, after all, a friend in the camp of mine enemies?

But the former owner had evidently foreseen my first act. The name had been most meticulously erased. But in fine writing in its place I discovered something had been written. The four words were difficult to decipher and they seemed to me to be growing more difficult as I looked. I made out, " Search in the C-a-r-e-e-n-i-n-g Cove." I thought I must have made an error, for it was not a name familiar to me. I was sure it was no place on the point of land which held the fortress. I had scanned the map too carefully not to have recognized it. I bent closer, intent on deciphering it anew, and was amazed to discover the writing was already gone. I had heard tales of secret ink which when exposed to strong light disappeared. This then was it. " Search in the Careening Cove." What could it mean?

For an instant hope soared within me. The one who had sent me that message must have expected me to escape. Then my spirits fell again. The one who had sent it more likely knew me as a spy and suspected I had ways of communicating with the enemy. But who, I asked myself, within the fortress, who with access to my cell, would bring me such a message? It did not now seem in keeping with the character of my visitor.

Altogether it was a strange business and kept me guessing for many hours, which was on the whole a fortunate thing. For it was two days more before the event I was ever suspecting about to happen took place.

I was scarce awake when I caught the sound of footsteps approaching my cell. I listened carefully. There were more than one pair of feet. My hour had come! I prayed for courage to meet my doom manfully.

There came now a greater congregation of light around the chinks of my door. In quicker time than I had expected, it was flung open. A detail filed in and surrounded me.

" Eben St. Jean de Gervais," a voice cried, " I bid you in the king's name come forth."

It always seemed to me a strange thing that in that moment fear left me. I made no doubt that I was being taken without trial to a firing squad. The hour suggested it. But all I could feel was a deep relief that at last my hours of waiting were over. After all, I told myself, this was a soldier's death, and many of our troops had already passed away.

I waited only long enough to secure the length of white linen with which Antoinette had bound my hand and which I had used for a towel and kept hanging on a knub of stone under my window. Slowly I folded it and placed it near my heart. I picked up my flute.

Certainly the days of my confinement had depleted my strength. I had to pause often for breath up the long flights. My guards were kind, a fact that seemed to make more certain my immediate doom.

When at last I passed through the great portal of the citadel, I was momentarily blinded with golden sunlight. On all sides my senses seemed assailed with strange odors and perfumes — the fresh salty tang of the sea, the sweet scent of phlox, and the pungent spice of the nasturtium. And suddenly I asked myself had I ever fully appreciated the glory of this daily largess of light? Had I

178

ever stopped to think of the prodigal wealth that freedom bestowed?

We proceeded toward the parade grounds. The sight of the governor's garden, where a woman tending her flowers amid a galaxy of color turned from them and smiled sweetly at me, moved me with emotion. I seemed to have died already and to have been reborn into a world of infinite kindness and beauty.

Suddenly the thought of facing death at a moment when life appeared so rich seemed terrible indeed.

At the foot of the steps to the parade ground my detail paused. I listened expectant of that order which would send me twenty paces back and six to the right. It did not come.

Then I discovered that we were but waiting for a like detail to cross our path. I glanced curiously at the other party and was startled to see in their midst a familiar figure, the straight warrior bearing of the sachem, the look of a bewildered child on his painted face. Now I had every cause to hate him for what he had done to Antoinette. I regarded him coldly. For one moment his eyes met mine. A warm flicker of those limpid brown depths told me he recognized me. It seemed to say, " Someday, white man, you will understand." But I like always to remember that even in that startled moment he made no sign to involve me in his trouble. I had to admit the sachem possessed elements of greatness.

To my relief, the other detail passed by us and the order was given to proceed again. I held my breath. Was I to be granted a reprieve?

Presently we passed to the edge of the town and the massive masonry of the Maurepas Gate with its carven coat of arms loomed above us. Joyfully I realized that by some strange stroke of clemency I was being allowed to go where I had petitioned. My spirits rose. Freedom seemed within reach. I would escape.

And then along the morning breezes came a sharp rattle of musketry — a single long-drawn-out report that lingered on as if loath to be forgotten. I knew its import. The sachem, with his guileless, childish face, was no more. I retold myself all his sins. He had reaped his just reward. In spite of Thundercloud's denial,

I knew he was wearing scalp locks. True, Antoinette still lived, but I could have wept for the beauty that was gone.

But it was not for that that he had died. I perceived now there was a kind of justice in his death. The thing he had coveted, and for which I imagined he had scalped, a childish little red hat — that thing had led him to his doom.

I could not miss its implication in my own case. I thought grimly, no wonder Morpain had been aghast at finding on me, a lad of Bostontown, one of the red hats. Undoubtedly he already had the sachem in custody. He must have thought the plot was widespread indeed, for Thundercloud had said that the sachem was of the horde of Indians brought down from the north for the taking of Annapolis Royal.

The detail handed me over to my new guards and marched away. I was shown to my new cell in the Maurepas Gate.

20: Of Some Merriment That Befell Me in the Cell in the Maurepas Gate

Whatever the future might hold, there was no question but that the present had been immeasurably improved. My new cell was on the main floor. It had a widely grilled door and two windows which, though too high to permit me to see out, were wide enough to let in two long, thin fingers of sunlight, warm and caressing when they fell upon my chilled body. They were also delightful to watch, as the morning progressed, in their steady march across my cell. But best of all the guardroom for the regiment was only a few cells away. They were a talkative company and, though I suspected they deliberately pitched their voices too low for me to distinguish the words, their tones were cheery, and now and then they burst into snatches of gay song. I was again in the land of the living.

Many times I blessed my strange visitor in the citadel under the

King's Bastion. Perhaps if I got friendly with my guards I might discover where and what was the Careening Cove. I longed for Aaron or Billy and Mistress Antoinette to help along my slow wits.

My first thought, of course, was of the carven lilies. I knew it was too much luck to have found them in my very cell, but I was well aware that in all life's problems much depended upon oneself. I had managed to get into the proximity of the lilies. I felt with care I might maneuver myself to and through that secret entrance. Hope rose high within me in my happy surroundings.

I thought that evening as I heard the voices of my guards singing lustily:

" *J'ai fait faire un beau navire, un navire, un bâtiment.*
L'équipag' qui le gouverne sont des filles de quinze ans.
Sautons, légères bergères.
Dansons-la légèrement! "

I would not have known that a siege was going on. And it occurred to me that what I had taken for a Swiss mercenary in the King's Bastion had in all likelihood been one of the original French troops of the king's army. No wonder he had been surlily minded toward me.

Now after some deep pondering I saw that two courses of action were open to me. First, I could acknowledge my understanding of the French tongue and question my guard in his own language concerning the carven panel and the Careening Cove. I was fearful, however, that this was some local French term known only to the natives themselves. I saw at once that in this method I ran great danger of putting my gaolers on their guard. They were not stupid fellows by any means. Indeed, two or three of them were possessed of very quick wits.

Therefore, I disregarded this idea completely and determined to deny all knowledge of their tongue. In this way I hoped they would be brought to trust me and talk freely within earshot. I realized it would probably take a good deal of time, time I could ill afford, but the information thus obtained, I did not doubt, would be much more accurate, and a great deal fuller.

So when my supper was brought to me, I was at much pains to have them understand I was quite ignorant of their language. I must have been more than ordinarily successful, for I heard the fact of my ignorance announced more than once that evening, with the result that their conversation rose to its habitual loud pitch and, to my great joy, was clearly audible in my cell.

I found that the guardroom in the Maurepas Gate kept a fire going all night, very warming to the men on duty on the salient. There was a constant coming and going, and a great loosening of tongues under the warm potions they managed to keep on hand.

Now while much of the news thus suddenly available to me was not such as to lift my spirits, still it was better than the stony silence, the terrible uncertainty of my state of mind in the cell in the depths of the citadel below the King's Bastion.

I listened intently for the two items in which I was most interested. To my disappointment, I caught no mention of either the panel of carven stone lilies or the Careening Cove. If I had been told to search there, why was it unknown to my guards?

However, I did find myself the recipient of some appalling, but at the same time extremely valuable, information.

There was a reason for their gaiety. Another great French ship had run the blockade and was unloading beside the other in the harbor. Supplies were coming in, how badly needed I could well guess by the exuberance of the guards. They were celebrating. I asked myself with beating heart what had happened to Admiral Warren's fleet during my incarceration.

My guards, it seemed, were of the Karrer Regiment. They kept their light-gray gaiters and red jerkins very natty. The collar, the great cuffs, and lining of the coat were of the blue of the sea. They were most likable fellows, but one in especial was very kind to me. I felt great reluctance in thus deceiving him, but when I recalled the condition of our own men, in the wet, cold marsh, illy clad and housed and some of 'them shoeless from getting the guns across the morass, I felt my first loyalty was to them.

Gradually I learned that our men were still keeping up a heavy but intermittent barrage from the four batteries on the Greene Hill. There had been but three when I left. Each battery had been placed a little nearer the West Gate with a little greater effectiveness. The intervals in the firing, they argued, and I knew they were right, were due to the enemy's lack of shot and shell which equaled their own. But this was the second occasion the blockade had been broken. They had great hopes it would be again. And then I learned something I was sure General Pepperrell did not know: Neither ship that had gotten in was the long-anticipated supply ship, but she had been sighted, repairing a damaged sail, and might be expected shortly. When she arrived, she would bring stores and provisions, guns and ammunition, in such quantities the fortress could undoubtedly hold out another six months. Now I noted that though they referred to her continually, she being ever in their thoughts, no mention in my hearing was ever made of her name, wherefore I realized they were very conscious of the use the enemy might make of such knowledge. It was, I knew, a deliberate omission, common to the mind of each and every one of them.

I was in a fever to get the word out. I did not think that if the general had this knowledge he would longer delay the assault. At all costs they would get on with it as Admiral Warren importuned. I became fair frantic to be thus inactive when I held such important information.

I learned further, with untold relief, that the Royal Battery was still in our hands, but it was cruel news, indeed, to hear that a third attempt to silence the Island Battery had met with the same dismal failure and with a most grievous loss of life on our side. I wondered if Billy had been of the party this time. My mind flew to Aaron suffering of his wound in the hospital. I had heard that the Sisters treated the wounded of both sides with great impartiality. I was glad he was out of the conflict.

But long after the guard had settled down for a few odd moments of sleep, I continued to ponder this evil news. The Island Battery must be silenced if the assault was to be a success. It was the general agreement. But how? Delay was become doubly dangerous.

Then I wondered about Admiral Warren's own re-enforcements. What of His Majesty's Ship *Hector,* the *Princess Mary,* the *Canterbury,* and the *Lark* — English ships, a match for any Frenchman? Had they been met up with ere ever they got here and been vanquished — no mention of them had come from my guards, or — I reminded myself of Dogood — had the English crown seen fit to order them elsewhere?

Two items of news came to me in those days which had also to be written on the growing debit side of the ledger. The French had new tales of disease decimating our troops. I judged it was the scurvy of which I already knew, but then I heard it was a flux born of the damp and the cold, well-known to the men in the fortress, and very mortal. My thoughts passed over our men and flew to the general himself. What would happen to the siege if Master William were taken ill? I knew no other so able to curb the turbulent spirits of our troops.

And then I had a thought which cheered my gloom mightily. I knew we had one advantage over the French that they could never take away from us. We had great faith in our leaders, and our faith was justified.

The second item of news caused me such horror that I was not like to get over it ever. It seemed that Beaubassin, one of the port captains, had sallied out and made a landing on the Point of the Lantern. A company of *Bastonnais* had been sent farther up the coast to a point called the Lorembec with instructions to cut him off. It was the thought of the New Englanders evidently that Beaubassin might be preparing to march around the harbor and attack them secretly in the rear. This landing had been attended with success. The two forces had met. But Beaubassin, being much the stronger, had forced the *Bastonnais* to surrender, whereupon the Indians with Beaubassin had promptly fallen upon the prisoners and murdered them in cold blood. Beaubassin had returned to the fortress and related the incident to the enhancement of his own reputation. But I could see that even my

184

guards were shocked. It was not their idea of waging honorable warfare.

A great fury against Beaubassin and his ilk possessed me. I must escape. I must get my information to General Pepperrell at once. And to do this, I saw, I must become friendly with my guards.

My flute was a friend indeed. One of the guards was a simple fellow much given to whistling little airs, but having no ear for music he always got lost in the attempt. I made him understand that if I had the notes, I could play for him. He was delighted and begged of the bandmaster some copies of some old Tirolese dance tunes. His joy was unbounded when I played them. Poor lad, he was no soldier at heart, but a great romantic who had signed up for the period only to secure enough money to buy a little farm for himself and his sweetheart on the green slopes of the Alps. Later I knew I owed much to his unwarlike turn of mind.

And now I discovered a strange thing. Much as I wished to hurry away, being fearful my own life might be snuffed out at any moment, I could not go without once more seeing Antoinette. This also must be accomplished. I had constant fear that she was dead.

I was pondering on some scheme to effect the matter one afternoon when I heard light, quick footsteps mingling with the measured tread of the sentry on duty at the gate. My heart stood still. Then a woman's voice I did not recognize, but passing gentle, accosted my guard, " Good day, good sir."

And I heard the prompt answer, " Good day to you, Sister."

" Are there any sick within, my good man? "

" Nay, Sister. We have but one in the cells and he is quite healthy."

The Sisters visited the prisoners! An idea assailed me. I picked up my flute and piped a few bars, then was silent.

" What is that? " a new, younger voice made query.

" Ah, *mademoiselle*," my guard replied, " it is but my prisoner passing his time."

Then the older voice urged quickly: " *Mademoiselle! Mademoiselle! We must be on our way.*" Undoubtedly the little minx had tried to see me.

Again I snatched up my flute. This time I played as I had never played before, a love song of the sea which I had played for Antoinette in the sailmaker's shop in Bostontown. Again I paused. The Sister was repeating anxiously: " Come! Come, *mademoiselle.*"

" Oh, but Sister," cried her young voice, " it is so passing sweet."

The good Sister was firm. " *Mademoiselle!* " she cried shortly. " It is most unseemly to linger near the abodes of men. The Good Mother would not like it. Come you back to the Congregation."

Then, like an answer, clear and unfalteringly my melody was returned to me in a low lilting whistle, sweetly true.

" *Mademoiselle!* " The good Sister was plainly shocked. Abruptly the whistling stopped. " I am sorry, Sister," a contrite voice replied. " I had great wish to remember it."

Now I made sure that the little minx was young and probably a gossip. I hoped she would chatter of my performance in the Home of the Good Sisters of the Congregation where she was undoubtedly being educated. If once it came to Mistress Antoinette's ears, she would quickly locate me. My longing for her had grown unbearable.

That night I demanded in halting French of my guard: " The Good Sisters! Come they often to the prisons? "

" Aye! If one is ill."

" Then am I *très malade,*" I hastened to make him understand. " I am like to die any day." I laid myself down and groaned.

Now my guard, as I have said, was not dumb. He thought it a fine piece of wit. " Ho! Ho! Ho! " he shouted, and that evening I heard him lustily retailing it to the shouts of the guardroom.

" By my hat! " cried a voice I knew as the night watchman's. " And I could wish he were sick. The goodies the Sisters bring. I have not had such sweeties since my mother's kitchen. I could wish I were sick again myself."

All that night I was in panic I would be led out to my death before Mistress Antoinette should come. I did not doubt she would. But I was still there the next afternoon, and so nervous I could not sit still but must pace my cell.

And at last her sweet voice reached me. I found myself near tears.

"Let us stop here, Sister," the voice came ringing through the doorway, the voice I knew and longed for.

"No! No! *Mademoiselle!*" the older voice made answer. My heart sank. "Sister Margarita stopped here but yesterday. There are no ill here, Mademoiselle Ignace."

"But what was true yesterday, may not be true today, Sister. It was told me on very good authority this morning there was a man like to have died here in the night." Did I imagine the quiver which seemed to linger in her voice: "Is it not so, *monsieur le capitaine?*"

At once I saw Antoinette's adroitness, for the guard, being only a poor sergeant at arms, was much elated over the new title. He acquiesced instantly. "But surely there is, *mademoiselle*. Come this way."

Instantly my panic returned. How did I look? Would she know me after my ordeal in the depths? Then disappointment almost overwhelmed me. My guard was taking them down the corridor in the opposite direction. Frantic, I picked up my flute and tremblingly played a plaintive note of the ditty I had piped the day before.

The next moment a swish of skirts sounded down the stone corridor. There came the patter of swift, light feet. Mistress Antoinette had pushed herself into the deep embrasure of my doorway and was poking her sweet face through the wooden slats of my barrier.

I flung down my flute and fled to her.

"O Eben!" cried Mistress Antoinette, hiding her face in my rough sleeve.

Then the voice of the Sister, greatly worried, echoed down the corridor. "Mademoiselle Ignace! Mademoiselle Ignace! Where are you?"

And I heard the voice of the guard saying ever so slowly, "I was mistaken, Sister, the sick man must have been moved to that cell in the other side."

They were headed toward us. Had Mistress Antoinette done for herself in communicating with me? But again as ever Mistress Antoinette's quick wits fairly took my breath away. She swept out her great skirts and swooped to the floor. I now saw she was carrying a basket of some weight. Deliberately she dumped its contents on the floor. Now the sight of such a wealth of good things spread out before my eyes on the stone floor was like to have done something to me. When Mistress Antoinette, screening her action from the Sister by her great skirts, picked up a jar of ruby-red jelly such as I had not seen in weeks and flung it crashing to the floor, I echoed the Sister's cry of consternation at sound of the splintering crash. But Mistress Antoinette, seemingly unconcerned, bent far forward again, sweeping her arms hither and thither in apparently wanton motion. The contents of the upset basket were gently rolling away in all directions. I did not catch her true design until a wave of bright yellow lemons and two glasses of jelly sought refuge under my wicket. Then my laggard wits caught up with her. I did the only thing I could: I slumped down on the floor and hid with my body that which had entered my cell. Not a moment too soon, either, for the guard and the Good Sister were upon us.

" O *mademoiselle!* What have you done? Such delicacies and all my poor sick in *l'hôpital*. Oh! Oh! Oh! " The poor Sister's knees seemed to sink under her as she dropped to the floor and tearfully rescued what was left.

" O Sister, dear! " my little witch made answer. " The great stupid I am. I am not to be trusted at all."

" Oh! Oh! Oh! " the Sister continued her wailing. " Three jars of the Mother's best calf's-foot jelly. Very strengthening it is! And a bottle of the best port wine. Oh! Oh! My poor sick soldiers."

Mistress Antoinette dropped contritely back. Her nimble fingers began reloading the basket, but meanwhile her foot, as the guard and I could very well see, had located that same bottle of wine which had rolled past her. She was propelling it into my cell.

I heard a faint snicker and looked up to find the face of my guard, high behind the figures of the two kneeling women, contorted with the merriment he could scarcely suppress.

Meanwhile the basket, such as was left of its contents, was repacked, my Mistress Antoinette keeping a becoming silence. Now the Sister firmly assumed responsibility of the basket. They were moving away.

Mistress Antoinette, however, lingered. " The poor sick man," she murmured. " But I have wasted so much through my foolishness. We cannot spare him aught, And he so weak, he cannot stand up."

Now I had been about to rise, feeling sure the errant goodies were well beyond their view now, but at that I was constrained to remain where I was and very foolish I felt about it all.

" Ah, well! " the Sister sighed reluctantly. " It would not seem right to leave without giving him anything. It was not his fault, poor fellow. This jar of potted meat, my poor man. Will you not accept it? "

I had had much more than my share, I knew, so I said in halting English with some bad French intermixed, which I saw the Sister understood, " Nay! Nay! Good Sister. I would not rob my comrades of the hospital."

But this only served to make the Sister think me a more deserving case and nothing would make her take it back. Indeed, she went away smiling happily. I wondered a little sadly, was gratitude to her so rare?

Immediately they were gone, my guard returned roaring with laughter. I displayed my great wealth. I will say this for him he would take only his just share.

" The young ones are always the most generous," he said with a wink. " I thought it best you should see her alone." He made himself clear by the addition of pantomime.

His action had been deliberate. He had taken them in the wrong direction well knowing that when he indicated his mistake, the girl would undoubtedly speed back and reach me far ahead of the slower, hard-working Sister. I felt ashamed of having had to deceive such a kindly fellow.

As my eyes regarded that tempting food I thought of General Pepperrell's remark — the pity of it that mere food could so move one. In spite of my evil circumstances, I was near heaven as I tasted its life-giving richness. The guardroom rejoiced over the extra potion of wine.

It was a merry incident, high-lighted against the tragic scenes of the siege, but that it was a definite part of it, I very soon knew. I had been much weakened by my incarceration in the cell in the citadel under the King's Bastion. I do not doubt that the sustenance and variety of all this unwonted store of food gave me, during the next few days, strength sufficient for the ordeal ahead of me.

21: I Am Ear Witness of an Engagement

That night I slept soundly until long after midnight. I doubt that I would have wakened then, so satisfying I found it to sleep on a full stomach, if it had not been that my cell of a sudden filled with a rosy glow. At first I thought I must be dreaming and back in Bostontown with the beacon burning on the hill. I noticed the peculiar rise and fall of the red light, and I was conscious of a peculiar smell reaching me through the open guardroom door.

I jumped up hastily, summoning my guard. He came down the stone corridor to my cell door and informed me in excited French that the enemy had sent over three fire ships in an attempt to fire the three boats which had run the blockade and were not yet fully unloaded. He told me proudly the attempt had failed. One had beached itself and the others were burning themselves out in the harbor near the Island Battery. For sea people, he blurted out, the enemy were most uncommon stupid. Anyone could see that the wind was against their success. Then realizing that they were my people he was denouncing, the poor fellow stopped in confusion. Whereupon he remembered I did not speak his language and had probably understood very little of it. His relief was evident, and he ambled off.

All I could think was we had failed again. Were we doomed to final failure in this tremendous, audacious, undertaking? I was like to sink down and give up. Then I recalled the general and how on being told at the embarkation in Bostontown that the English ships of war were not joining us, he had but braced himself anew and announced he would continue his course. I lifted up my head and stood gazing in amazement.

The whole interior of the cell opposite mine was lighted by a palpitating red light. Through the wide openings between the slats of the wicket I could see the farther wall. It comprised a stone panel! Carven in it were the arms of the Maurepas Gate. And below — below a dado of wild lilies of the field lifted their heads with shy grace! It was the panel to the secret passage.

Luck was still with us!

It was well for me that, with the whole town and the fortress awake, I decided it was no time for escape. In my eagerness to be moved to the new cell I would probably have given away the whole matter to my gay but vigilant guard.

Next morning I found the whole company so jubilant over the nonsuccess of the enemy's venture that they would have given me anything, short of my freedom. I made the excuse that by standing on my bed in the other cell I could see the burned ships, which I was curious to do. Somehow by pantomime I made them understand, and they let me move over. However, on getting there I found my height a few inches short, but no persuasion would make them understand. I could only suspect they were being deliberately dull and saw the danger of letting me see too much.

Now once in the cell I could scarcely contain myself until I had tried the tongues of the lilies. Surreptitiously I fingered them and at last I discovered one which seemed capable of moving. But I did not dare experiment with it until dark. I could not make my escape by daylight anyway.

All that day I prayed fervently that my life might be spared yet one more day. Fortunately for my success, I waited. For during that day I received information of great help to our side, and also I had a visitor who changed my plans somewhat.

During the morning an old woman came to my grilled door. She was almost smothered in woolen things and whined that she would do my laundry if I would but give her a few sous. In vain I told her I had no money. She persisted and at last, with a quick glance down the corridor, she stepped into the embrasure and hissed at me, "Seem to bargain with me, Eben."

My amazement was immeasurable. It was Feathertale John!

So, under apparent wrangling as to the price of washing a pair of socks and one cotton shift, Feathertale managed to note with satisfaction that I was in the cell with the carven lilies. Then he drew closer yet and whispered softly: "At two of the clock, Eben. Tomorrow night. A black shallop under a white hull."

Then he raised his voice and announced: "Two sous I say, *monsieur*. Only two sous. Would you cheat an old woman with a foot in the grave?"

Now my heart exulted. The most difficult part of my escape was being arranged for me. I had deliberately refused to let myself think what would happen to me once out of the tunnel. I knew I could only leave it to the chance of the moment. But now this was no longer a worry. It was too good to be true.

Then something made me demand how he himself had made entry. Very reluctantly, it seemed to me, he murmured that he and Asa had been fishing, and had met Captain O'Hara in a fog, who had boasted he could get them into the town, so much demand was there for a supply of fresh fish. He had offered to bring them in, then and there. Feathertale had accepted but sent Asa back. "It was the only way, Eben. I had to see you. Indeed, he brought me straight to you. I had no trouble at all."

Now I had never trusted Captain O'Hara. The whole affair made me gravely uneasy. Feathertale had returned to his bargaining, but my thoughts were afar. It seemed to me it might be a ruse on the part of Captain O'Hara to get Feathertale inside the fortress and keep him there. Then with the aid of Asa he could perhaps get into our encampment. I had no doubt he would sell the French information as readily as he seemed eager to sell us news concerning them.

"It is all right," Feathertale insisted. "He is friendly. Everything will be all right. Tomorrow night, Eben. At two! Tell me, Eben, which lily is it? I am fearful of some accident there, and I would know how to get in quickly. That is the only part that worries me."

I wished that I could say the same. Then I reflected I was in no situation to refuse anyone's help. " The thirteenth from the left," I whispered. He nodded to let me know he understood. Then I thought if Captain O'Hara could engineer so much he might well do more. " Antoinette goes with me," I insisted. Feathertale hesitated. Then he added, " If I can manage it, Eben." Feathertale quickly returned to his bickering to the amusement of the guard, who listened a moment, then moved away.

Now all this time I had been pondering a neat question. I had two items of news that I was most eager to get out. I reflected that Feathertale himself was most surely to be trusted, even if he told Captain O'Hara about the supply ship. It was news only the French themselves were cognizant of. The Careening Cove matter was a different thing. I had no idea what that referred to or why it had been given to me. I decided to entrust to Feathertale only the first.

" Listen, Feathertale, tell General Pepperrell," I saw his face light with interest, " one of the expected ships is a supply ship. If she gets in, they will be able to hold out at least six months."

" Aye, Eben. 'Tis valuable news, indeed. The general shall have it this noon." I wondered. Would Feathertale get away? Then I noted that Feathertale was leaving now and not to be in the vicinity at the time of my escape. What did this purport?

Our time was more than up. Once more Feathertale returned to his character. Giving me a last look of encouragement, he went down the corridor muttering his opinions of New Englanders in general and this enemy in particular. I could have found it in my heart to laugh with the guards had I not been so worried over the various ramifications of my own predicament.

That nothing happened to me that day, and I was left living, I believed was due to a new excitement in the fortress. To have been allowed to live through that day and the next would seem to have been too much luck otherwise.

Word was brought in that a great French ship was in the offing.

They had bespoken her in the fog. She was bearing in. Was she the supply ship? The fisherman had not been sure. My guards could not conceal their excitement.

I do not know how I kept silence as the time passed and I heard no sound of guns. A great bitterness against Admiral Warren and his ships of war welled up within me, and I quite forgot that the guarding of the harbor mouth had been given over to our own sloops because of the shoals there and the inability of the great English ships like the *Superb* to come in close without getting into point-blank range of the guns of the Island Battery.

All that afternoon I sat in my cell refusing to move for fear I might miss something. In their agitation my guards paced the corridor so I could not even distract myself by attempting to open the panel. Perhaps after all there were two panels, I tortured myself, and I was not even in the right cell.

Then the guards, returning from watch on the salient, announced excitedly: " She is bearing in. We saw her in a hole in the fog. Nothing can stop her. By her lines I am confident about her. Sixty guns! Our troubles are over."

Now a sixty-gun ship was of the *Princess Mary* class. She was more than a match for all but one or two of the English men-of-war. It was not only her armament which disturbed me. A ship of sixty guns was a city in itself. It could, as they said, provision the garrison for six months with food and ammunition.

At last we caught the sound of firing, somewhat weak at first it seemed to me. Brought up in Bostontown, I knew the sound of heavy cannonading. When at last a great broadside boomed out, my spirits cheered, for I thought, of course, she had met her match in one of our capital ships, but my hopes were promptly thrust down again. A guard, rushing in, announced excitedly: " The impudence of these besiegers. They send a third-class ship to annoy her." He followed with some pun on the name of our ship which he had recognized. The woman of the sea, he called her. Was the ship they meant the *Mermaid!* Aaron's ship! The *Mermaid* was engaging. A brave ship, but — only of forty guns. No match for the Frenchman. What of the others? What of the *Superb?*

By sundown my guards were confident. She was in the fairway

and punishing her enemy unmercifully. Each broadside made me weep for Aaron's comrades. Dusk came. We could hear the steady cannonading. Every time she let go with a broadside the latches of the doors of the fortress rattled. It seemed to me there was a dearth of answer. Each boom was a great hurt to me but the cause of congratulation on the part of my guards. They could see her. They watched the uneven progress of the fight. Even their admiration for the courage of the smaller ship hurt. It showed me so surely what was happening. And when that night the bells of St. Louis, St. Jean, and St. Antoine-Marie rang out their sweet song, it seemed to me it was a hymn of victory. My guards seemed to think so: they cheered lustily.

Then I thought of the men of the *Mermaid,* outgunned and outranged, spunkily standing up to their great opponent. It seemed to me magnificent. And yet tragic too. We were not in a position ourselves to lose a single ship.

But as the night passed I noted that in some strange way the jubilation lost its exuberance. The French were plainly worried. Their ship should have wounded her enemy to death by this time, and gotten in. But the firing had not stopped. And it seemed to me the detonations were heavier. Had they met the English fleet? And how were our allies faring?

Darkness fell. The great French ship still did not appear. What did it mean? A great silence cloaked the town. Certainly my guards did no singing. There came a remark which startled me.

" I do not think she was the *Vigilant.* I am sure of it now."

The *Vigilant!* That was the name of the supply ship. Anxiety had dulled their caution. Suddenly I thought she had need to live up to her name to get in.

And another murmured: " Undoubtedly we were mistaken. It must be that the *Vigilant* is in the offing and the stranger has stayed outside to protect her coming in."

And then in a tone sunk in despair: " If she was indeed the *Vigilant,* she is most surely taken, and we are lost. There is not store of powder to last another week."

And suddenly I knew their supplies were lower even than we had estimated. The loss of the *Vigilant* would be a blow indeed.

I prayed God we had taken her prisoner. And then an idea came to me. I had seen the direction of the fight in their discourse. Of a sudden it seemed to me in the direction of Admiral Warren's ships. Had the gallant *Mermaid* lured the *Vigilant* to her doom in the arms of the Admiral's squadron? I had blamed him often for remaining so far offshore. Could it be that in so doing he had hidden his strength from the chance fishermen who might pass that way and carry information?

At last, worn-out with excitement, the guardhouse quieted. I stole to the panel. I pressed the thirteenth lily. Slowly above me the panel began to open. A cold breath of air swept into my cell. It was the passage! I had a way of escape!

In that moment I do not know how I restrained myself, so eager was I to be gone. And so great was my desire not to put my trust in Feathertale's arrangements, dependent as they were on Captain O'Hara.

It was not fear of finding my way alone that held me back that night. It was the knowledge that with their anxiety about the *Vigilant,* a greater watch than ever would be kept on the harbor. My difficulties that night would be increased a thousandfold. I remembered my message, " Search the Careening Cove." I felt I must get this information at all costs to the general's own ears. I realized it was merely the better part of common sense to provide myself with food and water against the eventualities of the trip. We were very far north and the longest day was only just past. After two o'clock I had a very short time to make my way in darkness. I wondered that Feathertale had planned my escape so late, unless time had something to do with the watch. I did not see how I could get across without his help, and yet delay was dangerous. By another twelve hours I might be dead. Then I reminded myself I was in like position with the general, continually delayed, waiting for the fall of the Island Battery. Then I decided that I too would not be rushed into this undertaking unprepared. With great reluctance I closed the panel and sought my couch. I knew I would need all the rest I could get to prepare me for the task ahead.

22: I Engage in a Battle of My Own

All the next day my guards varied between hope and gloom, but when by the next night no word of the great white ship had come to them, I saw the beginning of something I had not suspected — a suggestion of despair.

Still they had not given up hope, but I had been given a hint of how hopeless they would become if time passed and the *Vigilant* did not get in.

It was great relief to me to find myself alive that second night. I laid me down early but not to sleep. I wanted to conserve the candle in the lantern with which the guards kindly supplied me each night, even though their own supplies, I knew, were low. I had in a water bottle a fair portion of fresh water, and in the piece of linen Antoinette had bound around my hand, which I had carefully washed and sun-bleached in the warm rays that stalked on fine days across my cell, I placed some bread against my night's ration.

Once more I wondered if I were walking into a trap. I reflected how much had come to me with seeming ease — my flute, then my change of cell, my spared life, and now my escape. Fear alternated with exhilaration. In a few hours, I told myself, I would be a free man once more. And Antoinette would be with me!

At last the appointed hour came. I counted the strokes on the parade-ground clock. My heart pounded with excitement as I picked up my flute and bundle, found the thirteenth lily, pressed, and encountered again that draught of ice-cold air. A space had opened wide enough for me to slip through. I stepped in, and suddenly I had great reluctance to close that door. Could I ever open it again? But I had no time to spare now. I closed it resolutely, and in spite of fear of Captain O'Hara it was great comfort to know that Feathertale knew the control. If anything happened to me, I felt sure he would find his way in again and contrive to investigate. Feathertale, I reminded myself, had never failed me.

Trembling all over, I felt my way ahead a few steps and stooped to light my lantern.

Some of my fear left me as I flung its light about me. I saw revealed a well-built passage with smooth walls and a solid floor. The damp wind surging up was not cellar damp, I decided, but the salty damp of the sea. The passage tended downward, and after a short distance began to bend to the left. This fact encouraged me. As far as I could tell, the bend was in the direction of the harbor, and not the Rochfort Point, that unfortified tip of the land on which the fortress stood. Presently a flight of steps interrupted my passage, leading down. This also checked with my expectations. The Maurepas Gate was several feet above sea level.

I heard a sudden sound. Chills went running down my spine. It was the pitter-patter of tiny feet. I told myself that if living things were in the tunnel, it was matter for satisfaction. There must be an outlet. I hurried forward as fast as I dared.

Once or twice I stopped and listened. It bothered me that I did not hear the pounding roar of the sea. Of a sudden new doubt assailed me. Could it be that the tunnel led only to some trap which would drop me into an abyss? Was it but a way to get rid of me? I had great difficulty in forcing myself to proceed and did so with much more caution. Only the thought of Antoinette waiting for me in the shallop under the white hull drove me on.

Then a second flight of steps appeared, a flight steeper and more crude. Indeed, I noticed that the walls were no longer sealed but suffered sadly from erosion. My tunnel was deteriorating. There was no question of that. Great chunks had fallen, almost blocking my path. It occurred to me that I might at any moment be pinned beneath one of these huge pieces of rock.

Then my spirits unexpectedly lifted. I caught the sound of water, water rising and falling. The fact lent wings to my feet. I forgot caution and fairly raced. The tunnel was running down to the sea as Thundercloud had said it would. A little later I found it lapping into my tunnel. If I would proceed, I must walk in it. I flung the lantern high and looked ahead. The tunnel continued, but I noted that here where the water started the passage had been widened into a kind of platform. The roof too was higher, and against the water's edge was a fine bar of shingle. I knew then something that was confirmed later as I felt the ebb and flow of the water about my feet, washing up and sucking down: it was tidal. And that was as it should be if it opened into the harbor. I waded in with new courage.

At first the water seemed icy cold, but gradually my body warmed a bit.

Then it seemed to me the floor of my tunnel was sinking under my feet. The water reached my knees, my armpits. At last I realized that if I would proceed further I must forsake my lantern and swim. I lifted the light high and flung its rays ahead of me. I almost gave up. The end of my tunnel was entirely under water! How far did it continue? It flashed through my mind that it was perchance a passage navigable only at low tide. I had no means of knowing how much the rise and fall might be, but I judged by the shingle it must be near flood tide. Should I wait? My courage began to ebb. But I knew I could not wait. I knew I must go on.

I sought a place to leave my lantern. I decided to leave it lighted even though it would give guidance to any chance pursuer. I heard nothing yet. Then I espied a narrow ledge running along the wall above the waterline that looked as if it had been built for just such a contingency. My courage returned. I felt sure the opening was not too faraway.

Setting the lantern down very carefully I took a few strokes which brought me to the roof of the tunnel. Then, taking a deep breath, I dived completely under and pushed myself ahead.

I was more conscious now of the tidal wash. At first it seemed to push me back. Then I was caught up by it and driven forward. I was flung against a barrier and could go no farther. My frantic hands touched a grating. At the same moment something wove itself around my fingers with octopus tenacity. I got a terrible fright, but it was only a piece of floating kelp caught in the grating. With dwindling strength I wrenched frantically at it, but in freeing myself I had used up precious time. All the force I could exert in one final effort failed to move the grating. Was I to get so far and be blocked? My eardrums were pounding a warning. My lungs were bursting. All I could do was to go back.

I fought my way against a falling tide and reached my ledge. There was joy for me in catching again the gleam of my lantern. I lay there panting and getting my breath. I thought of Antoinette waiting in the black shallop under the white hull, Antoinette who was in continual danger every minute she remained in the town — danger from her former connection with the Red Hats, danger from our shot and shell, danger of starvation if the fortress was as low in food as the gloom over the nonarrival of the *Vigilant* seemed to suggest.

I told myself the tunnel was here. It must have been meant to be used. There was some trick about the grating.

Once more I took a deep breath and plunged in. Again I felt myself rushed forward as I drew near the grating; indeed, this time I struck it with decidedly more force, and I knew the tide was changing. My fingers fell to exploring. Six bars. Three across. Three up and down. The horizontal bars wedged deep in the stone on the left — seemingly free on the right. I pushed frantically. No avail. I sought a latch. There was none. The uprights? Maddeningly I found they ended in arrows a good six inches short of the casement, at both top and bottom, too small a space to force my body through. I could not risk getting caught and drowned there. I had just breath enough left to push out with all my remaining strength. I pushed up. Nothing moved, and yet it seemed to me that two pins extending downward from the lowest horizontal were all that held it in place. I could feel hinges on the right.

My breath was gone. I had to return gasping to my ledge. I would not despair. I crawled back and lay by the lantern a few inches above the water level. I turned my face the way I had come. Was there no way but back? My whole body stiffened. Did I imagine it? Was there a bright star shining in my tunnel? There was! It grew larger! Then I knew it meant pursuit. I had been betrayed as I had suspected. Quickly I decided concealment on the ledge was my only hope of escape. I doused my lantern and waited. Perhaps it was but an inquisitive guard. In my effort to avoid noise, possibly I had not quite closed the panel.

The light approached, blinding me to what was behind it. The figure stooped at the shingle edge. It seemed puzzled. Then it put the lantern down. There was something familiar about that humped back. As the figure grew erect again I knew. It was Captain O'Hara. Captain O'Hara with his cold eyes, a knife between his teeth. What I had suspected had been true.

I was beginning to understand. Captain O'Hara had wanted to know the secret of the tunnel. He had tried and failed in Bostontown. For this reason he had offered his help to Feathertale John. That knowledge had been the price to bring Feathertale in. And honest Feathertale had argued that once I got out, as I undoubtedly would in a few hours, what did it matter what Captain O'Hara knew about the fortress? Perhaps the captain had given his word not to harm me.

Meanwhile Captain O'Hara stood by the shale, and, as if he had told me, I could see him figuring out my predicament. I was unarmed, probably half-dead from the meager fare being served to the prisoners. He had seen my light and knew I could not be far away. Where I had gone he could follow, catch up, and make an end of me. I knew that he had many a score to settle with me, not the least his banishment from Bostontown. He had had good pickings there in the information he obtained concerning the coming and going of our heavily laden ships. Perhaps he had been selling his knowledge to the French, or even operating in partnership with them. In that sharpened period of extreme terror, it came to me that no doubt he credited to me also his difficulty in getting through Admiral Warren's lines. I was sure now that the ragged seaman in his bundlesome muffler and cap that day in our camp had been Captain O'Hara himself.

But now his decision was made. He was wading toward me. He raised his hand, still confident in its power to mesmerize, and I saw again its huge proportions outlined against the candlelight. Perhaps it did mesmerize me. Certainly I lay there like one frozen. I wondered what he would do when he found the water reached to the roof. Did he suspect the grating and know that I was trapped, that I could not escape him? Undoubtedly he suspected I was hiding under water, and must come up for air. There was only one course open to me. We must fight it out.

I waited until he was even with me, a step or two beyond. Then I slipped off my ledge and started back to the platform of rock above the waterline. I knew this offered the best advantage. I had outwitted him, but, numbed with the cold, my limbs obeyed me clumsily. I bumped into the lantern, sending it into the water with a loud splash. Captain O'Hara wheeled around and saw me. He lunged after me, slipped, half fell. I sloshed heavily forward just out of reach and crunched over the shale at the water's edge, a step ahead of him.

One advantage came to me. In losing his footing he had given a slight gasp and lost the knife he carried between his teeth in order to keep his good hand free.

The fight was on. But we were more evenly matched.

Down in that pale lantern light in the depths of that subterranean tunnel we fought fiercely. Captain O'Hara was strong, but he was a heavy man. That I survived his onslaughts at all was due to my adroitness. Twice he slipped and all but fell. Nevertheless, he had tremendous endurance as compared to my prison-racked body. His huge wooden hand flew like a flail through the shadows, thwacking at me unmercifully. I wonder I survived. I felt sure he was armed, but his slip had saved me there too. He was shrewd enough to know his pistol had become ineffective and did not waste time trying to reach it.

Then in one of his lunges his wooden hand came in contact with my own. Furious at the punishment I had taken from it, I made a quick grab at it and twisted it sharply. Something seemed to give way. It came off in my hand. Instantly I seized upon it as a weapon. I rapped him smartly over the temple and he went down like a log. For a moment, I could only draw sobbing breaths.

Then in that dim light, I made a discovery that seemed to me unbelievable. I had looked to see the wooden hand leave an ugly stump. Instead I found myself gazing down upon a hand of perfect

202

proportions, absolutely whole. The truth was slow in coming to me.

I was puzzled too by the way the unconscious man was seemingly lengthening out. I looked at his hairy face, sopping from his fall. Something made me give the beard a yank. It came off in my hand. The hair of the head too. I looked down on the blond face of my dreaded enemy, Morpain! Captain O'Hara and Morpain were one and the same person.

In that moment fury possessed me. He was at my mercy. I thought of all he had done and might still do to me and mine — to my father and to Antoinette. A small piece of white Normandy stone caught my eye. It was hard and had a jagged edge. With it I could bash out his brains and be done. I stooped for it. Then something held me back. Some instinct stayed my hand. I had never killed and could not in cold blood. He was my enemy but he was helpless. Then I reflected he was the enemy of my country too. I raised my arm —

At that moment a shot reverberated through the tunnel and ricocheted against the roof above me. There was a splashing and a crashing of loose masonry.

I glanced up swiftly. Under a great flaming torch, Morpain's servant, the big Negro, was racing down the tunnel. I had had proof already of his devotion to his master when he had braved our shot and shell to drag the body of his wounded master into the fortress. There was only one exit open for me from his vengeance. I turned, plunged into the water, and, stopping only long enough to fill my lungs, dived under and to one side, swimming with all my might. Thankful I was to find the tide with me.

It seemed no distance at all until I was flung against the grating, which I grabbed at frantically, well aware that the same force would return to drive me back. I had no wish to have this strong tide wash me back and up into the clutches of the waiting Negro servant. I felt my body swept irresistibly upward as the tide returned. Still I clung to the grating, though the strength of the swell which flung me upward against the roof of the tunnel was like to have broken both my legs. Now, as I rose, I refused to let myself be parted from the grating, and suddenly I had an odd feeling it had risen with me. And when the backwash came a strange thing happened. I felt myself being rushed outward — without obstruction, and, weakened by the terrific strain of holding my breath so long, I let go. Immediately there came to me a sense of being shot upward, and I could hardly believe it when just as I was about to succumb to the pounding in my ears, a stream of water broke over my face. I drew in a mouthful of life-giving air, and saw above me the spangled heavens.

My first thought was I was free. True, danger was all about me still, but I was no longer incarcerated. I was abroad in the great, wide world — a free man.

For the next few moments all I could do was to turn over on my back and rest, gratefully filling my lungs and easing my bruised limbs.

As I lay there, gathering new strength for the swim to the boat, I seemed to understand a little of what had occurred. It was a clever trick and worthy of its French inventor. The opening was only a few yards below the surface of the water, perhaps at low tide a matter of feet. The grating was hinged on one side, but held in place by two pins extending downward into the masonry. The iron was rusted, and the grating, from the size of the bars, must have weighed no small amount. But to one clinging there, with perseverance, the leverage created by the lifting tide would be sufficient to raise it. My body had been flung up by a greater force than I could ever have imparted to it. I had refused to let go and the grating had risen with me. Once the pins were free, the hinges would work and the grating swing out with the drag of the tide. I wondered if a rising tide would swing it back into place, and if it would fall, letting its pins drop into the grooves again.

The numbing cold of that northern water warned me I dared no longer take my ease. Turning over, I looked across the shining water. Near by were the dark hulls of several craft, and here and there the gleam of a ship's red lantern.

I had no difficulty in finding Feathertale's white ship. Even in the starlight it rose in ghostly fashion much the biggest ship in the harbor. I sought and found the black shallop, clambered aboard her, and in the same instant heard someone splash over the other side. The boat rocked drunkenly. Our assistant, I perceived, whoever he was, was making good his escape.

My first thought, now that I was safely aboard, was of Antoinette. I saw a dim, dark figure huddled in the stern of the boat, and, I must confess, even though danger stalked sinisterly on every side, I was in half a mind to risk our necks for a moment's joy of holding my little maid in my arms. But in the end I was not a fool — in fact, said not a word or wasted a single motion — but took up the oars at once. I had taken two long, deep, quiet strokes, such as Pelletier had taught me to use, when crashing out of the night came the wild clamor of the bells of St. Louis, St. Jean, and St. Antoine-Marie. Lights flashed on the docks. Voices shouted from the gates. It was an alarm! For a moment I thought our assault had started, and then I knew. It was an alarm for me! Morpain's servant had returned for help and given the alarm. It was easy to imagine the consternation within the fortress. I thought with sorrow of my guard. I hoped he would escape blame.

Boats splashed noisily out from the docks. A lantern flashed above us. A voice challenged. I raised my flute and then had sudden inner warning. Was it for this it had been returned to me, that in the event of escape I could be traced? Instead, I bethought me of the password Pelletier had used and prayed it had not been superseded. " *L'ami du roi*," I repeated softly.

Instantly the answer came back to my listening ears: " *Passez-vous, l'ami du roi*." The chase swept to the other side of the harbor. I could scarce believe it — we were free!

When the boom grated under our keel I raised my oars just in time. I was indebted for the clamor of the bells of St. Louis, St. Jean, and St. Antoine-Marie. They drowned out the noise of my inexperienced hands on the oars.

As I swung the boat out into the swell of the channel from the Island Battery, my thoughts were busy. No wonder Morpain had been furious to find I was a Red Hat. Instantly he knew that he had been taken in. As Captain O'Hara he had known us all in Bostontown. He had known there was a map, but since he had not seen it he could not guess how accurate and how elaborate it was. In that instant it had become clear to him that the Red Hats was quite innocent, childish nonsense. But he had committed himself to his superiors, publicized his discovery, and asked all to be on the watch. No wonder I was never brought to trial! He did not dare risk what I would have told. But to dispatch me himself, and at the same time to find the secret of the tunnel — that would appeal to him! My escape had seemed in a manner easy. I smiled to myself. It had been deliberately planned, only the one who had planned it had never expected me to get away. And then another question came to me. By what means had he come by the map that he had put such faith in it? I did not think he had found it by chance.

But suddenly my heart was exultant. I was alive and on my way to General Pepperrell with information which might help him. When the great attack on Louisbourg was made, I would be of the party. And — my dear one was with me!

23: Dogood Leads Me to a Strange Discovery

The wind freshened. I began to feel a tug under the boat. We had pulled clear of the shipping and were in the open harbor. I knew we were getting the drag of the tide ebbing through the strait by the Island Battery. I pulled frantically. There was danger of our being swept out to sea, and, if we were, greater danger of our breaking up on the shoal which lay around the entrance. The sea was running high as I had had evidence earlier inside the tunnel. I threw the last ounce of my strength upon the oars, but it availed me nought. Steadily and surely we were being driven toward the Island Battery. I shuddered as I thought what would happen to Antoinette caught in such an enterprise. My own fate was already sealed, if I were caught.

The other figure in the boat made a quick movement. I thought she was coming to be near me for the last struggle, but instead another pair of oars were swiftly lifted and dropped into place. I felt the difference instantly. It seemed miraculous that in an emergency like this Antoinette's frail body should contain such strength. I began the battle anew. Somehow we pulled past the entrance and headed in under the lee shore of the Point of the Lantern. It was strange to move so quickly from such storm and stress to such deep peace.

I had planned to make land in the vicinity of the Royal Battery, hoping to attract the attention of our own lines, but day was coming apace. In the open harbor, after daylight, we would be a mark for either side, and too far away to be distinguished by our own men. It was imperative that we land soon. Did we dare land on the Point of the Lantern? Beaubassin, one of the port captains, had been holding it, I knew. But Beaubassin, I had been told, had returned to the fortress. Was it possible he had left the Point undefended? We had to take that chance.

" We will land now," I murmured softly, very grateful for that moment when I should see the face of my dear one again.

My companion stopped rowing, pulled in her oars, and faced me. I all but upset the boat.

" Dogood! " I cried, and I say it to my shame my voice was tinged with anger. It seemed to me I had been tricked into deserting Mistress Antoinette.

Dogood's lips quivered. " I know," she said, " I am not the one you think. But Antoinette could not well make the journey." She paused significantly, and new terror took hold of me. " She was needed to help to nurse," Dogood finished, somewhat lamely I thought. " The Sisters have had so many wounded since the shells began exploding in the town. Antoinette made me come in her place. She knew you could not get across in this weather alone."

" I will not desert her," I cried passionately. " I am going back." I swung the prow of the boat around and found that day was already breaking.

" You'll do nothing of the sort," Dogood eyed me sternly. She unshipped her oars and put them back carefully in the boat. " You would most certainly be shot at and this time killed. They would not wait to arrest you. Besides you are carrying out information of great value to the general."

Now this I knew was true, and I was at a loss to know how she knew it when she added quickly, " It was what Antoinette told me."

I knew that Dogood, as usual, had caught the gist of the situation. With such a mission I could not go back. Reluctantly I returned the boat. We proceeded on our way. I continued to ponder the matter, however. I could not understand Antoinette's knowing about the *Vigilant* unless she had communicated with Feathertale. I wondered if Feathertale had been allowed to return. As for the message, " Search in the Careening Cove," I could only wonder if Antoinette had sent that message. Was it information she had gathered in the hospital?

Then I found that Dogood was speaking. " If you sit beside me in the stern, the nose of the boat will be high and we can work our way inshore and seek a landing place. From what I heard at Beaubassin's there are no French on the Point of the Lantern."

I took Dogood's suggestion and using my oar as a paddle moved cautiously in along the rocky shore. The water over which we glided was mystically clear. I could see each separate rock on the bottom and the dark shadows of fish darting in and out. Overhead the air was filled with the sweet odors of spruce and pine and green bay. Life was good. A great exhilaration filled me.

Looking back, I gazed sadly on the fortress and its encradled town. The twin spires catching the gleam of the morning spears of light glittered like upthrust swords. Across the harbor the dew of the morning had thrown a diamond sheen over the scars of the ruin we had made of the settlements. It had been bloody work we had had to do, but already the scars were healing. It seemed to me a good omen of the future. Farther up, nearer the fortress, the Royal Battery stood like a child's toy on the water's edge.

I looked at Dogood, and the sight of her white face stilled my anger. " Tell me," I whispered, " all that happened, Dogood."

Tersely, she told her tale. Looking at her tightly bound head and white, drawn face, I realized a little how terrible the experience had been. It was much the same tale as Thundercloud had interpreted for the sachem, except that for some reason in sending the girls to the Reverend Mother of the Sisters of the Congregation, Morpain had told the sachem to say they were French. I guessed that he realized the value of a Stuart as a hostage and wished to keep the entire matter to himself. Stuart had died after they had been recaptured. He had contracted some fever and the sachem had been very kind. I realized then that whatever had happened to the girls had not been due to the sachem. Probably he had taken the scalps from the band who had carried them off, for Dogood spoke quite feelingly of his kindness. Indeed, so kind had he been and so childishly interested in the red hats that Antoinette had ripped hers off her coat and presented him with it. Of course it had occurred to them that it was a wise thing to leave some trail of their presence with him, some guarantee, if he ran into English hands, that he was the one who had saved them. They had learned of the expedition and of General Pepperrell's part in it, and judged I would be with him.

So Antoinette had parted with her red hat. Once at the House of the Sisters, Antoinette with her ability to speak French fluently had readily passed for a French girl. But Dogood's ignorance of the language made the Good Sisters suspicious. When they found on her the symbol of the Red Hats, the Reverend Mother had openly denounced her. She had summoned the authorities. For some reason that Dogood could not understand, the red hat was become the symbol of a spy. I was able to make that part clear to her.

But instead of putting Dogood in prison they had bound her out to Beaubassin's family where she was virtually a prisoner and had to work like a slave. She herself had probed the reason for that. They had expected the other Red Hats, sooner or later, to get in touch with her. Thus they hoped to capture the entire band. She had, however, one item of information which was very reassuring. She said that Beaubassin was in the fortress suffering with a wound. She was very sure that if there were any troops on the Point of the Lantern, they were the New England men.

And then Dogood sat up. She pointed. A great cove had opened up on our right. In it was an old ship's cradle. It smacked of the appearance of a rude repair dock. " It is the Careening Cove," she murmured. " We shall find good landing here."

Again I thought some unforeseen force was surely favoring our expedition, but for what was I to seek? Our eyes raked the shore — Dogood's in pursuit of any lurking enemy, mine seeking to find I knew not what.

The cove was still as a pool.

I sought the channel, and we drifted in. The peaked green trees showed in its glassy surface as in a mirror. It was difficult to tell where the real scene ended and the reflections began. Here and there a dewdrop, caught in the long fingers of a pine, glittered like a jewel on a woman's hand, and this also was repeated in the golden-brown depths. In my nostrils was the sweet clean smell of pine-carpeted pathways. I drank deep, forgetting that these same woods might hold our doom. I knew only that I was my own man again and the world was infinitely beautiful.

Now at the head of the cove was a strip of fine pebbly beach excellent for beaching the boat. I was making toward this, when Dogood who had turned her attention to the bottom, fascinated with its clear depths, cried out. " Eben! Look! On the bottom! "

I leaned over. And there right under our boat were some huge black shapes. They seemed to me the biggest fish I had ever seen. Sleeping whales, I thought, and gazed at them in amazement. But Dogood's mind was quicker than mine.

" They are guns, Eben! A whole battery of them! What does it mean? "

It was then we made our great discovery. The center of the cove was paved with sunken guns. We counted ten, but there were more. " Search the Careening Cove." He who sent me that message had known what I should find there.

With a long strong stroke, I sent the boat flying up on the shingle. If the French had left the Point, it must be, as Dogood said, because the New Englanders were in possession. We must find them and give them the news. The guns looked to me in good condition. They could not have lain there long. I was sure of that. Could it be that we could use them?

" Why, Dogood," I cried as I hurried her along the woody pathway, " such a battery on the Point of the Lantern might well silence the Island Battery."

" Do not get up your hopes," Dogood admonished. " Maybe they are utterly worthless. Undoubtedly they have been spiked and may not be usable."

Dogood was usually right, I thought dismally, and then remembered the guns of the Grand Battery. They had been spiked but so carelessly that we had had them playing on the town within twenty-four hours. It might be the same in this case. I refused to lose hope.

We came so abruptly upon our own men we were like to be shot before we were recognized. But we did manage to assure them just in time. It was a company of Colonel Gorham's. He greeted me as one from the dead, for he had heard of my disappearance.

He informed us they had been trying to build a battery ever since the French had evacuated the Point under their pressure. But he had had no guns. It was a long haul from the Royal Battery, and besides they had spared all they could to the Hill Battery. He knew about the overshotting and was most uncomplimentary toward the men who made up the battery. When I told him of the find I had made, he was at first frankly incredulous. Nevertheless, he and his company agreed to return with me.

" Ah, Eben," he said. " If only this could be true and they were in good condition, the success of the expedition would be assured."

I knew then how close we had been to failure in the minds of our leaders.

Very soon the gunners confirmed the find. There were ten good guns! The head gunner insisted they could be repaired in twelve hours, since they had been spiked in a most indifferent manner. The entire company cheered.

Then Captain Gridley informed me they had enough shot and shell for fifty rounds. " I hope the general can spare us some more. I shall send an express to him immediately. You shall take it, Eben."

Colonel Gorham now assured me that the woods around the harbor were at the moment quite safe. But I could if I wished take a

211

more venturesome route by sea. Dogood seemed much relieved when Captain Gridley invited her to remain. He was much in need of someone to direct the cooking for the camp. Her horror of the woods was hard to conquer. So we parted. I told her that but for her help I should never have gotten across. She seemed much pleased, especially since Colonel Gridley was listening. I hoped it made up in some small part for my rudeness when I discovered she was aboard.

I had not gone many yards on my journey when a loud intonation rent the air, and a shower of dust arose from the fortress. Our barrage had started again with the daylight. My heart sank fearfully. I shuddered for the safety of Antoinette and Aaron.

Then a new thought came to torture me during that long journey. Would the terrible experiences Mistress Antoinette had suffered drive her to seek sanctuary in convent walls? She was not a papist, but I could see that the sheltered life of the convent might well appeal to her after what she had gone through. I became as jealous of the Good Sisters as I had ever been of Aaron.

I stopped at the Royal Battery to impart and receive news.

Billy greeted me at the gate. " Eben," he cried weakly, " we thought you were dead."

I thought he looked closer to it himself — he had been wounded by a shell from the West Gate. He hobbled along beside me, leading me to Captain Waldo, who was now in command. He had great difficulty in manipulating himself up the stair and I thought, recalling how I had left him, that war was a terrible cruel business. Billy seemed broken.

Captain Waldo too seemed much thinner than I remembered him. His eyes were anxious. But they glowed with new hope as I told him my news. Then I pleaded with him to be more careful in the shelling of the town. I told him of Antoinette and Aaron there, and of the Good Sisters and the man who had fathered me in my trouble.

He frowned back at me. " I know, Eben," he said. " The women and children in that place trouble me greatly, though we did offer them a chance to leave at the beginning of hostilities. They felt safer in their casemates — terrible, dark places I understand. The real trouble is our marksmen. They are most indifferent gunners and I am afraid frequently hit what they do not aim at. I am writing the general even now in the hope we might obtain some more experienced gunners from the fleet. We have had some, and they are good. But two were badly wounded, and the admiral is a bit chary of sparing us more. Also, Eben, will you please tell General Pepperrell that I am most gravely in need of powder?"

It was the same tale, I reflected. How could they expect us to wage a war without the means of waging it?

But as I looked at the Dauphin Gate and saw the widening breach in the wall, I had to admit that, good gunners or not, we were accomplishing our purpose.

Somewhat cheered I bade good-by to Billy and resumed my journey. My next stop was the Hill Battery. As I neared it, I heard a gentle chink-chink, which wafted me back like a perfume to the governor's estate in Roxbury. I could not identify the sound until I had passed through the woods into a little clearing, and came, unchallenged, upon the battery. The garrison were playing quoits!

Our men playing quoits without sentries, and the French hourly expected with a huge force! As I neared them I perceived that they were ragged and ill-looking. The morass had taken a fearful toll of shoe leather. The camp was untidy. I wondered with a premonition of evil what kind of troops these would be in a drive against the impregnable wall of the great fortress, and yet, I had to admit that what we lacked in arms and numbers, we made up in courage. Not a one but was impatient at the delay and terribly eager to get at the job of assaulting the fortress.

The men cheered my news, then grumbled. Now perhaps the general would be willing to order them forward. But before I left they were back at their games again.

As I moved on I saw that three other batteries, making five in all now, each one nearer the Dauphin Gate, had been mounted, and though they were all taking continual punishment from the enemy's fire they were all intact and giving a good account of themselves. I understood they were being provisioned at night. It was my thought then that so long as the French ships did not come, we might be all right.

But each scout I passed seemed to tell a sorrier tale. The army was ill of dysentery, which seemed very prevalent. Rum and ammunition were most " terrible scarce." The greatness of my news seemed to be shrinking.

Weary of heart and greatly discouraged, I came to the morass and prepared to cross. And then I saw that which cheered me mightily. The camp had been palisaded. Perhaps we were not so careless of our own safety as it had seemed. In this mood I came to the general's camp. I felt my heart contract at sight of him. He was standing in the doorway of his tent sighting out to sea. His face was that of a man looking forward with grim courage.

" Why! " he cried at my greeting. " It is indeed young Eben. Pray God, lad, you are as usual the harbinger of good news. We are in most desperate straits, lad." Then he straightened up like the soldier he was and said quickly: " But we will carry through. Make no doubt, Eben. We will carry through." I perceived he had but spoken his thoughts at first and was already eager to obliterate them from my mind.

I entered the tent at his invitation and perched on a barrel top. The general dropped onto a wide platform, which I imagined was his bed. In prison, I reflected, he could scarcely have had less.

" I gave you up for dead, Eben, and was much worried about how to report the news to Governor Shirley and the good Mistress Merrie. Give me your news, lad. You look brimming over with it."

I related briefly the events of my sojourn in the fortress. When I told him that Morpain and Captain O'Hara were one and the same, he gazed at me in amazement. " Eben," he said, making a wry face, " I shall have to tell that to Admiral Warren. That sailor-man cannot be beat for shrewdness. I wonder if he is as right in other matters."

Then I gave him my news anent the supply ship. Feathertale, I was glad to hear, had got back, and brought my message. But it was news to the general that the name of the supply ship was the *Vigilant*.

" Why, Eben," he cried, " we have taken her already. That is the name of the great ship H. M. S. *Mermaid* engaged but a few days ago. Her captain, the Marquis de la Maisonfort is a very fine gentleman. I have met him. And you tell me the French do not know she is taken? Why, Eben, we must remedy that at once."

Then, having saved the Careening Cove discovery till the last, I made haste to tell him about the guns.

At that he sprang to his feet. " Eben! Eben! Why did you not tell me sooner? That outweighs everything else. The French are most careless. The guns will be all right, like the guns in the Royal Battery. The admiral is right! We must go ahead now! The fortress is ours! "

I had not the heart to tell him that since seeing our ragged troops I had made up my mind it would never be taken. I saw that his own depression had been great indeed. He was not one to wax so exuberant of a sudden for nothing.

" I will send a couple of gunsmiths and some tackle to Colonel Gorham at once," he concluded. " Colonel Gridley is already there."

That evening he sent for me again and asked me many questions concerning the fortress. I found I had gathered more than I knew, and all that I knew seemed of value.

Then he stopped and looked at me kindly. " I hope, Eben, that all will be well yet with Mistress Antoinette. I will issue orders that she is to be looked for and treated well when we enter the town. You should have told her we had much sickness and needed her same ministrations here."

I thought what folly it was that the idea had not come to me while I was in conversation with her. It was an argument she could not well have gainsaid.

Feathertale's joy at seeing me was unbounded. He admitted he had distrusted Captain O'Hara as much as I ever had. " But it was the only way, Eben," he assured me. " And I knew that you would be a match for him." Then I thanked him for his faith in me but assured him I would never have done what I did without all the instruction he had been at some pains to see that I got in the harbor of Bostontown.

The next day Admiral Warren came ashore, and all the leaders gathered in General Pepperrell's quarters. We knew immediately that great things were afoot.

When I saw Asa he shook his head over my news. " It is good to have something to cheer the men, Eben. They are sadly discouraged with all the delay. I am doubtful whether we are out of the woods yet. The Island Battery is the most solid of all. It will not fall easily, even to a battery on the Point of the Lantern. Here it has been but gray day after gray day. Fire our guns when we had the powder. Keep silent when we had not. The men started marauding, but the general stopped that. Some found a few small bags of louis d'or, but for the most part these peasants are poorer than the poorest in Bostontown."

I informed him that Morpain was Captain O'Hara, but to my surprise he only nodded. " I have suspected it for some time," he said and added scornfully, " A Frenchman is no match for a New Englander."

Then I began to ask for the men I had known. At mention of Thundercloud's name, his face sobered. " Prepare yourself, Eben, for a sad blow. Thundercloud is gone. He was a brave man and he went bravely."

Now though I had come to distrust Thundercloud, still he had been my friend for many years and the thought of his not being with us when again we gathered in Feathertale's shop in Bostontown gave me a strange shock.

" How was it? " I demanded.

" Well, it was one of the days on which the Hill Battery was out of shot. Thundercloud undertook to gather the French shells which had not exploded and were strewn over the hill. He had gotten in successfully with several when a French gunner got him. He had a shell in his hand at the time. It is hard to realize. Thundercloud just disappeared. He died bravely, fighting for us."

" But still I cannot understand his lying about the scalps," I said.

Feathertale nodded. " He was the most honest man ever I met," he murmured.

I thought of how Thundercloud had given me the secret of the fortress and how it had facilitated my escape. I could never give him my gratitude.

Two days later we caught the roar of the new battery on the Point of the Lantern. Working day and night, our men had got the guns ashore and mounted on the Point. By the sound of things they were working with good effect. The rumble of the cannonading could not drown the cheers of the men on the Greene Hill. But I could not join wholeheartedly in the general jubilation. Every now and then a shell from the Point of the Lantern missed its mark and landed in the town, doing untold damage.

That sundown I heard again the bells of St. Louis, St. Jean, and St. Antoine-Marie sending out their message, but it seemed to me much of their gaiety was gone. From the hill position I looked anxiously down into the town. The evening light played warmly on the roofs that were left. I thought then I had heard the bells in prison and out of it, but I doubt if my heart was any lighter in either case.

I wondered how long it would be before the spire of gold toppled and fell, silencing forever the bells' sweet song and crashing the roof into ruins over the heads of the Good Sisters of the Congregation and the Hospital of the Recollects, over Antoinette and Aaron. I was afraid of what was to come.

24: The Great Conquest

When I wakened in Feathertale's tent next morning I was as cold and chill as ever I had been in the prison cell on the floor of the moat under the King's Bastion.

I sought the canteen and Asa gave me a cup of warm liquor out of the soup pot. It refreshed me mightily. Instantly I was conscious of a new feeling in the air.

At last, it seemed, something was about to happen. Everywhere was excitement. I took up my flute, thinking to sooth the turbulent emotion which seemed abroad. It brought a sharp rebuke from the officer on duty. It was time, he said, to be all ears. Under cover of the fog, Beaubassin or Morpain or some other of the port captains might take it into their heads to sally forth. We might be murdered where we stood.

I could not help wondering if Morpain was sufficiently recovered from his engagement with me to conduct such a sortie, but if he were not, there were many others, I knew.

I was sent on a mission to the Royal Battery but not by General Pepperrell. He had already set out on the troubled waters in a small shallop to meet with Admiral Warren on board the H. M. S. *Superb*. It seemed to me a perilous undertaking in this fog. But Asa assured me it was no new thing. " I do not see how the general and the admiral work together. They continually miss each other." I hoped this time they would be more fortunate.

In the Royal Battery I found Billy much improved. Every man of the company was on the alert. They were on edge for the assault, which they felt was close at hand.

Again I saw that strange sight of the fog wisping away like floating veils, the roofs of the citadel afloat in it as if on a silver sea.

" Look, Eben! " Billy pointed. A shaft of sunlight had glorified the drifting veils. The spire of the Hospital of the Recollects was rising out of the mist like an upthrust sword, as if the mighty fortress knew it was doomed and was determined to go down fighting.

Our ears were soon to hear the cannonading from the Point of the Lantern. Evidently the fog had cleared a bit out there, in the strange way it had of rising and falling.

Before I left I visited again, with Billy, the little chapel. Master Moody was in the act of conducting service. To my sorrow the figure of the Virgin and Child had been removed. I was at some pains to account for my sudden desolation at the loss of these sacred relics belonging to men of an alien faith. Then I bethought me: such emptiness would be mine without Antoinette.

I said good-by to Billy, promising we would meet in the town. I returned to the Coromandière Cove. It was great relief to me to find that General Pepperrell was safely returned.

I went to my bed that night racked by doubt.

It was a different world that I awoke to. The camp was agog with news. Our fire on the Island Battery had been so hot and so devastating that the defending troops had rushed from it into the water. It would soon be silenced. Also there was a strange story about which all were talking.

Admiral Warren, on learning that the French in the fortress did not know the *Vigilant* had been taken, thought up a ruse. It seemed that the Marquis de la Maisonfort, captain of the conquered ship, and his crew had been given the honors of war. They had been taken aboard the English ships of war and given the treatment of honored guests. The admiral now complained to the French captain that our prisoners of war had been allowed to fall into the hands of the Indians and had been quickly annihilated. He asked the French captain to write a letter to Chevalier Du Chambon, telling of the fine treatment he was receiving. This the French captain promptly agreed to do. The letter had been written and sent into the fortress by a Major Macdonald. Major Macdonald had had the same idea as myself. He had pretended to know no French and had asked for an interpreter. At once their consternation over the news was apparent. They had not known of it. And their despair was as evident as that of my guards. It was in Major Macdonald's mind that they were in great mood to surrender.

And now plans went ahead apace. Trees were felled. Ladders were built to scale the moat. Heaps of brush were concentrated on the hill to use as signals between land and sea forces. A company was engaged in collecting moss with which the fleet could drape their hulls and bulwarks and thus soften any glancing shots. The fleet was stripped for action. We were building fascines.

Men whistled at their work. I wondered why I had ever thought them weak or ill.

On the morrow we marched to the assault.

Orders, that next morning, flew thick and fast. The men were lined up in front of the encampment. I had never seen braver sight than that battle array. We might lack shot and shell and gay French uniforms, and the discipline of a standing army, but abroad in all our whole expeditionary force was the indomitable spirit of the man who commanded it, General William Pepperrell.

Then amid our battle music we saw on the horizon a strange sight. I knew then that Admiral Warren had got his re-enforcements, and they were no small addition. Eleven great ships of the line, under full sail, surrounded by a host of smaller sloops and cruisers, swung in and took up their positions facing the town with military precision, the black guns of the frigates nosing out of the decks like dogs impatient at the leash.

It must then have been evident to those in the fortress that the hour had indeed struck and that the assault was a reality and about to begin.

With flags and banners Admiral Warren came ashore. Even I, gravely doubtful so long as to the outcome, was carried away with enthusiasm and joined in the wild huzzas. The drums beat a lively tune. Colors were gaily flying. I thought the admiral, for all he was so little, amply made up for his size in the dignity of his bearing and the forcefulness of his personality. His clear voice rang cheerily over the encampment: " My men, you cannot take the fortress with your land forces. We cannot take it with our sea forces. But, together, the impossible is become the inevitable."

Above the low growl of the guns on the Point of the Lantern, above the heavy boom of the sea ceaselessly pounding against the morass, his voice rang out.

From my high position I could see the Dauphin Gate and the roofs of the town. A louder rumble caught our ears. I saw the delicate upthrust point of the spire of the hospital bend crookedly, as if by magic, topple, and fall with a resounding crash. Heaviness returned to my heart. Had it crashed the roof? Was Antoinette there tending the sick? Were she and Aaron safe?

The general's voice rang over the waiting throng. He urged them to fidelity and heroism in the coming conflict. For once his kindly voice fell on deaf ears. A new sight held our attention. I did not need the poke of Asa's soup ladle to draw my attention to it.

The portcullis of the West Gate in the Dauphin Bastion had dropped open. A French officer, mounted on horseback, came

prancing out. He bore aloft a white flag. Our leaders saw it and waited.

A sharp order silenced our drums.

Admiral Warren ordered an express to meet the emissary.

Was it a request for parley?

Was the fortress, after six weeks of bitter siege, really succumbing without a fight?

Were we, after all, to be spared the bloody carnage of an assault?

25: The Bells of St. Louis, St. Jean, and St. Antoine-Marie

The admiral and General Pepperrell retired to quarters as the order, " Cease all firing! " went out.

A great weight seemed to be lifted from me until I noted that the battery on the Point of the Lantern continued its pounding of the Island Battery. We found out later that because of the distance the order to cease firing did not reach them until well into the night.

Admiral Warren returned to his waiting ships. We awaited with anxiety the articles the French might insist on.

When they arrived two special stipulations interested me greatly. One, I was much afraid neither the general nor the admiral would accept: the French demanded that they be allowed to march out with colors flying. They were not to be humbled in the dust.

Second, and this I thought a strange request indeed, that if any man wished, he was to go out masked!

I sat ready with my quill beside Master Greene while the general perused the document. I was in a fever to get inside the town and learn what had happened to Aaron and Antoinette. And it came to me that I had always heard the French were wily. Were they purposely delaying in the hope that a French fleet might still arrive? Was victory to be snatched from us at the very lip of the cup?

General Pepperrell took due thought. Then he said: " I do not

think, with the prospect of French re-enforcements still in the offing, we should be too harsh in our terms. Our own men are ill. Our powder is all but gone. Let us get inside the fortress by all means as soon as possible."

And so Admiral Warren was informed.

His answer was prompt.

"I am glad our sentiments agree with regard to allowing the troops the honor of war which they desire; the uncertainty of our affairs that depend so much on wind and weather makes it necessary not to stickle at trifles. I hope that all behave to the prisoners with the humanity and honor becoming English officers."

I bethought me they were both truly great men to have been willing to allow the French to go out pridefully and thus avoid a lingering bitterness.

It was the longest night ever I spent. However, I managed to get word to Mistress Antoinette to meet me on the King's Bastion on the morrow if it were possible. One of the men with the general's emissary was permitted to deliver it by word of mouth to Mademoiselle Ignace, in care of the Good Sisters of the Congregation. That night I learned to my great joy that both Aaron and Antoinette were safe.

By morning the affair was settled, and our jubilation knew no bounds. Billy and I entered the town as early next morning as we were permitted to do so. Billy was still weak. We were appalled at the wreckage we saw. No single house seemed to have escaped our bombardment. The delicate spire of the citadel, I knew, was no more, but it was with great shock I noted its loss. It seemed to me that the building, without it, was shorn of much of its architectural beauty. The stair to the parade ground, down which I had passed that night on my way to the new cell in the Maurepas Gate, was littered with fallen masonry, so that we had to pick our way most carefully. The English guard were already at work filling up the great gashes made in the earth of the parade ground. The French troops had need of a place in which to give up their arms.

Once again I looked at the carven shield of white Normandy stone which had formed the keystone of the arch over the wide

doorway. It lay in three great pieces on the stone threshold. The lilies of France were indeed in the dirt of the roadway. It seemed to me a sorry thing that in this great New World which harbored so little of man-made beauty we should have slain this single bit. I think perhaps I was the more conscious of it, knowing not what wreckage of my own personal hopes I was yet to encounter.

Then I perceived a ragged, weeping line of bent and dark-clad figures wending their way from the casemates. I knew it for the women and children, freed at last from their dark prison, but with fear — nay, terror — in their faces. For them, no matter how harsh the clime, how hard the struggle of the New World, this had held the security of home, and they were losing it, for what harder conditions they did not know.

I made for the ramparts and what remained of the King's Bastion. Feathertale had promised to bring Dogood there, and it was my appointed meeting place with Antoinette. I had but just attained the peaked embrasure when a dark figure glided toward me and Antoinette's sweet face was before me. In my great relief that she was still alive, I felt sudden emotion and could not touch her.

Mistress Antoinette cried out, " O Eben! Is it that you do not like me any more? "

And I, thinking of the terrible thing she had suffered, made haste to comfort her and had her in my arms before ever I was aware that the troops were assembling all about us and we were no longer alone.

Then Billy, who had stepped back, came at my call, and greeted her shyly. A stranger, swirling his navy cloak about him, stepped up to us and I had great difficulty in recognizing in this great tall man, albeit his face was still white from his wounding, my brother Aaron. Then did I have a sharp pang of jealousy, for it seemed to me that Antoinette clung overlong in his embrace.

As for Aaron, he looked down at me from his new-found height and said condescendingly, " Why, Eben, you have become quite a man."

Then I made Billy known to him and a little later Dogood and Feathertale joined us. Dogood and Antoinette clung together a moment, so that I realized something of what they had been through together. And I thought that although Antoinette's quaint face had become dearer to me than ever before I missed the dark radiance which ever had framed it, and which was there no more. I had great fear it was gone forever.

Now all this while the French troops had been massing on the plaza of the citadel. There was much piping and beating of drums as they moved to their places. Rank on rank they gathered below us, and I could feel only sorrow in my heart over their grave faces. I saw the Chevalier du Chambon, gorgeous in colored uniform and high hat. I thought had it been his victory he could not have borne himself more proudly. From his bearing none would have guessed how heavy must be his heart. With this great fortress his king had " betrusted him," and he had failed him.

Then on the ear came other martial music. The French forces were stilled. Nearer and nearer came the beating of the drums, filled with a new fervor. There was the pride of conquest in every drumbeat. Antoinette gripped my hand.

" Eben," she whispered. " It is the men of New England! The long siege is over. You have won."

And Dogood muttered shortly, " I wonder in what respect the crown holds us now."

Then filing through the ruins at the West Gate came Colonel Gorham's rangers in their picturesque uniforms, and Colonel Newcomb's regiment soberly clad. Man after man marched proudly up the slopes. I thought that General Pepperrell was the finest of them all, standing there without triumph but with a great peace written large upon his countenance. And beside him, Admiral Warren, in his natty sailor's blue and gold, looked monstrous dignified.

The French marched down to the parade ground and laid down their arms. The officers of both armies exchanged documents with becoming ceremony. And high on the citadel the lilies of France came fluttering down.

" See," cried Dogood. " General Pepperrell has been given the keys of the city fortress." Then she added bitterly, " Much good it will do our New England men, the general having forbid sacking the town."

And Aaron, twirling his navy cloak majestically about him, retorted, " We of the navy had great booty by the prize ships. Know ye all I am a rich man this day."

At which Dogood cried out angrily: " Aye! It is the most unfair thing ever I heard of. What did the navy do sitting aboard their great ships with a warm place to sleep and plenty to eat? "

Now I cannot say that I blamed Dogood, for it did seem to me that we of the land forces were likely to get the small end of the bargain. Still I recalled that Aaron had volunteered for the assault on the Island Battery and had gotten his wound thereby.

" Indeed," Aaron answered her coldly, " you know nothing whatever about the matter." Then he turned his back upon her, and I saw Dogood's mouth quiver. I could have cried for the glory of golden-yellow tresses, which, like Antoinette's, had seemed so much a part of her beauty. I perceived too that she had grown more sensitive since her experience. I was glad to note that Billy made haste to turn her attention to what was happening below.

I cannot say that I myself was much elated over the division of the spoils, for well I knew that Aaron was in a position to court Antoinette at once, while I was but a poor clerk of Master Pepperrell's warehouse and like to be so for some time.

A rattle of musketry brought my attention back to the massed throngs. The French had laid down their arms. They were a weaponless army now. The bugles uttered a clear call. The drums and fifes beat a lively tune. Rank on rank, shorn of all military equipment, but still in glittering array, proud-eyed and colors flying, the French troops wheeled and rightabout-faced and marched away to the waiting ships.

The governor and all his staff. The port captain, Morpain! The men about us whispered his name awesomely.

As the famous privateer, my enemy, passed, my spine seemed to shrivel in my body, so baleful was the glance he bent upon me. Then, with an oddly cavalier attitude, he flung up his head and raised his arm aloft. For one moment I seemed to see again the crouched body, the huge uplifted wooden glove by which he had effected so much of his disguise. The next moment something plopped in the dust at our feet. The troops marched on. Morpain was gone when we picked it up.

Dogood was the first to sense it was his wooden glove. " Morpain was Captain O'Hara," she cried hardly. Aaron looked amazed. " That was how the enemy had news of our ships! " she explained.

I could see that as a ruse of the enemy the idea intrigued him. War, I reflected sadly, was become his business.

Billy too was much interested in the glove. He thrust in his hand and drew out a small note. We gathered around as he deciphered it. It seemed to me there was something as sinister as itself in its meager message. " Perchance," the lettering ran, " it is not as dead as it would seem."

I knew then that Morpain had not forgotten; nor had he forgiven. I was glad to feel the comfort of Antoinette's hand stealing into mine.

" But I do not understand how he effected his disguise." Aaron's eyes were following the passing figures. " Morpain is a tall man."

Feathertale nodded. " It is a matter of mystery," he admitted. " Yet do I know how it was done. I have heard tell of a man who had a double joint in the lower knuckle of his spine and could make himself tall or short by several inches, taking, as it were, a tuck in his spine. I have sometimes thought Morpain was such a man."

I knew then that Feathertale had not been fooled. He had long suspected it. I wondered myself how Morpain had let him leave the fortress, and then I decided that Feathertale was his only available contact with our camp.

" The general thought," Feathertale seemed to read my unspoken conclusion, " since the admiral was suspicious I should keep in touch with him at sea. It was well to know what he was up to." So the general, though unsuspicious himself, had given heed to the warnings of his fellow commander. I wondered if that was not the secret of much of his success with men.

226

"Captain O'Hara as Morpain must have spent many uneasy nights thinking that there was a secret way into the fortress, known to his enemy and not to him," Feathertale continued. "He must have lain awake nights, thinking that at any moment a whole regiment might arrive inside the fortress."

"A kind of Trojan horse," Aaron supplied.

"Aye!" Feathertale was unusually talkative. "That is why you were allowed visitors, Eben, given your flute, changed to another cell at your request. Morpain knew you would undoubtedly request a change, and the change would be nearer, if not at, the secret entrance. Also, he may now suspect that the information regarding the hiding place of the guns which they had ready to mount on the Point of the Lantern, and did not accomplish in time, was supplied you, or gathered by you, within the fortress. In allowing you so much freedom he did not appreciate the use you would make of it."

I realized then that while I always thought of Morpain as the privateer, he was a member of their coast guard and as such responsible for the safety of the fortress.

We were all very thoughtful. The French continued to pass. I was glad to see in the throng my guard of the Maurepas Gate, the single happy-faced member of that sad gathering. He was going home.

One incident of the day, however, shocked and startled us all. Behind the governor's staff came a masked man. His eyes through the mask sought mine, not in anger but, it seemed to me, in pleading. A trick of his walk? I started.

"What is it, Eben?" Antoinette demanded.

It was Aaron who answered.

"My father!" He cried out, and there was pain in his cry. "My father leagued with the enemy!" I do not think that aught in all that great siege so completely overwhelmed me.

My father, the Captain St. Jean de Gervais, linked with the enemy! I still loved him. I would have run to him if I could, but in my heart was a great humiliation. I could not now think of Antoinette. I had lost her completely. I, the son of a man who had sold his country to the enemy.

Once again Feathertale John came to my rescue. He laid a hand on each of us. "Now listen to me, both of you," he said. "When Morpain captured your father, France and England were at war. The Captain St. Jean de Gervais saw that by pretending to go over to the enemy he could be of immense value to the New Englanders. And he certainly was. General Pepperrell knows it. And Governor Shirley knows it too."

Aaron was not to be appeased. "What did he sell them, Feathertale John?" he demanded. "What did he sell the shrewd Morpain which made him feel secure in the captain's faith?"

Feathertale nodded. "Aye," he murmured. "That will prove it. He sold them the map of the Red Hats." We all looked at each other. The map of the Red Hats! I recalled when it had disappeared. It had been my father, the Captain St. Jean de Gervais, who had first shown me the hiding place in the old figurehead. Yes, my father must have known the map was there. He had seen it. I remembered the night on the wharf when I had thought I had seen him and had found only Captain O'Hara. It had not been a dream. Truly I had seen him.

Feathertale was talking again. "But," he said, "he was much put out when he found that by so doing he had caught in the spy ring his own son."

Then light broke over me. The man I had thought a priest, who had befriended me and brought me such comfort, had been my own father. The message, "Search the Careening Cove," had been given me by my father at a time when he knew he himself was discredited with Morpain. He must have known my own straits were desperate indeed, but he supposed that having gotten myself in I had some means of communication without. No wonder he had started that night when at last I had spoken and thanked him. He knew definitely then that the mythical plot he had concocted to gain their confidence had caught in its cruel net his own son. Morpain, undoubtedly, had great satisfaction out of that. He had not been allowed to come again. Why he had been allowed to live, I could understand too. My father was a Frenchman, a gentleman, and no doubt among his own kind he had made friends easily, powerful friends, as evidenced by their eagerness to conceal his identity even in the surrender. And he, like me, could not be exposed, without exposing Morpain's stupidity. Something had watched over us.

"Do not forget," Feathertale concluded, "your father is a man well known to all our leaders, even Admiral Warren, and much commended by them, but he had to go out masked. There is still such a thing as French justice. The men of New England, like Aaron, would not have understood. He could never have moved among them again. Your father never lost touch with Bostontown." I knew then it was information, not money, Feathertale had feared Captain O'Hara would find in the figurehead, information of the enemy deposited there by Captain St. Jean de Gervais.

Then my thoughts turned to small Paul. His red hat had formed a trail for me to Antoinette. I had followed it into the fortress, and to news of the *Vigilant,* and out again, across the harbor waters, to the guns of the Careening Cove, so much a source of our victory.

I had much to think about as the Swiss mercenaries and the French troops paraded by, their gay uniforms of blue and scarlet brilliant in the July sun, the white and golden banner of the fleur-de-lis with its blue and scarlet flames flying gaily above them.

Then Aaron turned away peevishly. "I am aweary of all this," he said. "I would see this town I have heard so much about and have inhabited so long without knowing it. Come!" His eyes sought Antoinette's, and he moved away. He did not even wait, I noted, so sure was he that she would follow.

Antoinette looked at me. I nodded for her to go. I had no doubt where Aaron's suit was tending. And somehow I wanted at that moment to be quite alone.

Billy and Dogood followed Aaron eagerly. Feathertale too moved off.

But I turned my back on the marching columns and climbed again to the wreck of the King's Bastion. And when I arrived on the salient circling the great gun platform I came face to face with Antoinette, the old Antoinette, smiling mischievously at me.

"O Eben!" she demanded. "Is it that you do not like me any more that you push me off on that great brother of yours?"

I replied sternly, " He is a rich man and one you would do well to cultivate."

Then Antoinette came close up to me and cried out teasingly: " O Eben! You are jealous. I knew you were jealous." It seemed to afford her much enjoyment. Her silvery laughter rippled out over the deep moat as I had never expected to hear it again. I marveled that she could be so merry after all she had gone through; yet was my heart cheered thereby in a way I could not measure.

Mistress Antoinette ran to the edge of the battlement, and hooped herself up on the crumbling wall. And then she flung up her hands, and though I dared not look I knew she had bared her head to the breeze.

I held my breath as I dashed toward her. I wanted to gaze on her face and yet dared not, but I could not let her endanger herself on that battered wall. Holding her firmly, I raised my eyes, and was fair amazed. The long tresses were gone, but in their place was a mass of tumbled curls — appealingly childish. I gazed and gazed.

Then Antoinette hid her head on my shoulder, crying bitterly: " Please, please, Eben, do not mind. I could do nought else. It was impossible to keep long hair clean in the wilderness, and the Indian, Eben, was most uncommon pleased over the gift. And he had been so good to us. But," she added quickly, " he liked Dogood's flaxen locks best. Perhaps you do too." I could not speak, so great was my relief. " Indeed," continued Mistress Antoinette generously, " I thought it rarely beautiful myself, hanging from his belt."

" Aye," I said. " I saw it myself. And I thought — " I could not finish. I could only hold her close to me.

But Mistress Antoinette's quick mind understood. " O Eben! You loved me even then, when you thought I was quite hideous."

Mistress Antoinette rested in my arms at last, trustful as a small wild bird reared in captivity. I knew then there had come to me a richness I did not deserve.

Through my happiness flashed a memory of Thundercloud. Thundercloud had indeed known they were not scalps. Nor could he explain, not knowing how these things had happened. And now I could never tell him of my sorrow at doubting his faith.

Mistress Antoinette lifted her face from my shoulder. " What is it, Eben? " she said, knowing instantly my change of mood.

So I told her, and Antoinette said softly: " But he knows now, Eben. I am sure he knows now. Even as my father, the Stuart, knows too that all is well with us."

" Aye! " I said sweeping her off the crumbling wall into the safety of my arms.

Then the sound of bells came sweetly on the evening air. And I knew the drums and the bugles, the sound of marching men, had long passed by. The siege was over. Freedom to live our lives in the New World unmolested was surely ours at last. We had won it!

Antoinette held up her hand for silence. Her face took on a mystic beauty. " 'Tis the Angelus, Eben. Oh, the poor Sisters of the Congregation! I wonder what will happen to them now? "

Reverently we listened. The bells of St. Louis, St. Jean, and St. Antoine-Marie were summoning an alien people to prayer. As I saw Antoinette's lips form the familiar words which the Good Sisters had taught her, I thought of the motto which had carried us through — or how else had we accomplished this strange victory? — " *Nil desperandum Christo Duce.*"

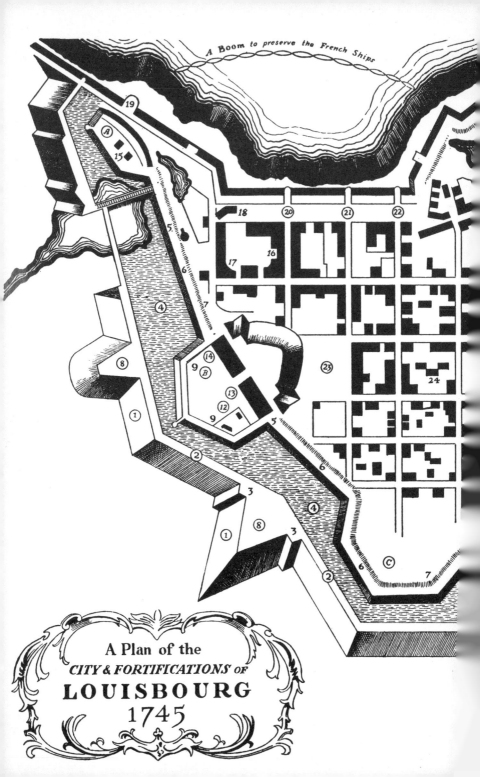

A Boom to preserve the French Ships

A Plan of the
CITY & FORTIFICATIONS of
LOUISBOURG
1745

EXPLANATION

A Dauphin Bastion
B King's Bastion & Citadel
C Queen's Bastion
D Princess Bastion
E Bowrillon Bastion
F Maurepas Bastion
G Batterie de la Grave
1 The Glascis
2 The Covered Way
3 Traverses
4 The Ditch
5 Parapet
6 The Ramparts
7 Slopes
8 Places d'Armes
9 Casemates
10 Guard Houses

11 Wooden Bridges
12 Governor's Apartments
13 The Chapel
14 Barracks for Garrison
15 Powder Magazine
16 Fortification House
17 Ordinance
18 General Storehouses
19 West Gate
20 Queen's Gate
21 East Gate
22 Gate in Quay Curtain
23 The Parade
24 Nunnery
25 Hospital and Church
26 Palisading with ramparts
27 Piquet raised during siege